BRIDE OF FINKELSTEIN

——— A RABBI BEN MYSTERY ———

MARVIN J. WOLF

MARVIN J. WOLF

Rambam Press, Asheville North Carolina

Copyright © 2020 Marvin J. Wolf

All rights reserved.

ISBN: 9798608796326

Disclaimer

This is a work of fiction. Certain communities, business establishments and other places named herein exist only in imagination. The names, identities, descriptions, and utterances of all characters bear no relation to actual people, living or dead and any similarity to person or events of real life is entirely coincidental.

Dedication

This book is dedicated to the many rabbis I have had the privilege of learning from: Harold Wasserman, Naomi Levy, Yitzchok Adlerstein, Daniel Shevitz, Matt Marko and Batsheva Meiri.

Also By Marvin J. Wolf

The Rabbi Ben Series

For Whom The Shofar Blows

A Scribe Dies In Brooklyn

A Tale of Two Rabbis

The CID Mystery Series

M-9

Papa Two-Niner (Summer 2020)

Nonfiction

They Were Soldiers (May 2020)

Abandoned In Hell

Where White Men Fear To Tread

Family Blood

Fallen Angels

Rotten Apples

Perfect Crimes

ACKNOWLEDGMENTS

I am indebted to Doug Grad for his sage advice and many fine suggestions; and to my daughter, Tomi, without whom I would be almost helpless.

Prologue

Steins Township, Illinois

About 6:00 pm, a slim-hipped young woman parks in a corner of Mariano's supermarket parking lot, then goes from car to car until she finds a battered, eight-year-old Hyundai with the keys in the ignition.

But the doors are locked.

Pulling a Slim Jim from her sweatpants, she opens the door and is out of the parking lot and heading west in under two minutes.

On her way home in the borrowed car, she stops at a hole-in-the-wall Chinese restaurant and leaves with dinner for two.

After dinner, she and her girlfriend watch television until 10:00, when they prepare for bed. By 11:00, both are asleep.

§

She arises at 5:00 and without bathing or applying makeup, silently pulls on a sweatshirt and sweat pants, grabs her purse, leaves the house and drives off in the stolen Hyundai.

Just before 6:00 am, she finds the long, curving street that is her destination, then parks at a place along the curb that offers an unobstructed view of the mouth of a short street leading to a cul-de-sac.

Leaving the car, she takes a pellet gun from her purse and with two quiet shots puts the streetlight out.

Back in the car, she cranks the driver's window down an inch, just enough to keep the windshield from frosting and waits, shivering in the morning cold.

About ten minutes crawl by before a thin, bearded man

wearing sweats and a watch cap strolls out of the cul-de-sac. Seemingly oblivious to her presence, he turns toward her. His long strides down the asphalt street propel him at almost a jogger's pace.

The woman remains behind the wheel, waiting. After half an hour she decides that her hitter isn't coming. She starts the engine—and then a light-colored, mid-sized SUV swerves off the street and parks a few spaces in front of her.

The stroller re-appears from the opposite direction.

Engine snarling, the SUV leaps into the street, accelerating as it hits the strolling man. His limp corpse flies down the street and lands against a parked car. The SUV speeds away.

"So that's that," says the woman.

She pulls a U-turn onto the street, leaving the dead pedestrian behind.

She returns to Mariano's, wipes down the car and leaves it with unlocked doors and the keys in the ignition. She finds her own car and drives off.

Dawn is breaking as she enters her bedroom, undresses down to panties and then slips into the king-sized bed next to a sleeping woman, who stirs but does not wake.

In minutes, she is asleep.

Chapter One

Jerusalem

Rabbi Ben Maimon glanced at his new watch, an ADI, the official timepiece of the Israeli Defense Force Paratroop Brigade and a gift from Miryam, his fiancé.

Ten past three. Rabbi Meir Farkas, secretary to Rabbi Menachem Wein, the president of the Israeli Rabbinate and the supreme authority on religious matters in the State of Israel, had invited him to his office.

And so far, Ben had been waiting for an hour and ten minutes.

"Five more minutes," Ben said aloud, in a half whisper.

He knew exactly why he was here. And he knew that he would regret walking out on as powerful and vindictive a man as Meir Farkas.

Nevertheless, when five minutes had passed, he got to his feet and approached the middle-aged female receptionist who had told him to have a seat and wait.

Speaking Hebrew in a pleasant tone of voice, Ben said, "Please tell Rabbi Farkas that I appreciate that he is very busy and that if he still wishes to speak with me, he knows how to find me."

"Rabbi Farkas will be very upset if you leave," replied the woman.

"Your concern for your boss's feelings is admirable," Ben replied.

As he turned to leave, a movement caught the corner of his eye and he felt the air pressure change, ever so slightly, as if a door had been opened. Without breaking stride, he headed for the elevator bank.

"Rabbi Maimon!" boomed a rich baritone from Ben's left.

Ben stopped and turned to face the man behind the voice. Ben was clean-shaven and his short, athletic but slender body was clad in a bespoke suit of cream linen over a light blue shirt. Knotted at his throat was a Royal Blue necktie sporting a muted silver Star of David pattern and atop his copper-colored hair was a small, dark blue *kippah*. In contrast, Rabbi Farkas was tall and heavy, a tanned forehead above a round black patch over his left eye, *a la* Moshe Dyan. His enormous salt-and-pepper beard was wildly untrimmed and he was clad in a wrinkled black wool suit over a soiled, open-necked white dress shirt. A wide-brimmed black fedora topped his head.

"I apologize for keeping you waiting," said Farkas. "Please come this way."

Ben smiled and followed Farkas to his office, a spacious top floor suite with a magnificent view of the Temple Mount. The walls were lined with bookshelves and Ben's quick scan noted that many of the volumes were rare and valuable. On the cluttered desk were an antique inkwell and a sharpened white feather quill.

"Please make yourself comfortable," Farkas said in Hebrew. "Would you prefer that we speak English?" he continued, switching to that language, which he spoke with a strong accent straight from the Bronx.

"Either is fine," Ben said in English.

"Please, sit there," Farkas said, indicating one of two comfortable chairs in front of the desk that faced a low table and a large sofa.

Ben took the chair and the older man sat down next to him. Ben noticed a long, thin white scar above the eye patch that made him wonder if Farkas had been hit by shrapnel. Had he served in the IDF?

A moment later the door opened and a young, pretty woman in the uniform of the IDF entered carrying a silver tray on which was a modern coffee service and an ornate dish piled with a pyramid of tiny almond cakes.

"Malachi Zeev speaks very highly of you," Farkas said as he poured coffee into a porcelain cup. "Cream and sugar?"

"Just a little cream," Ben said. "Have you spoken to Rabbi Zeev recently?"

"Last night," Farkas said. "He also spoke with great reverence of your grandfather, of blessed memory."

"I must see Malachi when I get back to America. He's very frail and I worry that he might die before we meet again."

"A good idea," replied Farkas and sipped his coffee.

After a long minute of uncomfortable silence, Farkas gave a short, unpleasant laugh. "I see that you are a student of the Japanese school of negotiation," he said.

Ben shook his head. "You are an important leader, a man of undoubted rectitude and if you wish to see me, you will tell me why when you are ready."

Again, Farkas laughed.

"Malachi didn't tell me that you were so maddeningly polite. He said that you were a man who could get things done."

Ben remained silent and sipped his coffee.

"You have a sister," Farkas began. "Marcia or Malka."

"My father's daughter, not my mother's, as you surely know."

"Your father was a very interesting man, Ben. "Very accomplished."

"My father, whom I never met, was a swindler, a thief, a confidence man. He was excommunicated by a Brooklyn *beit din*, a rabbinical court, in 1978."

Farkas looked surprised. "*That* I didn't know. How did you learn of this?"

"My grandfather, of blessed memory, left me a paper with the court's ruling."

"Astonishing!" said Farkas. "I've never heard of such a ruling in America."

Ben shrugged.

"What was the reason?" asked Farkas.

"I don't know," Ben said. "The ruling didn't mention it. But as I said, my father was a very bad man. He swindled synagogues and churches, Jewish charities..."

"But in his last years, he was a respected philanthropist."

Yet again, Ben remained silent.

"Let us speak now about Malka," said Farkas. "She is here to complete her education and become a Reform rabbi, which, as you are no doubt aware, is not the sort of title that the Rabbinate recognizes as an actual rabbi."

Ben declined to take the bait. "I don't know Malka very well yet but she is a fine woman, very *frum*, (observant) in the manner of the Reform movement."

Farkas frowned. "There is a problem," he said in a low voice, implying great seriousness. "We allow the Reform to teach rabbinical students here for their obligatory year of study. We do so in the hope that this will lead some of these students to more deeply inquire into Judaism and to find their way back to the traditions and laws of our ancestors."

Ben smiled. "And also, because most affiliated American Jews are Reform and collectively American Jewry raises about $7 billion a year for the State of Israel, not including what American Jews spend on tourism here."

Farkas inclined his head slightly in agreement but said nothing.

Silence filled the room for almost a minute.

"As I said, your sister has a problem," Farkas said. "She will not be allowed to continue her studies here because we, the Rabbinate, have learned that her conversion to Judaism was improper."

Ben said, "Very good of you to tell me, Rabbi Farkas. Is there anything else?"

He put his coffee cup down and got to his feet.

"Please sit down, Rabbi," said Farkas. "We are not finished."

Ben remained standing. "I shouldn't take too much of your time, Rabbi," he said.

"You are not interested in the way that Malka's conversion was improper?"

Ben shook his head. "I can think of a dozen reasons that a man in your position could raise, with or without cause, to challenge any individual's right to call themselves a Jew. Just tell me what you want and let's get on with this."

Farkas laughed. "Oy, you are one tough cookie! Sit down, this is not bad news. In fact, I think I can help you both."

Ben returned to his seat and looked expectantly at Farkas.

"I had a cousin, Shmuel. His mother and mine, of blessed memory, were sisters. He is—was—a rabbi, living in a Chicago suburb, for many years the spiritual leader of Congregation Beth Ohr of Steins Township. Three years ago he retired and remained at the synagogue as rabbi emeritus. More to the point, for about forty years, Shmuel was the guiding light behind *L'Dor v'Dor,* a charity that raises money for Yeshiva students in Israel. Every year they sent four or five promising boys to Israel to study and covered all their expenses for five years. Most of these boys become rabbis and most return to the United States."

Ben said, "You said that he *was* a rabbi. Did he die?"

Farkas frowned. "About two weeks ago, while taking his morning walk—he took a different route from one morning to the next but he was very well known in the community. If you were looking for him on the streets around Beth Ohr during the hour before sunrise, you wouldn't have much trouble finding Rabbi Shmuel Rubin."

"You believe that he was murdered."

"Exactly."

"How?"

"The local police called it an accident. He was struck by a car, which did not even stop. We have no description of the car but the police claim to have some forensic evidence."

"You want me to find his killer?"

"That would be a bonus. I want you to wind up his charity, liquidate its assets, find the major donors and ask them to contact me and send all cash and other assets, all records and papers, to the Rabbinate. To our scholarship fund.

"I would go to the States and do this myself but Rabbi Wein requires my presence here at several important meetings over the next six weeks and I don't want to wait that long."

Ben nodded to show that he understood.

"While you are doing that, you will serve as the interim rabbi of Congregation Beth Ohr, until they can hire a replacement. I will see that your sister is allowed to remain here until she returns to Los Angeles and resumes her studies at the Ziegler School. But... I suggest very strongly that she finds a proper rabbi here and undergo conversion to our faith at her earliest opportunity. I can give you a list of rabbis with whom she might consult."

Again Ben nodded his understanding. "This Congregation— Beth Ohr. They are without a rabbi since Shmuel retired?"

"Not at all. He was replaced by Rabbi Emanuel Shevitz, an able but much younger man. Rabbi Shevitz disappeared the same day that my cousin was murdered."

"And am I to find him as well?"

Rabbi Farkas shrugged and spread both hands, palms up. "Only if it proves necessary to complete the task that I have set you."

"Is there anything that you haven't told me that I should know?"

Farkas spread his hands, palms up. "I suspect that there is much to learn but I have told you what I know."

Chapter Two

Jerusalem

Blinking in the early spring sunshine, Ben stepped out of the seven-story sandstone building housing the Rabbinate, crossed the avenue and walked three blocks down HaHavaselet Street, then turned the corner and entered a tiny café. A petite, pretty woman in her late twenties waved from one of the tables. Her hair was copper, almost the same shade as Ben's; on her face, a spray of freckles framed blue eyes that matched Ben's. A scarf covered her hair and her arms were encased in the long sleeves of a loose, wine-colored blouse above a long, dark green skirt.

She rose from the seat and they exchanged hugs.

"Coffee?" said Marcia Bender, widow, rabbinical student and Ben's sister.

"No, thanks. Just had some."

"So tell me! Do I get to be a rabbi or not?"

Ben said, "I think it'll be okay. Rabbi Farkas has a task for me and he will withhold any action to remove you from rabbinical school until I get him what he wants. Oh, and he wants you to find a 'real' rabbi here and convert again."

"What?"

"He claims to have found something in your first conversion that is wanting. I didn't press for details, because this whole thing is some kind of power play. I'm certain he just invented a reason. You are, I'm sorry to say, only a pawn in this, merely his way of getting me to do something for him."

"To do what, Ben?"

"I'm to take a pulpit in suburban Chicago for a few months and meanwhile close down a charity that was his late cousin's little fiefdom and forward any cash and all the records and papers to him. Let the principal donors know. And if I have time, find out who killed his cousin. Oh and maybe find the rabbi who replaced his cousin, who has disappeared."

"That doesn't sound so easy."

"I'll need a lawyer to shut down the charity but if it's on the up and up, that shouldn't be a big deal. As for the rest, I might hire a local investigator to help."

Marcia shook her head. "Ben, if it's really that simple, he wouldn't need you. He could hire a lawyer by email. And an investigator, too."

"That thought has also occurred to me," Ben said. "But either way, I can make sure that what he wants of me will take—what? Four months?"

"Almost," agreed Marcia.

"So then just forget about all this. Go see one of his recommended rabbis and tell him whatever he needs to hear. Make sure you offer his synagogue or school a healthy donation."

"So this is really just a shakedown?"

"Not *just* a shakedown. He's also hired my services without compensation. Welcome to the land of the *Haredim,* the ultra-orthodox who have taken power and the things that come with it."

"What if I just ignore the demand to convert a second time?"

"I think you'll be okay in the short run. But if you need to return to Israel at some time, Farkas could cause you trouble if he cared to. But—I think this was a one-off and you're just a means to an end. If he comes back at you after I wind this up, I'll expose him as a corrupt official."

"Why not do that *now*?"

"Do you want to graduate on time?"

Chapter Three

Jerusalem

The woman behind the wheel of the baby-blue Mercedes coupe was a knockout.

Barely five feet tall, twenty-five years old but looking younger and a little too busty for her otherwise perfectly proportioned figure, her clear olive skin glowed with good health. A short mop of curly dark hair topped a cover model's almost symmetrical face, including huge brown eyes and long, naturally curly lashes. A small, pickle-shaped patch of white hair above her left eye lent an air of exotic mystery.

As the taxi arrived, Miryam Benkamal opened the door and got out. Wearing a loose T-shirt and walking shorts that displayed her spectacular legs, she ran to the taxi. As Ben and Marcia alighted, she flew into Ben's welcoming arms.

"What took so long?" she said and before Ben could reply, bestowed a passionate kiss that lasted nearly an entire minute.

When he could breathe again, Ben looked at Miryam and smiled. "Rabbi Meir Farkas decided that he would have me cool my heels in reception for an hour or so before he told me what he wanted," he said.

"And what was that, my beloved?" Miryam said.

"Nothing much. How do you feel about living in Chicago for a few months?"

Miryam's face lit up. "How about Chicago for two *years*?"

"What haven't you told me?"

"We got a pile of mail today, at the hotel. You have a letter from Abe Smolkin in Pittsburg. And...I was accepted as a doctoral candidate by the Department of Comparative

Human Development at the University of Chicago. I could start summer classes this June."

Ben's smile was as wide as the four-lane street. "That's wonderful!" he said.

"Congratulations," said Marcia and moved in for a hug.

Ben said, "Why are we meeting here, instead of at the hotel?"

Miryam smiled. "I'm thinking of buying a house," she said and turned to indicate a spacious walled villa with a red-tiled roof. "This one."

Ben and Marcia turned to look.

"That's an awful lot of house," Ben said.

"About 14,000 square feet. And completely furnished. We could rent it out as a vacation home or conference center for most of the year. And maybe someday…"

"What are they asking?" said Marcia.

"Seven million new shekels."

"My God," Marcia said, in a whisper. "It's a steal."

Ben shot his sister a look that said, not for most people.

Marcia said, "Dad left Mort and me a fortune. His half is in trust—he gets some when he's 25 and the rest when he's 35. And Ben, don't get started on where Dad's money came from. I know that it makes you angry. But he repented. He turned back to God and pursued godly ways. He saw to it that his children got a Jewish education. When I was growing up, he bought and sold commercial real estate all over Los Angeles. He did very well and he left half his estate to charities— Childen's Hospital of Los Angeles, the Anti-Defamation League, Hadassah Medical Center here in Jerusalem, the Jewish Federation of Los Angeles, the American Jewish Joint Distribution Committee and several others."

Ben nodded and said, "Marita, mi corazón, you started to say something, 'maybe someday…'"

Miryam smiled. "Maybe someday, in the not too distant future, this could be a school for the children of working mothers. Our foundation could probably..."

Ben smiled. The charitable foundation that Miryam had started began after she inherited a priceless artifact, along with several million dollars. She donated this artifact, a codex of the Hebrew Bible written by a legendary woman scribe, to the Jewish Museum of New York. In return, they had endowed a foundation that was still in its formative stages. When fully staffed and funded, it would provide grants for early childhood education in low-income communities.

Ben gestured toward the villa. "Let's have a look inside."

The ornately carved front door opened into an enormous room with a tile floor, expensive Middle Eastern rugs and a towering ceiling with four skylights. Overstuffed chairs, couches, and love seats were artfully arranged around a very long, low table. Bookshelves lined the walls and a staircase rose in a gentle arc to a second- floor balcony.

"You must see the kitchens," said Miryam and led the way down a corridor into a bright, expansive space. Three Wolf industrial ranges, each with six burners, were spaced along one wall. Copper pots and pans hung from the wall and despite an industrial dishwasher, three long benches, two big sinks, and a walk-in refrigerator, plenty of floor space remained.

Miryam opened a swinging door and Ben and Marcia followed her into a second kitchen that has about half the size of the first—but still enormous.

"This is for dairy," she explained. "The big one is for meat."

Thus could be observed the Biblical commandment not to eat milk with meat.

Miryam opened a door that led to an expansive grassy circular courtyard with a stone fountain at the center. Around its perimeter, Ben counted twelve doors.

Miryam took his arm. "Each one is a bedroom suite with its own bath. One for each of the Twelve Tribes."

"We could have our wedding here," said Ben, feeling a little overwhelmed.

"Of course," said Miryam, as though she had just that minute realized it.

Ben was laughing as she led the way up a second staircase to the upper floor.

"How many bedrooms here?" said Marcia.

Miryam said, "Six, including the master suite. So, eighteen in all."

Ben and Marcia exchanged meaningful glances. Each letter of the Hebrew alphabet carries a numerical value. The letters *hai* and *yud* form the word "hai," which means life. Their numerical value adds to eighteen. Thus in Hebrew, eighteen is shorthand for life.

The second floor offered a view of the Temple Mount, although not as grand as the one from Rabbi Farkas's office. The master bedroom suite had two separate baths, a king-sized bed and an antechamber with a half bath and a comfortable sofa. Down a corridor were five bedrooms, each with its own bath.

"What do you think?" said Miryam, looking at Ben.

Ben shrugged. "For a family of five or six or even ten—way too much. But for a school or a conference center—a splendid space. Why not let the foundation buy it and we'll donate the purchase price."

"Beloved Ben," Miryam began. "I had you take your last clients, in Pittsburgh, *pro bono publico*. And now Rabbi Farkas demands another job without a paycheck. I know you have some savings but I will buy this little palace with part of my inheritance, that money obtained by murder and fraud may be cleansed by going to improve the lives of poor children and their families."

Chapter Four

Jerusalem, the King David Hotel

Ben kicked off his shoes, hung his jacket from the closet door and threw himself down on the bed. A moment later Miryam joined him and they lay side-by-side, silent but communicating nevertheless.

After several minutes, Ben rolled on his side to face Miryam.

"What's troubling you?"

"My wonderful family. They love me so much that they insist on paying for our wedding and choosing the rabbi to perform the ceremony."

Ben said, "How can that be? Your father's family is here, the Benkamals. Your mother's siblings and cousins are in Buenos Aires—the Moshons."

Miryam said. "Exactly. They both want to take charge of our wedding. Also, the Benkamals want us to marry right after Pesach but the Moshons can't come to Israel until May."

Ben reached for Miryam and gently brought her to him. "I suggest a compromise," he said.

Miryam said, "New York in May. We pick the rabbi. Rabbi Zeev, if he's up to it."

"How did you get to be a mind reader?"

"You're trying to teach me to think like a rabbi. So…"

"You pitched the compromise?"

"This morning, on a conference call. The Benkamals are amenable to New York but they insist on picking the rabbi. Or rather, bringing their own."

Ben hugged Miryam tightly and for several minutes they were

silent, kissing, stroking, hugging one another.

Three months earlier, before leaving Pittsburgh for Buenos Aires, Ben had surrendered blood and bone marrow to Doctor Gilbert Rao, chief investigator for a university patient trial of an innovative approach to combatting HIV. Ben had been infected nine years earlier, in the aftermath of a terror bombing in Jerusalem. His face and arms covered with superficial cuts, Ben had assisted first responders and in the process became covered with blood from several other victims.

While Dr. Rao had found no trace of the virus in blood or marrow, he cautioned Ben that his instruments could not detect extremely small levels of the pathogen. Ben had himself tested again when he arrived in Israel, with the same result.

When he came up for air from a long kiss, Ben said, "How do the Moshons feel about New York?"

Miryam said, "Kiss me again and I'll tell you."

A little later she said, "They have no friends in New York—only in Los Angeles—and their rabbi detests New York. He says it's full of Ashkenazi Hasids."

"Is it that they don't like Ashkenazi or that so many New York Jews are Hasids?"

"I didn't ask."

"So where are we?"

"Nowhere."

"Call back. Tell both the Moshons and the Benkamals that we are moving to Chicago and we will invite them all to our wedding but *we* will choose the rabbi and they can come or not come but we are getting married in Chicago after Pesach."

"They won't like that," Miryam said.

"Then we'll have a small wedding. We can send them each a

video to cluck over. I have several good friends in Chicago. And my son is buried there."

Miryam began to weep, almost silently.

After a moment, Ben said, "What's wrong? Why the tears?"

"Your son. He lived only a few hours. It's just not right. You didn't deserve that."

"Thank you, dearest woman. But now I have you."

"Do you ever think about that, Ben? How God punished you for no reason?"

Through Ben's mind flashed a verse from the Book of Job, as the Voice of God calls to Job from a whirlwind:

> Then the LORD answered Job out of the whirlwind and said,
>
> "Who is this that darkeneth counsel by words without knowledge?
>
> "Gird up now thy loins like a man; for I will demand of thee and answer thou me,
>
> Where wast thou when I laid the foundations of the earth?
>
> Declare, if thou hast understanding.
>
> Who hath laid the measures thereof, if thou knowest? Or who hath stretched the line upon it?
>
> Whereupon are the foundations thereof fastened? Or who laid the cornerstone thereof;
>
> When the morning stars sang together and all the sons of God shouted for joy"?

"Earth to Ben," said Miryam. "Come back to me."

Ben smiled. "Sorry, I was pulled into Torah. Listen, I don't believe in a God that punishes the righteous. I don't believe in a God who sends suicide bombers to murder innocents.

We are granted free will; therefore, evil men will do evil deeds. I believe in the God that saved me from that bomb. The God that after many years trying to live a righteous life, sent you to me."

Ben kissed Miryam, a long, passionate kiss that lasted for several minutes.

Miryam said, "You *tried* to live a righteous life? Only *tried?*

"I'm human. Sometimes, especially when I was younger, I was unable to resist the evil inclinations that are always present in mankind."

"Tell me."

"It's a long story."

"Tell me, Ben Scheherazade."

Ben sighed. "My zaide, may his memory be a blessing until the time of the *Moshiach*, was chair of the Talmud department at the Jewish Theological Seminary. He had a good salary but he gave most of it away. To tiny, struggling synagogues, to the poor, to the hungry, to hospitals. People came up to him on the street, men and women he didn't even know and recited their tales of woe—their children were hungry, they were being evicted, their mother was dying—and he never turned them down. Once a well-dressed man came to his office and said, 'You won't remember me but during the Depression when I was out of work and my child was sick, you paid for her doctor—saved her life. Tomorrow she graduates from Harvard Medical School.' He gave *Zaide* a check for $5,000. He gave all of it to a Harlem food bank.

"More than once, *Zaide* came home in the middle of winter, once even in a snowstorm, hatless and coatless. He had given them to someone he'd never seen before, someone who couldn't afford a coat or a warm hat but needed them.

"My *bubbe* was not always happy with such generosity. We lived, then, my grandparents, my mother and me, in a two-bedroom apartment on the fifth floor of a Brooklyn walk-up."

Miriam said, "What's a walk-up?"

"No elevator."

"Oh."

"My *bubbe* told my *zaide* that he shouldn't be so generous. That it wouldn't be terrible if we had a third bedroom, instead of one where my mother had to sleep on a roll-away in the living room. That we could afford to live in a building with an elevator. That it was no sin to have meat once in a while. My *zaide* said, 'We have more than enough and there are many who don't know where their next meal is coming from. There are sick children with no money for a doctor. People live on the streets in the rain and snow. God expects us to help them.' That was my *zaide*.

"But I wanted more," Ben continued. "One summer I went to a camp in the Catskills. One summer only and only for two weeks. A boy in my cabin, Rafi Lobenfeld, had his birthday there. His family came—his parents, aunts, uncles, cousins. Everyone gave him an envelope.

"His wallet was stuffed with cash. He left it in his locker. I got up in the middle of the night and took twenty dollars from that wallet. I don't think he ever noticed."

Miryam stroked Ben's face. "That doesn't sound so terrible."

Ben shook his head. "That was only the beginning. I hid the money in my underwear drawer. When school started—my mother packed me a good lunch every day. Egg salad or tuna, sometimes salmon loaf, tomato and cheese and always fruit and cookies. No meat, because the school gave us milk. There was a kid in my class, a black boy named Nathan. We called him Nate. Every day he brought for lunch one slice of baloney with white bread, not even a *shmear* of mustard. And nothing more. Sometimes he had nothing at all. Sometimes I gave him half my sandwich or an apple and a cookie."

Miryam said, "Like your zaide."

"I wanted to be like him. But I had this money, this stolen loot and it began to bother me. So, one day I gave my lunch to Nate and I snuck out of school and went to McDonald's. I bought a Big Mac, fries, a Coke."

"A Big Mac has cheese."

"Yes. Milk and meat together. A terrible thing for the grandson of a *tzadik*. I was consumed with guilt as I ate every last crumb and then licked my fingers."

"Moshe Binyamin, you're telling me that eating a Big Mac and stealing twenty dollars are the worst things you ever did? That you are a terrible person?"

"No, not a terrible person. But human. One who feels the evil impulse and gives in to it. But I did try to make atonement. I stayed in touch with Rafi Lobenfeld. I sent his son $500 for his bar mitzvah. And I gave the rest of the money that I stole to Nate."

"So you repented. You made things right."

Ben shook his head, no. "I made them worse. Nate gave that money to his mother and she beat him for stealing and made him give it back. I put it in the poor box at our shul."

Miryam said, "I thank HaShem for making you atone for your sins by tricking a phalanx of bossy nuns, charming the ferocious mastiff Samson and leaping into my backyard dressed as a Roman Catholic priest."

Ben shook his head, smiling. "God didn't do that. That was all me." Then he laughed, recalling the moment and a moment later so did Miryam.

Miryam said, "We still barely know each other, yet I feel so close to you. But I have many little questions to ask."

Ben smiled. "For instance?"

"Do you have any special skills that I should know about?"

"I can wiggle my ears."

Miryam giggled. "Show me!"

Ben twisted his torso so Miryam could see both ears. He wiggled first his left, then the right. Then both together.

Unable to contain herself, Miryam howled with laughter.

Ben lay down again beside her.

"Now you," he said. "Show me your special talents."

Miryam said, "Pull the covers up until you can see my toes."

Ben doubled the pillow under his head and slowly pulled the blanket and sheet up.

"I can cross my toes," she said and proceeded to put the little toe on each foot over the one next to it. And then the third toe over the fourth.

Ben giggled. "Never know when that might prove useful."

"I can also sing song lyrics backward."

"No! Really?"

"Try me."

"'America The Beautiful.'"

"That's easy," Miryam said.

And she sang,

"Skies spacious for beautiful O

Grain of waves amber for,

Majesties mountains purple for

Plain fruited the above!

America, America,

Thee on grace his shed God

Brotherhood with good thy crown And

Sea Shining to sea From!"

Ben broke up. "And in perfect pitch! How about, "'*Hotel California.*'"

Miryam smiled. "One of my favorites." And she sang:

"*Hair my in wind cool highway desert dark a On,*

Colitas of smell warm Air the through up rising

distance, the in ahead up Light shimmering—"

Doubled over with laughter, Ben raised an arm for her to stop.

When he could find his voice, Ben said, "How on earth did you learn to do that?"

"I had a music teacher and I guess she was a nice lady but you could smell her bad breath. from the fourth row. So, when we were supposed to learn lyrics, a bunch of us taught ourselves to sing them backward, just to get back at her."

Miryam said. "What else can *you* do?"

"I'll have to get out of bed for this one."

"Don't be long."

Ben rolled out of bed, went into the bathroom and came back with half a glass of water. He looked around the room.

"Do you see the vase with the orange flowers on the table?"

"Sure."

Ben took a long sip from the glass.

He faked pulling his shorts down.

"Ben!"

He pursed his lips and squirted a stream of water halfway across the room to land on the flowers.

Laughing even harder than before, Miryam clapped her hands in delight.

Ben made a little bow, set the glass on the nightstand and slid back into bed.

"My turn," Miryam said. "How did you learn to do that?"

"In the second grade, right after my permanent teeth came in, a big kid grabbed a piece of pie right off my plate in the lunchroom. I jumped up and tried to hit him but he punched me in the mouth and that was the fight.

"That punch pushed my two front teeth a little apart. My mother wanted me to get braces but there was no money. And my grandfather said that the space between my teeth would add character to my face.

"About a year later I saw an older kid, a teenager, with a gap between his teeth, spitting tobacco juice. He showed me how to do it but I hated the taste. So I use water."

Miryam said, "That punch. Is that why you learned to fight?"

"Pretty much. I got tired of being pushed around and there was a dojo in Brooklyn that enrolled kids under ten free.

"Anyway, those are all my special talents," he said.

"No, no," Miryam said, "What about all the women who want you in their bed? Did you ever want to do that?"

"All the time. But I never do. I stop myself."

Miryam smiled. "Except with me. But it took you long enough."

Ben said, "I don't get it. I don't approach these women. I try to distance myself and yet so many think I'm being coy. Why me? I'm short, not particularly handsome and have red hair."

Miryam pulled Ben closer. "We—women—know who you are. We sense it. We know that you are kind and that you'll never harm us. And we know that you are very brave—you have the heart of a lion—and you will do whatever task you set yourself, no matter how dangerous or difficult."

Ben shook his head. "Thank you, Marita but I don't see how you can know that."

"Because we are women. We know things that men do not. And every day I thank HaShem that of all the women on the face of the earth, you chose me."

Ben smiled and again they held each other for several minutes. Then Ben moved away to look into Miryam's face.

"We are together," he said. "We have our health, we are not poor and the rest of our lives is before us," Ben said. "I would like to have your entire family witness our marriage but most of all, I want us together under a *chuppah* [wedding canopy] to observe the commandments and the customs of our ancestors as we are joined together."

Miryam said, "I'll handle my family. Now let's take a shower and then... And afterward, we can read our mail and order room service."

§

Ninety minutes later, Ben and Miryam sat down at a table full of delicious food. Ben tasted the cucumber salad, ate a slice of roast chicken and opened the first of a small pile of mail that had caught up with them after weeks of international travel.

At that moment, Ben's phone rang. He checked the caller: Rabbi Farkas.

Annoyed, he turned the phone off.

A few minutes of eating and reading went by before the suite's phone rang.

Sighing Ben left the table and picked up the phone.

"This is Rabbi Farkas," said the voice in his ear. "Rabbi Shevitz's wife, Leah, has disappeared. You must go to Ben Gurion [airport] immediately. A ticket is waiting at the El Al counter, along with a set of instructions. When you get to Chicago, you are to contact Special Agent Pat Gilmore of the FBI. At Beth Ohr, they will help you find a kosher hotel."

Ben said, "Rabbi, I'm in Israel to get married. I didn't agree to be at your beck and call for everything about Beth Ohr."

Farkas said, "Leah Shevitz is Rabbi Shevitz' wife. She's an accountant. She keeps the books for L'Dor v' Dor. Your plane leaves in three hours. If you're not on it, be assured that your sister will be on the next flight to Los Angeles."

The line went dead.

Ben turned to find Miryam standing behind him.

"I heard," she said. "Go. I'll stay, buy the house and hire a school administrator and then try to get some agreement between the Moshons and Benkamals."

Ben said, "I love you, Marita."

Miryam said, "And I love you. Be careful. Come back to me soon."

Chapter Five

Aboard El Al Flight LY7

In a middle seat two rows from the back of the plane in Economy, Ben was squeezed between a large, older woman with a peculiarly offensive body odor and a tall, bearded young man who passed the time playing video games that emitted strange, annoying sounds. He tried to make the best of the situation, pushing his seat back and closing his eyes but it was a losing battle.

Abruptly he sat up, retrieved the typewritten page of instructions that had been waiting with his ticket and tried to make sense of it.

Mrs. Shevitz was 31, employed as an accountant in a small manufacturing company near Beth Ohr. She also kept the charity's books. Her car had been found at an intersection about 6:30 am on the previous day. Both doors were open, the engine was running and a small amount of blood matching her type—B negative—was found on the steering wheel. Police entered her unlocked home and found no one there. A bedside lamp had fallen from its place on a nightstand and its bulb shattered. There was no evidence that anything had been taken from the home.

Two days earlier, the couple's two children, ages two and four, had been sent to stay with Mrs. Shevitz's mother, Sharon Gordon, in Skokie, another Chicago suburb.

Police interviewed Gordon and learned that the children had arrived the afternoon of the day that Rabbi Shevitz vanished.

The FBI agent running the abduction case was Special Agent Pat Gilmore. A handwritten Chicago phone number was the last thing on the page.

But what was his mission? Ben wondered. Was he to find Mrs. Shevitz? Rabbi Shevitz? Or continue with his original instructions to close down L'Dor v'Dor, notify the donors and send all records and funds to Farkas.

He decided that his first task, upon reaching New York, where he would change planes for Chicago with a two-hour layover, was to call Farkas and confirm his instructions.

He folded the paper and returned it to his coat pocket. Then he took the unopened letter from another pocket and carefully tore one end off. The sender was Rabbi Abe Smolkin, his Yeshiva classmate, close personal friend and just then the director of the Pittsburgh Jewish Community Center. Abe was also a lawyer.

Inside the envelope, he found a handwritten note from Abe, a typed page of what looked like the minutes of a synagogue's board of directors meeting and a fancy vellum certificate issued by Banker's Life, a giant Chicago insurance company. The certificate was proof that an endowment policy had been purchased by the Sanoker Home for the Aged and the Sanoker Congregation of Berona, Pennsylvania. The endowment would pay Mark T. Glass of Cambridge, MA, the sum of $105,412 each January 3 for the next thirty years.

While Rabbi Ben Maimon was his Hebrew name and title, Ben's legal name was Mark Thompson Glass. It had also been his late father's name. No one, including his beloved grandparents, could or would tell him how his father had come by Thompson as a middle name.

But he, Rabbi Ben Maimon, was indeed Mark Thompson Glass and this certificate guaranteed him a substantial yearly income for the next thirty years.

With wonderment and joy, he read Abe's note:

Hey Ben!

The cash that you recovered came to a little over $21 million. I incorporated the retirement home and the synagogue into a single not-for-profit and after an extended negotiation with our friendly IRS dudes, it was agreed that this cash had been stolen from the nonprofit and as far as could be determined, it was chiefly life insurance payouts. We made a token tax **payment ($100,000) to save everyone's face.**

I have every reason to believe that the Sanoker, in the next few years, will partner with a local builder to develop some of the land on the western slope of Mt. Sanoker for residential usage. Per a unanimous vote of the board of directors, half will be set aside for low-income buyers and renters. The board, which is chaired by your pal Abby Silverblatt, RN, also voted to award you ten percent of the sum that you recovered, as a reward for recovering it. At my suggestion, this comes in the form of a 30-year endowment, which should save you a bundle in taxes and allow you to take more pro bono cases.

One more thing: Mrs. Lois Seligman, in gratitude for you recovering her Rembrandt sketch, at my suggestion has endowed a school for artists and musicians, to be built on land adjacent to the existing board and care. It will be open to all children ages six to 18, at low or no tuition. Until they get more funding, they can accommodate eighty kids for after-school and evening classes.

Stay in touch, my friend!

Abe "Whatchoo" Smolkin!

PS: The shul is looking to hire a rabbi. The job is yours if you want it.

Ben carefully folded the three papers, returned them to the envelope and then to his coat pocket. He couldn't wait to tell Miryam, who had encouraged and all but committed him to take a missing person case in Pittsburgh as his civic duty.

He sat back in his seat and tried to ignore the incessant beeping and the odor emanating from his seatmate.

Chapter Six

Chicago O'Hare Airport

"Mr. Glass?"

Ben looked up from the baggage carousel where he waited to claim his suitcase.

"Mark Thomson Glass?" said a very pretty woman in her thirties. She was tall and well proportioned, clad in a conservatively cut charcoal suit. Her coat was open, revealing a belt holster with a badge and a 40mm Glock pistol.

Ben said, "That's me. I usually go by my Hebrew name, Rabbi Ben Maimon."

"Please come with me," said the woman, flashing an FBI credential.

"I need to be able to read and inspect your ID," Ben said.

The woman approached and held the card case where Ben could see it.

Ben said, "Special Agent Pat Gilmore. I was going to call you when I found a place to spend the night."

"Come with me," she said.

"What about my luggage?"

"We'll take care of it."

"Where am I going?"

"First, to my office. Then, we'll see."

"Am I under arrest?" Ben said.

"Not yet. I could arrange that, if you like."

"What would be the charge?"

Agent Gilmore frowned. "I don't have time to play games. Come with me now or I'll have you in handcuffs."

"What is the charge?" said Ben in a voice loud enough to carry to the hundreds of people clustered around the carousel. "I'm not going anywhere until I know why I should accompany you?"

Agent Gilmore frowned again. "It's in connection with a kidnapping."

"The kidnapping of Mrs. Manny Shevitz? I've been in Israel for the last two weeks. Before that, I was in Argentina. I know nothing about the kidnapping except what I was told by Rabbi Farkas, in Jerusalem, several hours ago."

"We can help you," said Gilmore. But if you want to make a scene, I'm glad to oblige you."

Ben decided to see how this unexpected turn of events played out.

"If you let me get my baggage, I'm happy to go with you."

"A woman is missing. She has two young children."

Ben nodded. "There is nothing that I know that could help you find her. But just give me a few minutes and I'll gladly go with you."

"You have five minutes and then you're in handcuffs."

Three minutes dragged by before the baggage carousel sprang to life. Less than a minute later, Ben's suitcase came into view and he grabbed it.

Ben turned to Gilmore. "Let's go," he said.

Chapter Seven

Chicago

Under a threatening early March sky, with strong gusts off Lake Michigan and a few drops of wind-borne rain spotting its windshield, a dark blue SUV turned off Roosevelt Road onto South Leavitt and then into a broad driveway that led to underground parking. In minutes Ben was riding an elevator that stopped at a top floor. He followed Agent Ed Roberts, tall and husky with a salt-and-pepper goatee, down the hall, with Agent Gilmore almost on Ben's heels. They stopped at a small, well-appointed conference room and Roberts held the door.

Ben took the seat at the head of the table, drawing a frown from Roberts and a smile from Gilmore. "It's not often that I meet a man with your kind of chutzpah," said Gilmore, pronouncing it "chuts paw."

Ben smiled back. "Now that I'm here, what is that you wanted so urgently?"

Gilmore swiveled toward Roberts and said, "Ed, why don't you ask Marcy to bring in some coffee?"

Roberts sighed and left the room.

Gilmore and Ben remained silent until Roberts returned.

"Why are you in Chicago, Rabbi?" said Gilmore.

Ben said, "Rabbi Meir Farkas, a very influential member of the Israeli Rabbinate, threatened to deport my sister, a rabbinical student, unless I helped him wind up a charity that his late cousin, Shmuel Rubin, ran. Rabbi Rubin died recently."

"Are you being paid for this?" Roberts asked.

"No. In effect, I am paying blackmail to a powerful, almost

untouchable, government official."

"Why were you in Israel?"

"To marry my fiancé, whose family lives in Israel. Well, about half of them. The rest are in Argentina."

Gilmore said, "And that's why you were in Buenos Aires for more than three weeks?"

Understanding that the agent had just revealed that she had accessed either his email or the ICE files that recorded exits and entries to the country, Ben nodded his agreement. "To meet her family. Before we married."

"What do you know about L'Dor v'Dor?"

"The words mean something like, 'from one generation to the next.' It relates to the Jewish obligation to educate our children not only in worldly matters but also in the language, history, and customs of our ancestors."

"And that is what the charity does?"

"My understanding, which comes entirely from Rabbi Farkas, is that it raises funds to send young men to Israel to study to become Orthodox rabbis."

"And you are an Orthodox rabbi?"

Ben shook his head, no, "There are four 'streams' of Judaism today. The Orthodox, who seek to preserve intact the customs, practices and societal mores of early 20th Century Judaism, which were pretty much the same as 18th Century Judaism. The Reform Movement seeks to reconcile Jewish worship, practices, and customs with the reality of the modern world that we live in. The Conservative Movement, which is my stream, seeks to strike a balance between these two extremes. Finally, Reconstructionist Judaism grew out of the Conservative Movement and seeks a somewhat different path of dealing with the modern world."

Roberts nodded his understanding. "Why would Farkas send you, a Conservative, to perform a service for an Orthodox organization?"

Ben shrugged. "Hard to say. But seeing as you are FBI agents and that I have a very thick FBI file which presumably you have read or at least skimmed, then you should know that I'm a freelance troubleshooter. You might call me a Jewish paladin."

Gilmore opened her mouth to speak but before she could, Ben continued.

"And as there is also an even thicker FBI file about my late father's exploits, I wish to make you aware of two things: Although we have the same name, my parents divorced when I was a few weeks old and I never laid eyes on my father. And I do not hold my sister Marcia responsible for the crimes that our father committed over a long and ugly career."

Gilmore smiled again, this time a genuine one. "That will certainly save us some time, Rabbi."

"If you're telling the truth," added Roberts.

"When it comes to lies," said Ben in an even tone of voice, "It is against the law for *me* to lie to the FBI. The FBI, meaning its agents, can lie to me as much as an agent cares to and without penalty. So, I will believe you until I don't and you can believe me until I prove otherwise."

This time Roberts laughed. "You're some piece of work," he said.

Ben shook his head. "Piece of work—because I'm not afraid of you?"

Roberts just stared at Ben.

"I have no reason to lie to you," Ben said. "And if you've looked at my file, you'll see that while my methods are often unorthodox, I usually get along well with law enforcement, as long as we are straight with each other. Now tell me why I am here."

Gilmore said. "Some of the people associated with L'Dor v'Dor are persons of interest to us, in a variety of ways."

Ben spread his hands, palms up as if to say, So what?

"It would be helpful if you could tell us in what way these people are associated with the charity."

Ben said, "I've never met Rabbi Rubin. I'm told that Rabbi Shevitz's wife, Leah, is an accountant and who keeps the charity's books. Those are the only two names that I am aware of that are associated with L'Dor v'Dor."

"But you will undoubtedly learn more about this outfit as you begin to look around," said Gilmore.

"Which I have not been able to start, because you snatched me up at the airport."

"Don't get smart with us, Glass," said Roberts.

"Or? There is a law against getting smart? You and your colleagues are anti-smart? You're pro dumb?"

Gilmore guffawed and Roberts shot her a warning glance.

"What Agent Roberts means," began Gilmore, "Is that it's better for everyone if you cooperate."

Ben shook his head. "No. It's better for *you*. You could get a subpoena and go through the charity's books—which I have yet to see—but instead, you dragged me down here and threatened me. Is it because getting a subpoena for a Jewish charity is difficult? Or because a judge will want some evidence and all you have is a hunch. Or some hope. Or a deep-seated anti-Semitism."

Roberts looked like he could cheerfully throttle Ben. Gilmore shook her head, sending dark curls flying.

"This doesn't have to be adversarial, Rabbi. And nobody here is anti-Semitic."

Ben shook his head. "Most anti-Semites don't even know it. My guess is that two out of five FBI agents believe one or more untrue and unflattering Jewish stereotypes.

"I don't care how you feel about Jews," Ben continued. "I cannot work for two masters. You can threaten me, you can probably have me jailed if it suits you but I am not a threat to the FBI. I will do as Rabbi Farkas asked. In the process, if I come across anything that might be of legitimate interest to the FBI, I will do my duty as a citizen and share that information with you. And by the way, I would do that if I had never met either of you and if you hadn't dragooned me from the airport.

"Now, if you'll excuse me, I haven't slept in nearly two days. I must find a bed, I'll be in touch when I have something to tell you."

Ben got to his feet. "Please have my suitcase out in front. I'm going to call an Uber car."

Roberts said, "We haven't released you."

Ben said, "Then you'll have to arrest me because I'm leaving."

Chapter Eight

Chicago

The Uber car was waiting in front of the building. Shivering from the cold seeping through his semi-tropical clothes, Ben stowed his suitcase in the trunk and climbed into the back seat. "Skokie," he said and promptly fell asleep.

"Hey!" said the driver and Ben opened one eye. "*Where* in Skokie?"

Ben gave him an address.

Twenty minutes later he felt the car stop. He sat up.

He got out of the car, waited while the driver popped the trunk and hauled the suitcase out.

The car drove off. In the street, Ben knelt and opened the suitcase. His fingers explored the bag's inner wall until he found what he was looking for. He pulled out a metallic, dime-sized device and dropped it down a nearby storm drain.

Then, dragging the wheeled suitcase behind him, he walked three blocks to the home of Rabbi Mitchell Katz, MD, Ph.D.

Stopping at the two-story house behind a neatly trimmed lawn, he pulled out his iPhone and found the message Mitch had sent the previous day.

"*Lag b'Omer* + *life*. Second floor, third door."

On his phone, Ben used a Hebrew app to look up the date of Lag b'Omer, a minor feast celebrating the end of a plague that killed many disciples of Rabbi Akiva, a First Century sage. This year it fell on March 30, so he converted that to 0330, its numeric equivalent, then added 18—life—which yielded 0348

Ben climbed three stairs to the front porch, tapped 0348 into the Schlage keyless entry lock and twisted the deadbolt back.

Inside, he climbed two short flights of stairs to a hallway, then found the third door and entered the Katz's guest room. Five minutes later, after undressing and brushing his teeth, he was asleep.

Chapter Nine

Skokie, IL

Five hours after falling into bed, Ben sat up. The odor wafting under the door caused his mouth to water. Grinning, he got out of bed, showered, put on fresh clothes and made his way downstairs to the dining room, where Marcia Katz, Mitch's wife, was placing a platter with a roasted chicken on the table.

"Ben!" she said, squealing with joy. She set the platter down and embraced Ben, a tall, lean woman with a big "Jewfro" of salt-and-pepper curls.

"It's been too long," Marcia Katz said and hugged Ben a second time.

"Agreed," said Ben.

"And you're getting married! Wonderful! When do we meet this lucky woman?"

Ben pulled out a chair and sat down. "Soon, I think. She's in Jerusalem, buying a giant house that we'll never live in, hiring a school administrator to start a daycare center and trying to cajole the Israeli and Argentine halves of her family into attending a wedding at a place of *our* choosing. And by the way, *I'm* the lucky one. Miryam is brilliant, gorgeous, funny and kind of rich, although I don't care about the last thing."

Marcia Katz said, "You should wait and tell both us all about her. Mitch is taking a shower but he'll be down in a minute."

§

"Do I understand that you now have a sister and a brother?" said Mitch Katz. He was well over six feet, nearly bald and working on a paunch. Ben's closest friend and for two years at M.I.T. his roommate, Mitch had completed rabbinical school, found an associate rabbi's post on the pricey end of Long Island—and after a year quit and enrolled in medical school. He now practiced psychiatry in a suburban medical group.

Ben said, "That's right. Marcia is 28, a rabbinical student in Israel and Mort, just starting first grade. We are all half-siblings."

Mitch said, "What brings you to Chicagoland?"

"I was hired to shut down a charity whose founder has died," Ben said and explained the circumstances, omitting his visit with the FBI.

"Is there anything we can do to help?" Marcia asked.

"Maybe. Are you still active as a CPA?"

"Oh yes. I have eleven employees now. Why do you ask?"

"The wife of a rabbi connected to the charity is missing. I'm told she was an accountant. Is there a professional association that she might belong to?"

Marcia said, "Money Minders of Greater Chicago. I'm executive VP this year."

"If you could find someone who knows Leah Shevitz, I'd like to talk to them."

"It could take a few days," Marcia said. "I'll put out an email tonight."

"Thanks," Ben said. "Have either of you heard of a charity called L'Dor v'Dor?"

Mitch nodded, yes. "Through our shul. We get a brochure or something every year. Something about sending high school seniors to Israel, I think."

"That's it," Ben said. "Have you ever contributed?"

Marcia said, "I think we send them fifty dollars every year."

"Would you have a canceled check?" Ben said.

"We can get that online," Marcia said. "Maybe right after dinner, if that's okay."

Mitch said, "Why do you need that?"

"It will tell me what bank they used to deposit the check."

Chapter Ten

Steins, Illinois

Ben turned off Finkelstein Boulevard onto Epstein Road and a block later the synagogue came into view. It was a very large modern building that as Ben drew closer resolved itself into a complex of three similar and adjacent structures. He turned into the driveway, threaded his way past half a dozen cars in a lot that could easily accommodate 300 and parked near the Flora Orenstein Community center, a three-story building with a gymnasium and a natatorium.

Ben walked past this building until he encountered a somewhat smaller and slightly newer structure. A modest sign announced the Rifka R. Mermelstein Child Center. Judging by the ages and apparent ethnicities of the children in the fenced playground, this was a preschool facility that served the entire community. Finally Ben found the main entrance to Beth Ohr Synagogue and as he entered the building spied two dedication plaques: Joseph Bodenstein and Yakov Rosenstein were the buildings' principal donors.

Bodenstein, Rosenstein, Epstein Orenstein, Finkelstein—a lot of –steins, Ben thought before realizing that perhaps this was why this small city near the Wisconsin state line was called Steins.

The door to the synagogue office was open. Inside Ben found three women of various ages, races, and sizes.

"I'm Rabbi Ben Maimon," he began and the oldest of the trio, a white woman in late middle age with thinning, reddish-brown hair falling to her chin, frowned.

"Oh dear," she said. "We weren't expecting you until the end of the week."

Ben shrugged.

The youngest of the three women stood up, a chubby, ebony-skinned woman a few months shy of delivering a baby and smiled.

"Rabbi, we have a problem."

Ben waited.

"Rabbi Shevitz's office is locked and we can't find the master key."

Finally, the third woman, a dark-haired, olive-skinned beauty in her thirties, spoke up.

"We called a locksmith but they want a fortune to come out and drill the lock. We just don't have a budget for that."

"I understand," Ben said, not fathoming how a big, busy synagogue with new buildings and an enormous parking lot couldn't round up a hundred dollars.

"What about Rabbi Rubin's office," Ben said.

"The same thing," said the older woman. "I'm Mollie Levy," she said. "Acting synagogue administrator."

Ben turned to the obviously pregnant one and they exchanged smiles.

"Tracey Washington," she said. "I'm a temp. Although Mrs. Levy thinks…"

A glance from the older woman stopped her in mid-sentence.

Ben turned to the slim, dark woman, noting the sparkling diamond ring and wedding band on the third finger of her left hand. "And you are?"

She blushed. "Julie Morgenstern, president of the Sisterhood."

Concealed in the cuff of his left trouser was a set of lock picks but Ben decided not to reveal that he could open almost any locked door. He reached instead into his trouser pocket and came out with a roll of hundreds. He peeled three of them off and laid them on the nearest desk.

"Call the locksmith," he said. "While I'm waiting for an office to use, where can I find Josh Green?"

Morgenstern looked at Ben, a note of alarm in her voice. "Why do you need to see Josh?" she said in a low voice.

Ben now realized that all three women were behaving oddly. Something must be terribly wrong—and then he knew what it was.

Ben said, "He must be in hiding—is that right?"

Levy said, "Then you know why."

Ben shook his head. "I can guess. Rabbi Rubin is dead. Rabbi Shevitz and his wife missing, possibly abducted. Mr. Green fears that he might be next."

Morgenstern gave a tiny nod. "We're all a little spooked. And for that reason, I should ask you for some identification."

"Of course," Ben said and took out his passport and his wallet, then extracted his Massachusetts driver's license and a photocopy of his diploma from the Jewish Theological Seminary.

Morgenstern looked both over. "So, you go by your Hebrew name?"

Ben nodded, yes. "I bear my father's legal name. He was a scoundrel and my parents divorced while I was an infant. I prefer the name that my mother and grandparents, of blessed memory, called me as a child."

Morgenstern handed the papers back. "I'll try to locate Josh," she said. "Do you need a place to stay?"

"I have friends in Skokie," Ben said.

"We keep a small apartment here. Upstairs," she added.

"For visiting scholars?"

Morgenstern smiled, revealing flawless teeth and charmingly

mismatched dimples. "You should stay here, in the shul. It's probably safer than going back and forth to Skokie."

Ben nodded. "Thank you. I'll move in tomorrow—my friends are expecting me for dinner tonight."

Morgenstern turned to Mrs. Levy. "I'll show him the apartment," she said and Levy opened her desk drawer, hunted through it for several seconds and came out with a set of keys.

"Don't be too long," Levy said. "We've got to finish the mailing before 5:00."

Before they could leave, the door opened and a tall, bearded man with skin the color of tea and wearing a bright green turban over stained denim overalls stepped inside.

Morgenstern said, "Rabbi this is Mr. Singh, our maintenance supervisor. Mr. Singh, this is Rabbi Ben Maimon, who is filling in for Rabbi Shevitz."

Singh smiled, displaying large, very white and even teeth. "A pleasure, Rabbi," he said with no discernible accent. "Please call me Ujjal, my given name."

"Bright, clean, holy—a fine name," Ben said and Singh's eyes widened.

"You are knowledgeable about the Sikh?" he said.

Ben shook his head. "When I was just out of rabbinical school, I worked part-time in a school, teaching Hebrew. The maintenance supervisor, an older man, was a Sikh and he satisfied my curiosity about your people by teaching me a few names and sharing a little of your history."

"I would be honored to teach you more," Singh said.

"If we can both find the time."

Morgenstern said, "We were just leaving, Mr. Singh."

"Peace onto you both," said Singh.

Chapter Eleven

Steins

Morgenstern led Ben to a small elevator down the corridor. They rode to the third-floor side-by-side in silence. The door opened and Morgenstern brushed against Ben as both started forward at the same time.

"Sorry," she murmured and Ben considered the possibility that the brief meeting of their bodies might not have been accidental.

"You're not married?" she said as they moved down the corridor.

"Engaged," he replied.

She stopped at the end of the corridor and unlocked a door of dark wood. Inside Ben found a small, well-lit bedroom with a full-size bed, dresser, and a nightstand. A bathroom, kitchenette with a half-sized refrigerator and a microwave oven. A book-lined study with a writing desk completed the apartment.

"Very cozy," Ben said and held his hand out for the keys.

"I'm sure you'll be comfortable here," Morgenstern said, placing the keys in his hand their fingers touching for just a beat too long.

"If there's anything you need, please call me," she said and took a business card from her pocket and pressed it into his hand.

Ben looked at the card.

"You're an attorney," he said. "What sort of practice do you have?"

"I'm a sole practitioner," she replied. "A little of everything, I guess. Wills, estates, probate, divorces, adoptions, civil litigation. Real estate, that sort of thing."

"And your husband?" Ben said.

Morgenstern looked down. "He's also an attorney," she said and turned to leave.

Ben said, "Thanks for everything, Mrs. Morgenstern."

"It's *Ms*. Morgenstern. You can call me Julie."

§

Ben found linens and blankets in the closet and began making up the bed. As he worked, he heard music that seemed to come from his floor. The sound was muted but Ben could make out the melody, a traditional Hebrew hymn.

Locking the door behind him, he made his way downstairs to the Sanctuary. One of the doors was open and Ben slipped in and sat in a shadowed back row on the men's side of the room.

Arrayed before him on the bima was a choir of a dozen men and women. From the women's side, one voice was heard above the others, a pure soprano that rose to an almost impossible pitch. The singer seemed to be in early middle age, very tall, with an astonishing hourglass figure and long, dark hair streaked with gray piled high atop her head.

An elfin man in a chauffeur's uniform sat down next to Ben, who could not help noticing the man's prominent walleye and that he had advanced kyphosis—the condition known as hunchback. "I.M. Falkenberg," he said, extending a small, pale hand. "Mr. Finkelstein's chauffeur."

"Rabbi Ben Maimon," Ben replied. "Call me Ben or Rabbi Ben."

"You can call me Igor," replied the hunchback. "I'm here to fetch Mrs. Finkelstein."

"Which one is she?"

"The tall one," he said.

"She has an amazing voice," Ben said.

"I'm also her bodyguard," Igor said, opening his coat to reveal an elaborate harness that Ben imagined was designed to help straighten his spine.

"Bodyguard?" Ben said. "You're armed?"

"Yes, I'm strapped," Igor said, fingering the butt of a pistol in a shoulder holster almost invisible among the leather of the harness.

"Why does Mrs. Finkelstein need a bodyguard?"

Igor shrugged. "I just do what Mr. Finkelstein tells me. And Mrs. Finkelstein, of course."

As the musical prayer drew to a close, Ben found himself muttering the Hebrew aloud for a few beats.

"Good meeting you, Igor," he said.

"Likewise," he said.

Chapter Twelve

STEINS

Before 7:00 the next morning, Ben had breakfasted on a bran muffin and coffee in the Katz's kitchen, drove himself to Steins in an inconspicuous black two-year-old Honda Accord that he'd rented the previous afternoon, carried his suitcase up to the tiny apartment and had begun to unpack.

But when he opened the small closet, he found it full of banker boxes. Peering at the boxes, each box was marked with a year in the 1940s, plus the word "synagogue records." Probably, a historical research project of some kind, Ben decided.

Improvising, he hung his two extra suits and six dress shirts from shelves in the library and put the rest in a dresser drawer.

Wearing dark slacks and a light blue shirt, he took the elevator down to the office just as Mrs. Levy came in the front door, lugging a pair of bulging paper shopping bags. Ben hurried to the door, relieved her of the bags and after she unlocked the office, followed her inside. "I'll be back in a little while," she said, taking the bags and heading down the corridor in a slow, painful, arthritic walk before turning into what turned out to be a large kitchen. Ben followed and from the kitchen doorway, watched her stow several bundles of something wrapped in waxed paper in a refrigerator, followed by tubs of cream cheese. The second bag held dozens of frozen bagels. She began setting bags of a half-dozen each out on a stainless-steel table to thaw.

"I have to do everything now," she said over her shoulder. "Ellie Evans, our executive director, quit the day Rabbi Shevitz disappeared. I was her assistant. Now the board will probably offer me her job but I tell you, Rabbi, I don't want it. Let them hire someone with administrative experience. I'm a high-school graduate and a born follower, if you know what I mean."

Ben said, "Mrs. Levy, how many members do we have?"

Levy stopped unpacking bagels and turned to face Ben. "Two weeks ago, we had 497 family units. About 1100 adults, give or take. Before Rabbi Shevitz came, we had about 550 families. When Rabbi Rubin retired, about fifty families left and joined Anshe Yakov, the other Orthodox temple. And then, when Rabbi Shevitz and his wife disappeared, more people canceled their memberships. Three families just yesterday. About fifty altogether, so far."

"Have they a demanded dues refunds?"

"Most. Technically, they have no claim on a refund, because we're more than sixty days into the fiscal year. But Dr. Green and the board decided to give a refund to anyone who asked. We're hoping most of them come back when all this *mishegas* is over."

Ben nodded. "That's why you have no cash to call a locksmith?"

Levy finished her work and turned back toward Ben. "According to our treasurer, Mrs. Singer, we're draining our emergency fund just to meet payroll and utilities. We have a pretty good endowment, I've heard more than $5 million, but it's not liquid. Stocks and bonds. And real estate. But I let the bosses worry about that."

Down the hall, an office phone rang.

Mrs. Levy started down the corridor.

"I'll get it," Ben said and loped down the polished tiles to the office.

"Congregation Beth Ohr," he said into the mouthpiece.

"Rabbi Ben, is that you?" said a female voice.

"Yes. Who is this?"

"Julie Morgenstern. We met yesterday?"

"Of course. What can I do for you, Mrs. Morgenstern?"

"Ms., if you please. Or Julie. If you want to meet Dr. Green, Josh Green, our congregational president, go to the public library on Finkelstein and Fourth, in one hour."

"The library in one hour. How will I know Dr. Green?"

"See the Reference Librarian."

"Thank you, Ms. Morgenstern."

"It's Julie," she said, with an awkward little laugh.

"Thanks, Ms. Morgenstern," Ben said and eased the phone back onto its cradle.

The last thing he needed, Ben told himself, was another woman trying to attract his romantic interest.

Chapter Thirteen

Steins

The Dorothy and Samuel Finkelstein Memorial Library was an imposing, three-story yellow brick building with an adjacent parking structure. Ben left the Honda on the first parking level and entered the building through a mezzanine door. Directly below him, on the ground floor, was the Reference Desk.

"I'm here to see Dr. Green," Ben told a petite, gray-haired woman of perhaps sixty, who smiled through ill-fitting dentures and pointed to an unmarked door.

"In the staff lounge," she said in a pleasant, Midwestern voice.

Ben pushed the door open and stepped into a long, narrow room with dark green carpets. A few chairs, a small table and a couple of floor lamps were the only furniture. On the far wall were two doors, labeled "Men" and "Women."

In the middle of the room stood a tall, heavy man with skin the color of milk chocolate. He wore a dark suit and a gray fedora.

"Dr. Green?" Ben said.

Without answering, the man approached, then grabbed Ben's shoulders with both hands and spun him around.

"Stay put," he said, in a high tenor voice that belonged to a man half his size.

Ben brought his right leg up behind him and struck the man's groin, hard.

He uttered a deep grunt and released Ben's shoulders.

At high speed, Ben took two steps forward, whirled on his left foot and delivered a second blow to the groin area.

The big man staggered and fell. He produced a large-caliber automatic pistol; another kick sent it flying across the room.

The big man got to his feet, slowly.

Ben said, "Are we done?"

The man launched a roundhouse right at Ben's head.

Ben spun to his right as he bent backward, seized the man's right bicep in his own left hand and his wrist with his right hand. In a single, swift movement he pushed the bicep and pulled the wrist and a sickening sound of tearing cartilage came from the elbow. The man staggered and fell.

Ben moved to the wall and retrieved the handgun.

The woman's restroom door opened and a tall, thin man with a neatly trimmed gray beard stepped into the room, holding both hands, palms open in front of him.

"There's no reason to kill us," he said. "I'll pay you! Twice—no, three times—what you were promised."

Ben ejected the cartridge in the automatic's chamber, removed the magazine and then with two quick moves of his hands separated the slide and barrel from the grip and trigger mechanism.

"I'm not here to kill anyone," Ben said. "If you're Dr. Joshua Green, we have an appointment. This guy"—he pointed at the man writhing on the floor—"attacked me, then pulled a gun. Maybe *he* was trying to kill you."

"Oh, no," Green said. "That's Morris. Morris Jefferson. He works for me."

The door to the library opened and the reference librarian stuck her head inside.

Ben said, "Mr. Jefferson needs an ambulance,"

The librarian withdrew.

Ben approached Jefferson and squatted on the floor next to him. "Do you have medical insurance," he said.

Jefferson gave a tiny nod.

Ben said, "I apologize for breaking your elbow. But, you should have identified yourself before attacking me."

A strange, inchoate sound issued from Jefferson.

"I'll cover whatever your insurance doesn't, including the deductible," Ben said and stood up.

"Dr. Green, I'm Rabbi Ben Maimon and I need to speak with you about Rabbi Rubin, about L'Dor v'Dor and about Rabbi and Mrs. Shevitz."

Green was slack-jawed. Abruptly he closed his mouth. "You're a rabbi?"

"I was sent by Rabbi Meir Farkas of the Israeli Rabbinate."

"I was expecting someone much older. Someone..."

"Someone dressed in black, with a big black hat? Someone who looks like your *bubbe's rebbe*?"

"I wouldn't put it exactly like that but..."

"Call Rabbi Farkas and ask him what the man he sent looks like."

"Yes, that's a good idea," Green said.

Ben took out his cell phone, found the number and dialed it, then handed the phone to Green.

The conversation, in English, lasted less than a minute.

Green looked like a whipped puppy. "I'm sorry that I doubted you, Rabbi."

"How is it that you are acquainted with Rabbi Farkas?"

"Through Rabbi Rubin. They're cousins, you know?"

Ben nodded.

"Well, Rabbi Farkas comes three or four times a year and stays for a week or so. That's how we met."

The door to the library opened and two men in paramedic uniforms entered, pushing a collapsible gurney cart. Ben waited until they had placed Jefferson on the cart, strapped him in and left the room.

§

"Have a seat," said Ben and pointed at a chair next to a table. Green sat, nervously looking around.

"You're not a physician, so what kind of doctor are you?"

"How do you know I'm not an M.D.?" Green said.

"Because you failed to tell that rookie paramedic to immobilize Jefferson's arm before putting him on a gurney."

"Ah. Rabbinical logic. I'm an Ed.D, a doctor of education. I'm an independent scholar. I do research and every year or so I get a paper published."

Ben rewarded Green with a searching look.

"I never worked in education," Green said. "I was a second child and my parents were very wealthy. They expected my elder brother to take over their business."

"And he didn't?"

Green shook his head. "He died on September 11, 2001. Meanwhile, I was a professional student. The doctorate and three master's degrees. I was—am—totally unprepared for any management position. My election to the synagogue's presidency amounts to a compromise to make peace between various factions on the board. Anyway, when my father retired, he brought someone in to be CEO. I have a seat on the board and chair the ethics committee."

"Why are you in hiding, Doctor?"

"You should call me Josh," Green said.

Ben nodded and waited.

After a long pause, Green cleared his throat. "I had long suspected that Rabbi Rubin was up to something with that charity, L'Dor v'Dor."

Ben said, "Up to *what?*"

Green shook his head. "No idea. It was the people that he surrounded himself with. His major donors. They were—are—all quite well-to-do and have various business interests. But rather than involve themselves in the life of the temple, serving on committees, leading prayer services, even participating in the Brotherhood—they gave a little money to the shul but they did almost nothing else. But while Rabbi Rubin was our spiritual leader, these men were often singled out for their generous contributions to his charity."

Ben said, "And that bothered you?"

"What kind of Jew doesn't involve himself, even in small ways, with the community, a holy community, but wins a rabbi's praise for donating funds to send rabbinical students to study in Israel? Better they should send their own sons to study in Israel. Or go to Israel, maybe once or twice, to see what they were supporting."

Ben waited but Green had nothing further to say.

"So, what do *you* think happened to Rabbi Shevitz and his wife?"

Tears came to Green's eyes. "I'm afraid they're dead. We might never even find their bodies. Maybe they're in a landfill or were burned in a crematory, dissolved in acid—something."

Chapter Fourteen

Steins

Ben said, "Do you read a lot of mysteries, Dr. Green? Thrillers?"

Green nodded agreement. "I enjoy them. Yes."

Ben said, "That's fiction. In the real world, most murder victims are found, usually quite soon after their deaths. Not always, of course."

"Oh, certainly. Of course. I know that. It's just that Rabbi Rubin...."

"Go on, please."

Green shook his head. "It's not right to speak ill of the dead. But the men that he surrounded himself with—these were not honorable men. I am very uncomfortable around them, singular and plural."

Ben said, "Did you have much to do with Rabbi Rubin or L'Dor v'Dor?"

Green slowly shook his head. "Not at all. L'Dor v'Dor is separate from the synagogue and in any event, I wasn't serving as president before he retired."

Ben said, "Did you donate?"

"Yes, of course. I gave him, I think, $50,000 at least four times, that I recall. He knew that I could afford it and that in fact. I have to work hard to find the right causes to support."

"So you are a philanthropist?"

Green beamed. "I guess I am. I never thought of myself that way. I have a tremendous tax liability every year and it pleases me to support worthy causes as they reduce my tax burden. And it gives me something useful to do."

"You inherited a fortune?"

"I inherited a controlling interest in a privately-held investment bank, Green & Green. My father and my uncle. My uncle sold his shares to my father years ago."

"So besides your duties as Beth Ohr president and giving away money, how do you spend your time?"

"One of my master's degrees is in library science. So I help out here, several hours a week, wherever I'm needed. I suppose I could have found a job as a librarian but there are very few well-paying positions in libraries these days and if I took such a job it would mean that someone at least as well qualified would be forced to take a lesser position or leave the field. I don't need more money, so…"

Ben said, "Very commendable, Josh. I'm quite impressed."

"Thank you, Rabbi."

"Can we talk about L'Dor v'Dor for a few minutes?"

"I've already told you as much as I know."

"Can you give me a list of the men that you described? His major donors?"

Green answered with a slow nod. "Some of them, anyway."

Ben took out his iPhone and opened a notebook app.

"Go ahead, please," he said.

"Well, Joe and Michael Stern. Brothers. They're in the scrap metal business."

"Go on."

"Ivan Chubatovsky. Some kind of wholesaler—produce, I think."

"Jewish?"

Green shrugged. "So he says. Then there's Mordecai Kuznetzov. Another Russian, I think, a developer. He also owns several hotels."

Ben said, "Anyone else?"

"Several thugs, whose names I don't know but who I have reason to believe are criminals of one kind or another."

Ben said, "And that's all you can remember?"

Green shook his head. "I'm hesitant to name this man. Outwardly he seems perfectly ordinary, even a little shy. If you met him a dozen times, you wouldn't be able to recognize him if you passed him on the street."

"Why is that?"

"He's very ordinary looking. Wears forgettable suits and nondescript ties. Average height, average weight, a round face that sometimes looks oval and other times kind of square. Speaks softly, no noticeable regional accent. And he's a direct descendant of one of this city's most esteemed founders."

"So he would be a Finkelstein?"

"Exactly. Randy Finkelstein."

"What does he do? His business or profession?"

Green frowned. "I'm told that he has a company that sells spare parts for obsolete appliances and such."

"So if I needed a part for a 20-year-old microwave oven?"

"Yes, that sort of thing. A refrigerator door. A burner knob for an old stove."

Ben shook his head. "I can't believe he could make much of a living that way."

Green smiled. "He doesn't need to. His parents left him a lot of real estate. Commercial and residential, even some factory buildings. I think the parts store is more like a hobby. And he has two city lots on which he grows vegetables. Gives most of them away to the poor. Half the kids in this town have had one of his pumpkins or some corn or tomatoes from his field."

Ben said, "Seems like a model of rectitude."

"And yet he used to hang out with that other bunch."

"Used to?"

"He found something else to do. Lilian Golden, an artist."

"This is a romantic attachment?"

"It appears that way. There's Sisterhood buzz about a wedding."

"What do you know about her?"

"Not much. Apparently, they've known each other for many years. Finkelstein was married, until last year, when his wife asked for a divorce."

"You've been very helpful, Josh. My advice to you is to come out of hiding. I don't think you're in any danger."

Chapter Fifteen

STEINS

Brilliant sunshine bathed the Beth Ohr parking lot as Ben pulled in. As he got out of the Honda, a man in workman's clothes got into a locksmith's truck and drove away.

Mrs. Levy rose from her desk to greet Ben.

"It's really a nice day," Ben said. "Have you been outside?"

Mrs. Levy shook her head. "Don't be deceived. In ten minutes it could be snowing. You know what they say about Chicago weather?"

Ben shook his head, no.

"If you don't like the weather, wait for half an hour and it'll change."

Ben smiled.

Mrs. Levy said, "Did you speak with Josh? Dr. Green?"

"He's fine," Ben said. "A very interesting man."

"But he's okay?" Levy persisted.

"Yes. Can I get into Rabbi Rubin's office now?"

"Second floor, next to the elevator. It should be open."

Rubin's office was a suite of rooms with a bathroom, a tiny bedroom with a narrow bed and a small dresser. The bed was a bare mattress on a base of springs. In the dresser were two blankets, a set of sheets and two pillows. The rest of the unit was an expansive study with a large desk. A row of filing cabinets huddled along one wall, blocking the window.

In the bathroom, towels hung from bars. A tiny closet held more towels, bath soap, shampoo, and conditioner. The medicine cabinet held only an electric toothbrush with a worn head, two replacement heads, a tube of toothpaste and an unused container of dental floss.

Ben returned to the study and started with the computer on the desk. He switched it on and after several seconds a message appeared on the monitor: Insert boot disc. Ben suspected that the hard disc had been wiped to destroy its data.

He shut it off and turned to the desk itself. Like many of its type, locking the center drawer also locked the other drawers. Ben straightened a paperclip and with a few minutes' work unlocked the desk.

The L'Dor v'Dor corporate seal and articles of incorporation were in the lower right drawer, inside a locked steel box that yielded to Ben's luggage key. Papers showed that the charity was established in 1991 in Dover, Delaware. Three corporate officers were listed: Shmuel Rubin, president, Deborah Rubin, treasurer, and Meir Farkas, secretary.

Farkas had never mentioned that he was an officer of the corporation. Ben wondered if that was an innocent omission. He also wondered why, if he was a corporate officer, he needed Ben to shut the corporation down.

The file cabinet drawers were half empty. What remained was to Ben's eyes the minutia of a nonprofit corporation: Minutes of the board of directors, memos of all sorts sent to or from various board members and three years of tax returns. The most recent, from the previous year, listed $2,751,043 in receipts and operating expenses of $298,563, including salaries for Shmuel Rubin, Deborah Rubin, Meir Farkas, which accounted for all but a few thousand dollars. The balance of the expenses was $1,000 honorariums to seven different board members, the purchase of a cell phone and petty cash expenditures.

Ben was not too distressed to learn that the two Rubins had been paid $125,000 each and that Farkas got $40,000 for his duties as a corporate officer. All three had attended the quarterly board meetings of the previous year. If the charity was performing as intended, executive salaries of less than six percent of revenue were not excessive.

In the bottom drawer of a filing cabinet, Ben found Rabbi Rubin's wallet and keys; one turned out to open his office door. There was also a baggie containing a sandwich of what smelled like spoiled tuna salad.

Ben decided to leave the other cabinets for another time.

Rubin's car key opened a dark blue Lincoln MKS in the synagogue lot. In its trunk, under a blanket, was an aluminum Halliburton case. The initials JD were scratched on the back. Another of Rubin's keys opened the case, which contained, to Ben's trained eye, perhaps half a million dollars in hundreds, fifties and twenties.

What was a retired rabbi who ran a nonprofit doing with that kind of cash?

Chapter Sixteen

Steins

Ben put the Halliburton case in Rabbi Rubin's office, locked the door and took the stairs down to the office, where he found Julie conferring with Mrs. Levy.

"Did you find what you were looking for, Rabbi?" said Levy.

"Not yet," Ben said. "Do you know if Rabbi Rubin was married?"

"His wife died several years ago," Levy said. "He has a sister, Deborah, who lives in Chicago."

"Thanks," Ben said. "Do you have a phone number or address for her?"

"We've been sending Rabbi Rubin's pension to her, since he retired," Levy said. "Give me a moment and I'll find that address for you."

Levy turned and headed for a filing cabinet and Morgenstern smiled at Ben. "Is your little apartment comfortable?" she said.

Levy turned and headed for a filing cabinet and Morgenstern smiled at Ben. "Is your little apartment comfortable?" she said.

"It will do for now," Ben said. "I'd like to chat with you for a few minutes. Do you have time now?"

"Actually, no. I've got a meeting downtown at 4:00 p.m. What about tomorrow?"

"Do you know a quiet, casual restaurant where we could have coffee and talk?"

"There's one in my building. I mean, the building where I rent an office."

She took out a business card and wrote the name of a café, Banners, in a neat yet distinctive hand.

"Tomorrow morning at 10:00?"

"That's fine," Ben said.

§

Deborah Rubin's address was in a triangular lakefront high-rise on North Sheridan Road in the trendy Edgewater Beach neighborhood. Ben parked Rubin's Lincoln in a visitor slot, then entered the lobby. A polite, uniformed young woman at a circular security desk typed Deborah Rubin into a computer, waited, then shook her blonde curls. "No Deborah Rubin living here," she said, frowning.

"What about Shmuel Rubin?"

She typed the name and smiled. "Yes. Is he expecting you?"

"That's Apartment 2006?"

"Yes. Shall I call up?"

"You know what, I think I'll go out to the car and call him. He hasn't been feeling well, you know?"

The blonde curls shook again. "No, sorry, I'm new. Don't know many of the residents yet."

"Thanks for your help," Ben said and left the building.

Back in the Lincoln, he thought for a long moment, then took the keys out of the ignition and searched through them until he found one that might fit the door of an apartment in a swanky high-rise.

Or not.

He opened the glove compartment but found little besides a folded roadmap, a Lincoln owner's manual and a pair of compact binoculars.

Ben's phone rang and he looked at the caller ID: Miryam!

"My love! How are you, my sweet Marita?"

"Frustrated. There are so many handsome men around and none of them is you."

"Be patient. We will be back together soon."

"I think I have the wedding solved. Almost."

"Tell me."

"First, you tell me what's going on in Chicago?"

Ben gave her a quick summary of what he knew, what he guessed and what he thought the outcome would be.

"Are you safe? No guns, no burning houses, no sexy women with designs on your body?"

Ben laughed. "Maybe tomorrow. Now tell me about our wedding. And did you buy that enormous villa?"

"In progress. The paperwork, including a title search back to the Ottoman era, will take a few weeks. Anyway, here's where we stand: The Benkamals and the Moshons—or most of them—will come to Chicago. You need to rent the largest wedding venue that you can and find a kosher caterer that can meet the approval of two foreign rabbis."

"When?"

"Dates are still fluid. Make firm reservations for any Sunday in May or June. Earlier is better."

Ben said, "Wonderful. What about the rabbi?"

"That's still sticky. The Moshons want their rabbi and the Benkamals want theirs."

"Then let's have both. Let them figure the service out between them."

"That means bringing both rabbi's families, Ben."

"Can we afford it?"

"Yes, but there might be problems with visas."

"What kind of problems?"

"Rabbi Yosef ben Abadi, two words, is in Buenos Aires and shares a name with Yusef Benabadi, one word. He's a Palestinian terrorist who was recently released from an Israeli prison. The American authorities…"

"Get all the information that you can on Rabbi Abadi. Where he was born, his age, all his identification data. I have a friend in the Israeli government who might be able to help."

"Who is your friend? Should I go see her?"

"Him. Yossi Bar Tzvi."

"The President of the State of Israel is your friend?"

"It's a long story but it starts with him asking me to find the missing pages of the Aleppo Codex…"

"Oh. My. God. How come you never told me?"

"Not important, my dearest Marita. By the way, have I told you lately that I love you more than anything or anyone in this world?"

"Not lately, Romeo Ben. Tell me again."

"I love you more than anything or anyone in this world. And now I have to go. I'm working."

"Doing what?"

"I'm about to drop in on Deborah Rubin at her swanky highrise apartment."

"What does she look like?"

"No idea. But she's in her fifties or sixties, I think."

"Be careful, Casanova Ben. You attract women like flies to doggie doo-doo."

"Thank you, I think. Bye, sweetie."

"Be careful. Be safe. Don't pretend to be a priest or get trapped in another burning building."

"I promise. Bye."

"Love you."

§

It took Ben several minutes to regroup his thoughts.

Then he tried the console between the car's front seats and found a pair of sunglasses, three parking tickets, and a pocket-sized notebook. He riffled through its pages and found lists written in some incomprehensible code. Incomprehensible until he realized that the characters were cursive Hebrew, instead of the more formal fonts that appear in printed matter.

He took a second look and then a third, before realizing that some of the characters might represent numbers, not text. "Ezra, 18400, 17-04-23, 12" was a typical entry. A name, amount, date and something else? Perhaps, he thought. Food for thought and study.

He put the notebook in his pocket, closed the console and lifted his eyes. Several compartments protruded from the overhead panel. He pushed one lightly and it fell open, revealing what looked like a compact version of a garage door opener.

Ben put the remote on the seat next to him, started the engine and backed out of the lot. He drove around the block and found the residents' parking entrance. One click and the heavy steel mesh door slid upward.

Ben circled the structure, climbing to the twentieth floor. There he found a space marked 2006 A. He parked in 2006 B, next to a year-old Mazda Miata hardtop convertible in fire engine red.

The remote opened a steel door from the parking structure

that led to a corridor with a plush rug. Seven doors down he found a door marked 2006.

Ben found the key that might open the apartment, then put it back in his pocket. He rang the doorbell.

After almost a minute he heard footsteps. The door opened a crack.

"Who are you? What do you want?" said a young beauty, considerably south of thirty, clad only in an enormous bath towel and with a shower cap covering long red tresses.

"It's about Shmuel Rubin. Rabbi Rubin," Ben said. "I'm Rabbi Ben Maimon, from Beth Ohr, in Steins."

"You mean *Sam* Rubin?"

"Of course, that's what his friends call him."

"Well, what about him?"

"I'm very sorry that I interrupted your bath," Ben said. "But this is very important. Could I possibly come in and wait while you get dressed?"

"Wait outside," she said and closed the door, softly.

§

Ten minutes dragged by before the door opened and the woman, now barefoot and clad in a pair of tight jeans and an untucked silk blouse with two buttons fastened, revealing that she wore nothing underneath. She was tall and curvy and had used the minutes while Ben waited to apply lipstick, mascara and eye shadow.

In her left hand, she gripped a yellow taser gun.

"Sorry," she said with a tight smile, "but I don't know you. How did you get into this building?"

"With Sam's clicker and his key. They were in his car."

The woman retreated half a step. Trembling, she said, "What the hell's going on?"

"Sam was hit by a car several days ago," Ben said. "While he was out walking, He died at the scene."

"NO!" she shrieked. "No, no. No, that can't be right. He made a deposit in my account just yesterday."

"The account that you share with Deborah Rubin?"

"Who is she, anyway?"

"I'm pretty sure that's Sam's sister."

The woman's face registered shock, then suspicion.

"Who are you again?"

"Rabbi Ben Maimon. You can call Congregation Beth Ohr and ask them if I'm who I say I am."

"I'm gonna do that," she said.

"By the way, what's *your* name?" Ben said.

"Kylee. Kylee Dugan. What's that Beth thing again?"

"Congregation Beth Ohr, in Steins Township."

Kylee took a cell phone from her pocket, hit a few keys and repeated the information that Ben gave her, then waited while the connection went through.

"Do you have a Rabbi Ben My Mon there?" she said into the phone.

After a brief pause, she said, "He's out, okay. What does he look like?"

"Uh-huh. And he's really a rabbi?"

A pause.

"What about Sam Rubin? Is he there?"

A pause.

"Yes, Shmoo-el Rubin, that's what I meant."

A longer pause.

"Oh, no. So he's really dead? Wait—was he about sixty and kind of short, with white hair and a small beard? Like that old painter, Van Dyke?"

Kylee put the phone down, dropped the taser on the rug and fell back on to a sofa, weeping.

Ben allowed her to cry for a few minutes.

"Did you love him?" Ben said.

"Love him? No! Noooo. Well, he was okay. Better than okay. He was always very nice to me. Very gentle. He paid me really good and all he wanted was that he could come over two nights a week and on Sunday afternoons."

Ben nodded. "And now what?"

"Well, I'm going to have to get out of this lease. No way I can afford the rent without Sam's help."

"Do you have savings?"

Kylee nodded, wiped her eyes with the back of her hand and seemed to pull herself together. "I guess I should find a cheap apartment, finish college and find a good job," she said.

"What kind of a job would that be?"

She began to cry again. "I don't know," she wailed. "He wasn't supposed to die."

"How long were you and Sam together, Kylee?" Ben said.

"Almost three years."

And again she burst into tears.

Ben got to his feet.

"I'm very sorry for your loss," he said and turned to go.

"Wait!"

Ben turned back to face Kylee.

"Why did you come here?" she said.

"To tell you that Sam had passed away."

"He was really a rabbi?"

Ben nodded. "Very well respected. His death is a shock, I know, but death comes to us all."

He turned toward the door again, then turned back to Kylee.

"One more thing. Well, two. Can I get your phone number?"

"Why?"

"Sam might have left you something. In his will."

"You think so?"

Ben shrugged. "It's possible."

She found a scrap of paper on the kitchen breakfast bar, scribbled a number and handed it to Ben."

"You said *two* things?"

"The car that hit Sam—it was a hit-and-run. The police think that he might have been murdered."

Kylee was wide-eyed, frightened.

"Can you think of anyone who might have wanted to hurt Sam? Kill him, even?"

Still wide-eyed, she shook her head, slowly, processing this information.

Ben turned toward the door.

"Wait, hang on," Kylee said.

Ben stopped and half-turned to look at her.

"Are you married?"

"Engaged to a wonderful woman," he replied. "Maybe you could find a roommate?"

"It's a one-bedroom," Kylee said.

Ben offered a small, sad, smile. "I'm afraid that you'll either have to learn to support yourself or find another boyfriend. Speaking as a rabbi, you might do better with someone who you really care about, rather than a guy with a lot of money."

"I *have* a boyfriend," she wailed. "I really love him. And he loves me."

"Then I suggest that you try to make that relationship work. Maybe you could move in together and you could find some kind of job."

Kylee began to weep again. "No, no. He's married. And he doesn't have any money. And all I know how to do is make men feel good."

She began to cry again. Mascara made black streaks down her lovely face.

Again, Ben turned toward the door and again he turned back to Kylee.

"What kind of car does your boyfriend drive?"

"A Subaru."

"What color?"

"Stephen doesn't even know about Sam," she said.

"What color?"

"Silver."

"Good luck to you, Kylee."

"You'll call if there's anything for me in Sam's will?"

"Of course."

Chapter Seventeen

Chicago

In the parking structure, Ben opened the door to Rubin's Lincoln, then stopped. He took out his phone, brought up the camera app and took a photo of the Miata's license plate.

The top was down and Ben found the Illinois registration certificate behind the driver's sun visor. The car was owned by Shmuel Rubin, 204 Sunflower Road, Steins. He took a picture of the registration.

Ben got back into the Lincoln and headed north.

§

He left the Lincoln in the same Beth Ohr parking space where he had found it and drove his rented Honda two blocks past the yellow-brick library on Finkelstein, then turned into the self-parking entrance of the FSC Financial building, one of Steins' few skyscrapers. He parked and walked down to ground level, then entered Banners. His mouth began to water from the smell of fresh bread, Ben realized that he hadn't eaten since the previous evening.

A hostess in a starched uniform seated him at a table for two. Ben took the seat facing the entrance and then glanced at his watch: He was almost twenty minutes early. He ordered a pumpernickel bagel with lox, cream cheese, tomato and lettuce, and a cup of coffee. When the food arrived, he began to eat.

Ben was more than halfway through the bagel when Morgenstern appeared, carrying a newspaper. He stood, she sat, he sat. She laid the newspaper on the table.

"I was hungry," Ben said, by way of explanation.

"Go ahead," she said, smiling. "Eat."

"In a minute. The reason I wanted to talk to you concerns L'Dor v'Dor."

Julie nodded her understanding.

"It's a nonprofit, 501(c) 3 corporation. I need an attorney to wind it up or maybe the correct phrase is "shut it down.""

Julie nodded again. "I could do that. Where is it chartered—what state?"

"Delaware," Ben said and Julie cocked an eyebrow.

"Interesting," she said. "But not a problem."

"First thing, find the checkbook—it should be somewhere in Rabbi Rubin's office—find out what the cash situation is, then get started on shutting it down. Bill L'Dor v'Dor at your usual hourly rate."

"Okay, I can do that. What bank? Who can sign checks?"

Before he could answer, Ben's phone beeped.

"Excuse me," he said and read a short text message from Marcia Katz.

"First National of Steins," Ben said.

"That was the text message? How did you know I was going to ask that question when I did?"

Ben smiled. "The secrets of the Zohar may not be shared with the uninitiated," he whispered.

Julie giggled. "Seriously?"

"Seriously, this was from the wife of my best friend. They live in Skokie and last year made a contribution to L'Dor v'Dor. Two days ago I asked her to find out what bank their check was deposited in."

"So it was serendipity that she answered just now?"

Ben knit his eyebrows together and whispered, "The secrets of the Zohar…"

A large white-haired man wearing a worn and dirty suit appeared at their table and reached across Ben to take the remaining fraction of his bagel off the plate. The coat reeked of garbage and stale urine.

"You're not going to eat this, right?" the man said while grabbing a napkin from the table and wrapping the food in it.

Julie stared, shocked. "What are you doing?" she said.

The man took the newspaper and folded it under his arm. "Thanks," he said.

Ben pushed his chair back, got to his feet and turned to face the man.

"That's very bad manners," Ben said. "You don't grab food off people's tables."

"I'm hungry," he said. "No job, no place to stay."

Ben dug in his pocket and came out with a fifty.

"Get yourself cleaned up—"

The babble of café conversation was pierced by a woman's shriek. Ben turned to see Julie being marched toward the front door by a tall man with a death grip on her throat. His left hand held an automatic pistol, jammed into her spine.

Zigzagging between tables, in five long steps Ben reached the man and in one swift movement snatched the pistol away.

As the man turned to face Ben he produced a large knife to hold at Julie's throat.

"I'm leaving with your girlfriend," he said. "Try to shoot me and I'll cut her throat."

As he lowered the gun, Ben thumbed the safety off, then fired a single shot.

The man screamed and fell backward, blood pulsing from his left foot. Ben made the gun safe, left it on a table and after wrapping his hand in a linen napkin, retrieved the man's knife, which he also laid on the table.

All this took less than ten seconds.

"Someone call the police," he said, loudly, and as Julie began to shudder and cry, he took her in his arms and held her tightly.

"It's all right now," he said, in a low voice. "You're safe."

Chapter Eighteen

Steins

The cop spun Ben around and removed the handcuffs that held his arms behind him. "Sit," he said, indicating a chair at a scarred table in a cramped, claustrophobic room with a big mirror on one wall and no windows.

After several minutes the door opened and a balding, middle-aged black man in a rumpled blue suit and a clean but worn white shirt entered. A gold badge graced his belt.

"Detective Edison Gray," he said.

"Rabbi Ben Maimon, which is my Hebrew name but legally I'm Mark Thompson Glass. Am I under arrest?"

The detective shook his head. "Not yet. Tell me what happened in the restaurant."

"A heavy-set older man dressed as a vagrant distracted my attention by snatching food off my plate and then taking Mrs. Morgenstern's newspaper. While I was talking to this man, my back was turned to Mrs. Morgenstern. A second man stuck a gun in her back and started to march her out of the restaurant.

"I ran to this man, took the gun out of his hand and when he produced a knife and threatened to kill Mrs. Morgenstern, I shot him in the foot."

Gray nodded his understanding. "That's pretty much what Mrs. Morgensten said. But I have a few questions."

Ben nodded in turn. "Proceed," he said.

"Were you not afraid that by taking the gun from his hand it would go off, thus endangering Mrs. Morgenstern?"

"No," Ben said. "The gun is a copy of the US Army 1911 Colt

automatic. It has a thumb safety that can only be pushed up—safe—or down—fire—from the left side of the receiver. He gripped the gun in his left hand which meant his thumb was on the right side of the receiver. He could not make the gun ready to fire with one hand. I knew that I could take it from him safely."

"How did you come by this knowledge of firearms?"

"I took a shooting course while I was an undergraduate student and then made it my business to learn about handguns."

"Do you own a handgun?"

Ben shook his head. "No."

"Mrs. Morgenstern, I'm sorry to say, does not yet understand what you just told me about the safety on the gun. She's kind of shook up."

"Perhaps you could explain the safety to her, Detective."

"I'll ask my boss to do just that. Where do you live, Rabbi?"

"I have an apartment on the grounds of Congregation Beth Ohr."

"What is the nature of your relationship with Mrs. Morgenstern?"

"I don't see how that is any of your business, Detective."

"It's the business of the Illinois State's Attorney for Kishnef County."

"I don't see how that could possibly be true."

"His name is Leonard Morgenstern."

"That will be Mrs. Morgenstern's husband?"

"He is."

"Then I will tell you that we met in the building where she has her office so that I could decide whether or not to engage her services as an attorney, in connection with a Jewish charity that I'm associated with. I'm also the interim rabbi at Congregation Beth Ohr and Mrs. Morgenstern is the President of the Sisterhood of that synagogue."

"You don't have a personal relationship? A romantic relationship?"

Ben shook his head. "She's married and I respect that. As it happens, I am engaged to a wonderful woman and we plan to marry soon. My relationship with Mrs. Morgenstern is entirely professional. I've only known her for two days."

Gray got to his feet. "Stay put. I'll be back in a few minutes," he said.

Chapter Nineteen

Steins

A short, balding white man in a well-tailored suit entered the room.

"Captain Finley Peters," he said and extended his hand for Ben to shake.

"Rabbi Ben Maimon," Ben said and they shook hands.

"I appreciate the fact that you shot the perp's foot instead of killing him. Seven witnesses in the coffee shop and Mrs. Morgenstern, of course, back your version of events, so you're free to go," said Peters. "But I'd like to ask a few questions first if you don't mind."

Ben sat back down. "I'd like to ask a few myself," he said.

"You first, then," Peters said.

"Who was the man that I shot? What was he after?"

Peters nodded. "His name—one of them—is Pytor Sapozhnik, aka 'Pete the Rusky.' A long record of arrests, small-time fraud, strong-arm stuff and two convictions: assault with a deadly weapon and attempted murder. He does odd jobs for the Russian Mafia."

"What did he want with Mrs. Morgenstern?"

"That remains to be seen. He's in the hospital. Doctors are trying to save his foot. Do you know how many bones there are in the human foot?"

"Twenty-six and more than a hundred ligaments, muscles, and tendons."

Peters stared at Ben, then laughed. "I suppose I shouldn't be surprised. You're a doctor, too?"

Again, Ben shook his head. "No, but over the years I have collected an enormous amount of mostly useless trivia. Try as I might, I seem to retain most of what I read. It's a real problem sometimes."

Peters laughed again. "Anyway, he's under police guard and will be charged with assault with a deadly weapon and attempted kidnapping. You might have to testify."

"I will do my duty," Ben said.

"I'll have someone take you home," he said.

"What about Mrs. Morgenstern?"

"Her husband took her home."

Ben said, "Captain, this isn't the right time but I would like to come back tomorrow and ask you a few questions about another case. What time would be convenient?"

"What case?"

"The hit-and-run death of Rabbi Shmuel Rubin."

"There isn't much to tell but I'll be happy to share what I know. Why don't you come at about noon and we can grab lunch. I'm told that you're a very interesting man."

Ben smiled. "I hope you won't be disappointed. I'm just a rabbi."

"Noon," said Peters.

Chapter Twenty

Steins

Ben awoke an hour before sunrise, put on his running clothes and let himself out of the synagogue. After ten minutes of stretching, he started a slow jog around the neighborhood. It was overcast and chilly but after several minutes his exertions warmed his extremities and he no longer felt the cold.

He made a wide circle from Beth Ohr, crossing streets that ran both north and south and at angles between. After he had gone what he judged was close to three miles, he looked for a place where he could turn around without breaking stride. He turned into a dead-end street and almost stopped when he saw the sign: Sunflower Road. He jogged past 204 and to his surprise, there was a light in a window. A flash of movement caught his eye.

§

Ninety minutes later, having showered and eaten a bagel from the synagogue's refrigerator, Ben parked his car around the corner from 204 Sunflower Road. He watched the apartment in his rearview mirror but saw no movement.

He waited for almost an hour until most of the cars parked on the street had been driven away.

He climbed the back porch steps and went in through the kitchen, using a key that he supposed would also open the front door. A harsh odor that he identified as a mixture of animal feces and urine assaulted his nose. Peering around, he saw an overflowing cat box.

"Oh, shit," Ben said.

He shut the door and moved slowly around the apartment until he spied the tip of a gray feline tail peeking out from beneath an easy chair.

Ben returned to the kitchen, opened the windows, then looked around the floor until he found a pair of bowls that had once contained water and cat food, respectively. He rinsed the bowls in the sink before opening cabinet doors until he found a stack of cat food cans. He filled the water bowl and put it back where he'd found it, then opened a can and emptied its contents into the second bowl, which he placed on the floor near the water.

He found a half-full bag of kitty litter in a corner and a plastic garbage bag in a kitchen drawer. Grimacing, he emptied the cat box into the bag, which he sealed and put out on the porch.

After refilling the cat box, Ben made a quick inspection tour of the house: Kitchen, pantry, breakfast nook, living room, bathroom, two small bedrooms and a stairway leading to a basement. One of the bedrooms was outfitted as an office, with a desk, computer, printer and a filing cabinet.

He returned to the kitchen to find an emaciated cat lapping water from the bowl. It paid him no attention and when the bowl was nearly empty, it began eating from the food bowl.

"Poor kitty," Ben said and made his way to the office. The desk was unlocked and yielded little beyond a day planner, a stack of household bills—electricity, gas, credit cards, etc. A quick survey revealed that they were all recent and that the accounts were current. Rubin's three credit cards held small balances totaling less than $1,000. Deeper in the drawer he found a small LED flashlight, a few pens and two checkbooks on Chicago banks.

The center drawer held the big surprise: A 9mm Glock Model 19. It held a 15-round magazine. A sixteenth cartridge was in the chamber.

Ben left the gun where he'd found it and started on the filing cabinet. One file folder contained family documents: Rubin's birth certificate, his parents' *ketubah*, death certificates for both parents, a younger brother and Shmuel's wife, Bella.

There was also a hand-drawn genealogy that spanned four legal-sized sheets of paper.

A close reading revealed that his mother's three brothers had perished in the Holocaust. His mother had no sister. His father, also a rabbi, had one brother, and he had also been a Holocaust victim—he died in Sobibór. So Meir Farkas had lied: He was not a cousin of the late Shmuel Rubin.

Ben's second glance drew a closer look. Shmuel's father had married twice; Shmuel's only sister was the child of the second marriage. She was twenty-two years his junior. Ben returned to the death certificates and saw that Shmuel's father, Avram, passed away when his daughter was four years old.

Another folder contained photos, including a black-and-white 8x10 of a robust young man in an old fashioned tuxedo and his bride, a tall, slim, top-heavy beauty with a face that Botticelli or Romney might have painted. Ben didn't know much about women's fashion but her wedding dress seemed more Jazz Age than Rock'n'Roll. There was no date or other information. A young Shmuel and his wife? His parents? It was hard to tell.

The third folder dealt with real estate. Apparently, Rubin owned seven homes in Chicago's northern suburbs, including the one on Sunflower. There was no mortgage information and the duplicate deeds of trust in the file listed no lien holder. An Arlington Heights Realtor collected the rents and maintained six of the seven properties. Judging from the previous month's statement, Rubin was collecting almost $15,000 a month in rents.

Ben cocked his head, an unconscious act, while he thought. Shmuel seemed to have a lot more money than one would expect from a retired pulpit rabbi. So much money that he had given his pension, a little over $4,000 a month, to Kylee Dugan. Was there more? Cash in savings accounts or certificates of deposit? Stocks and bonds?

Ben put that aside for the moment and opened the third folder. It contained documents that belonged to Deborah L.

Rubin, including a bank savings book, driving license, diplomas, life insurance policies, birth certificate, marriage and divorce papers, and many others. The driver's license photo showed a strong resemblance to the woman in the mysterious wedding photo.

Deborah had married Richard Golden at 22 and divorced him six years later. There was no indication of a child. Deborah's driving license had expired several years before and the address on it was the high-rise apartment on North Sheridan Road where Kylee Dugan now lived.

It seemed unlikely that Deborah was still alive. Did she die of natural causes or was she murdered? What happened to her remains? Ben decided that he didn't like Shmuel Rubin one bit.

The last folder confirmed Ben's earlier notion: The late Rabbi Rubin had cash in four banks, including two in the Bahamas. His securities portfolio, owned by Kylee Comforts, LLC, Freeport, Grand Bahama Island was highly diversified and valued at over two million Bahamas dollars. A quick Google check on his phone revealed that a Bahamian dollar was worth a U.S. dollar, one for one.

Where would a man like Rabbi Rubin get money like that? Ben thought that he knew the answer and he didn't like it any more than he liked "Sam" Rubin.

He took out his phone, moved a lamp on the desk and set about photographing everything in the four folders.

When he had finished, he spent another half hour looking for a will but found nothing of the sort.

Chapter Twenty-One

Steins

After dropping the cat at an animal hospital for a checkup, Ben returned to Beth Ohr. He was surprised to find Julie Morgenstern waiting for him in the office.

She smiled warmly and got to her feet. "My hero," she said and both Mrs. Levy and Tracey Washington, the temp, applauded.

Ben's face burned. He held up both hands and after a while, the clapping stopped.

"I owe you my life, Rabbi," Julie said. "You are the bravest man I know."

Clearly embarrassed, Ben shook his head. "I did no more than any man—any person—would have done, were they able to do so. I was able, so I did. This is what God expects of us, no more, no less.

Still smiling, Julie got to her feet. "Your modesty is very becoming, Rabbi but we both know that that thug could have killed you. And he would have. And I'd be dead or a hostage. Thank you, from the bottom of my heart."

Levy and Washington applauded again.

"I'm not used to this," Ben said. "Please, let's not make a big deal of it."

"Too late," Julie said. "Josh spoke to the board and this Shabbat we'll have a *Birkat HaGomel* service to celebrate our escape from danger."

Ben knew that this was entirely proper but he shied from personal publicity. He did whatever he did out of a sense of justice, of being obliged to do so because it was necessary and proper. He felt strongly that he would be morally deficient if he shirked his responsibility to act when an occasion arose.

"*Birkat HaGomel* is appropriate and welcome," he said. "And also very brief. Is Dr. Green still in hiding?"

Mrs. Levy shook her head, no. "He said he'd be in late this afternoon if you'd like to chat."

Ben smiled. "Excellent," he said.

"Do you have time now to talk about winding up L'Dor v'Dor?" said Julie.

"Let's use Rabbi Shevitz's office," he said and followed her out the door and around the corner to a large office. Ben pulled the door open and held it for Julie.

It was a large office with beautiful wooden paneling, big windows, and a very large mahogany desk. Ben took a seat in front of the desk and Julie sat next to him.

"There's something I need to tell you," she said. "It's important."

Ben shrugged. "Sure," he said.

"Leonard and I have been separated since late last year. I filed divorce papers last week."

Ben shook his head. "I'm very sorry to hear this," he said. "Marriage can be difficult but it is the desirable state for adults."

Julie dropped her head. "I wanted to make it work but his girlfriends, plural, had other ideas. I cannot abide the notion of being faithful to a man who doesn't know what the word means."

Ben nodded to show that he understood. "I understand the necessity for faithfulness in marriage. It can be difficult, sometimes, because the world is full of temptation and it requires a strong commitment to resist what the ancient rabbis called "the evil impulse."

Julie said, "My husband thinks that we are having an affair."

Ben smiled. "Neither of us has done anything to foster such a notion. So the idea of unfaithfulness originates in your husband's mind. I will have a word with him."

"Not a good idea," Julie said, shaking her head. "He's a violent man."

"Be that as it may, I'll find a way to make it clear. Now, let's talk about L'Dor v'Dor. Do you still want the job?"

"Of course."

"I think that you may find that certain documents are missing. Do your best and put together a list of what should be there and isn't."

"Okay. What else, Ben?"

"Do you know a good private investigator?"

"I use Hilly Lippman. His office is in the same building as mine."

"Good. I may go see him today. How are *you* holding up? Getting abducted, even for a few minutes, is a major trauma. I recommend that you find a psychologist or a psychiatrist, with experience in trauma and make an appointment as soon as possible."

"But I feel fine."

"Please take my word on this. I have experienced severe trauma. Early intervention is your best and first choice for heading off problems down the road."

"Okay. I'll look into it."

"Promise?" said Ben, smiling.

"Promise," said Julie. "And by the way, I find you almost irresistibly attractive. We could have an affair. Or maybe something more."

Ben was momentarily tongue-tied.

"Well?"

Ben frowned. "I'm flattered. You're beautiful, smart and kind. If I was not committed to marrying a woman whom I believe will be the best wife in the world for me, I would certainly be very interested. But as it happens, I'm not available."

Julie offered a sad, small smile. "I was almost sure of that. The good ones never stay single long."

Chapter Twenty-Two

Steins

Captain Peters welcomed Ben to his office with an effusive handshake and together they went across the street to Katz's Kosher Deli. One look at the menu, however, told Ben that the food was kosher *style*. There was no indication that a rabbi had supervised its preparation, so he couldn't be sure that the meat on the menu was kosher. He ordered a potato knish and a bowl of vegetable soup, while Peters went with a corned beef sandwich on Russian rye.

"I've been reading your FBI file," Peters said. "You should be an agent," he said. "Or a cop."

"Because it pays so well," Ben said with a smile.

"Yeah, there it is."

They ate for a few minutes in silence.

"Why did you come to Steins?" Peters said, eyeing Ben.

"To oversee the shutting down of a charity run by Rabbi Rubin," Ben replied. 'Is there any evidence that he was murdered?"

"Possibly. The car was going about sixty and it threw his body almost eighty feet. It was a narrow road, half an hour after sunrise, he was dressed in black and it's just as likely that somebody was driving too fast and didn't see him. We have no motive."

"What kind of car, if you know?"

"We've got it down to a late-model Japanese make, because of the type of paint. I think we sent samples to the FBI lab or maybe downstate. Eventually, they'll get back to us."

"What about Rabbi Shevitz and his wife? Do you have an open case on them?"

Peters shook his head. "It's kidnapping. The FBI has that case."

Ben said, "What can you tell me about Pete the Ruskie? Who does he work for?

"I can talk to Quinn, our OC sergeant. He's pretty much up to date on which thug works for which bigger thug."

"Or I could talk to him. After lunch, you think?"

"He's in Chicago for an FBI class but I'll check when he's back."

"That would be very kind of you," Ben said.

Again they ate in silence until Peters put the remains of his sandwich down.

"I eat way too much red meat," he said.

"Learn to like fish," Ben said. "And vegetables."

"Fish is so expensive these days. I remember that when I was a kid, only poor people ate fish because it was cheap. Now it's more expensive than chicken or beef."

"Supply and demand Captain."

"Call me Fin."

"Ben."

Philips said, "Your old man—he was a big-shot crook?"

Ben nodded. "That he was. He and my mother split up when I was a few weeks old. I never got to meet him."

"That's kind of good news, bad news."

Ben shrugged. "I can't think of any reason that I would have wanted or needed to meet him. He hurt a lot of good people."

"Don't take this personally, Ben but are you actually a rabbi?"

"I am. Eight years ago, I graduated first in my class from the Jewish Theological Seminary, in New York. For a long time, I had a medical condition that precluded me from a rabbi's pulpit. I just finished a long medical trial; I might be cured. It will be a few years, with follow-up tests, to see if I am in remission or completely cured."

"You happy doing what you're doing?"

"More or less. I'm about to get married. That puts another spin on banging heads with bad guys—I'll always worry that someone will come after my wife to get at me. I'm hoping to find a permanent pulpit. Maybe after this job. But we'll see."

Peters pushed his plate away. "I should get back to work," he said, grabbing the check. "Call or come by in a day or two and I'll have something to tell you about Pete the Ruskie."

§

The name on the door was Lippman Investigations. Ben pushed a button and a few minutes went by before the door opened a crack.

"Help you?" said a deep male voice behind the door.

"Hilly Lippman?"

"You are?"

"Rabbi Ben Maimon."

The door opened, revealing a tall man in his late twenties with a receding blond hairline, a lot of muscles and a big smile.

"Mrs. Morgenstern said you might call," he said. "I'm in the middle of something but come in," he said.

Ben came through the door and watched Lippman bolt it behind him.

"I have a lot of sensitive stuff here," he said.

"I can only imagine."

"Can you wait a few minutes while I finish this test? My client needs this as soon as possible."

"No problem."

"Would you like to watch?"

"What are you doing?"

"ESDA. Electrostatic Detection Apparatus."

"I think I know what this does but how does it work?"

"It lays an electrostatic field across a piece of paper and then I add very fine particles of ink and that reveals any indentations in the paper."

"So, if I wrote a note on the top sheet of a pad of paper, the sheet below would register very subtle indentations and this would reveal the writing?"

"That's it. Faster, more accurate and more sensitive than going back and forth on the sheet with a soft pencil."

Ben watched as Hilly laid a blank sheet of special paper across the ESDA grid, then pushed a button that charged the sheet and then sprayed dry ink evenly across the page.

A single cursive sentence, seven words running diagonally from the center of the page toward the upper right corner, was revealed.

"What does that mean?" Ben said.

Hilly shrugged. "I don't know. The client—in this case, an attorney—will decide if it's relevant to his case or not. I just run the tests."

"Got many more of these?"

"Just a few. Why don't you go around the corner, find my fridge and help yourself to a cold drink?"

§

Ben had just taken a sip of Vernor's ginger ale when his

phone rang: Mrs. Levy.

"What's up?" Ben said.

"You had a call from a Kylee Dugan. Do you know her?"

"Yes. A friend of Rabbi Rubin, I believe."

"She sounded very young."

"Did she say what she wanted, Mrs. Levy?"

"She said you have her number."

"Okay. Say, on a different matter, do you have Rabbi Rubin's Social Security number? And one for his sister Deborah? Also, what bank account do we send Deborah's checks to?"

"Let me find that for you. Are you going to give a sermon tomorrow?"

"Of course."

"Okay. Hold on while I get those numbers for you."

Hilly entered the room.

"Done. What can I for you, Rabbi?"

"I'm waiting for some information but we can talk until Mrs. Levy comes back on the line. Did Mrs. Morgenstern tell you what I do for a living?"

"She said you were a rabbi."

"I'm also a kind of investigator. But I don't have the resources or, frankly, the know-how to do all the things that a licensed P.I. should do."

"What do you need?"

"I'm trying to find out if a particular woman is still alive."

"Tell me more."

Ben took several sentences to explain the basis for his suspicion that Deborah Rubin was dead.

Hilly nodded. "I can do several things that won't take much time. There's a searchable database of deceased Social Security numbers—actually, *you* can access that, it's public. Then, and this takes a few days, I can find out if a person with that Social owns any property, a car, has a driver's license, a bank account, is a patient in a nursing home or hospital, is incarcerated in a state or federal prison or has left the country on a valid passport."

"In all fifty states?"

"And Puerto Rico, Guam, American Samoa, and the American Virgin Islands."

"Excellent. I hadn't considered that she might be in jail or a nursing home or had left the country. I'll do the Social Security search. What do you charge for the rest?"

"I get $500 a day, plus out-of-pocket. This shouldn't take more than two or three days."

Ben took a roll of hundreds from his pocket and counted out ten. "That enough for a retainer?"

"Sure. Do you have any documents?"

"Rabbi, are you still there?" said Mrs. Levy in Ben's ear.

"Yes. Do you have that information?"

Silently, Hilly passed a pad of paper and a pen to Ben and he wrote as Levy dictated the numbers.

When she finished, Ben said goodbye and hung up.

Ben said, "I have pictures of documents. Can I email them to you or upload them directly to your computer?"

Hilly pointed to a PC on a nearby desk. "You'll find a transfer cable in the drawer."

Chapter Twenty-Three

Steins

Ben took the elevator down to the parking structure and headed up the ramp toward his car. He found the car and agent Gilmore waiting.

"Long time, no see," Gilmore said.

"A few days. How have you been, Agent Gilmore? Your parents? Your husband and children?"

Gilmore giggled. "Nice move, Rabbi."

"What brings you to my humble parking space?"

"You had an encounter with Pytor Sapozhnik and you never bothered to bring us up to speed," she said.

Ben laughed. "He and another guy tried to abduct an attorney friend of mine and I stopped it. We exchanged a few words. Actually, he did all the talking. Not much to report, Agent Gilmore."

"You can call me Pat."

Ben said. "You can call me Ben. Seriously, why are you here?"

"We agreed that you'd share any information that you have on L'Dor v'Dor."

"What I have is precious little. Most of the records seem to be missing, although they may be in some storage facility. I hired a lawyer to help me shut it down. What else do you need to know?"

"No sign of anything strange or illegal?"

"With the charity, not yet. I don't know much about it yet."

"What about Rabbi Shmuel Rubin?"

"He's still dead, last I heard. I've asked the Steins police to share what they have on the crime scene and what they told me was what I already knew: Hit by a speeding car, the driver failed to stop, Rubin was DOA."

'What about Rubin's personal life, his finances?"

"Why do I get the idea that you already know more than I do about that?"

Again, Gilmore giggled. "The broad strokes, then."

"Well, he kept a young woman in a fancy Edgewater Beach high-rise. Which shouldn't be of any interest to the federal government, as long as she reported the income."

"She has not."

Ben shrugged. "Rubin seems to have been wealthy. More than I would have expected from a retired rabbi. Bank and brokerage accounts in the Bahamas. Half a dozen rental houses. But maybe his family had money. Perhaps his late wife left him a bundle. Or he hit the lottery. Not my business where the money came from unless it came from the charity."

"Not bad for only four days, Ben," Gilmore said. "It took us weeks to find his offshore accounts."

"So you don't do black bag jobs anymore?"

"Not without a warrant. But I understand that you have a talent for burglary."

"I had a key to Rubin's house. It was in his office, which is in the synagogue that now employs me."

"How are you and Mrs. Morgenstern getting along?"

"We are not lovers and we will never be intimate. I have a fiancé whom I am devoted to and we will soon be married. Furthermore, my personal life is not the FBI's business."

"I agree. But here's a heads-up: Leonard Morgenstern is

about to sue you for alienation of affection."

Ben laughed. "They have been separated for months and I've been here four days. Is there an Illinois law against frivolous lawsuits?"

Pat said, "There is."

"Then I should have a chat with him."

"He's pretty big."

Ben shrugged. "I'm not going to fight him for the hand of the lovely Mrs. Morgenstern. I just want to assure him that there is nothing but business between me and his wife."

"Good luck with that, Ben."

"Pat, what can you tell me about Pete the Ruskie? Who does he work for?"

"Pete and his uncle Nicolai—"Tricky Nicky," are small-time grifters. Everything from the pigeon drop to the Spanish prisoner to real-estate scams. Pete also does freelance strong-arm for some mobbed-up guys, mostly in the suburbs. Hard to tell who sent him to snatch Mrs. Morgenstern or why and it's unlikely he'll talk."

Ben nodded his head to show understanding.

The agent turned to go. "Stay in touch, Ben," she said and headed for an exit.

Ben said, "Wait, I've got one more question."

Pat turned back. "You're supposed to feed me information, not vice-versa."

Ben said, "Shmuel Rubin's sister Deborah seems to be missing. Does the Bureau have anything on her?"

Pat shrugged. "Why are you looking for her?"

"She's still listed as an officer of L'Dor v'Dor. Treasurer."

"If I hear anything, I'll let you know," said Pat and continued up the ramp.

Chapter Twenty-Four

Steins

Ben stood next to his rented car, watching Agent Gilmore leave, thinking.

Abruptly he put his keys away and returned to the elevator. Seven minutes later he again stood in front of Lippman Investigations. He rang the bell.

As before, several minutes elapsed before the door was opened a few inches and Hilly peered at him. The detective smiled and opened the door to admit Ben.

"Forget something, Rabbi?"

Ben shook his head. "I think I need more of your services. Mrs. Morgenstern and I are in the process of winding up a nonprofit charity. How can we get copies of its tax returns for the last several years?"

"Their accountant or CPA should have them."

"She's missing. So is her husband. Abducted or hiding, I don't know."

Hilly said, "I imagine that an officer of the corporation could request them from the IRS."

"How long would that take?"

"A few weeks to a few years."

"Is there another way?"

Hilly frowned. "There might be. It's expensive and possibly illegal."

"You'd have to bribe an IRS employee?"

Hilly frowned again. "I don't discuss my methods."

"Hypothetically speaking, then, if someone requested such service from, say, the Ace Detective Agency of Chicago, how long would it take and how much would it cost?"

"Hypothetically, the Ace Detective Agency would likely want about $10,000."

"Do you happen to know anyone at the Ace Detective Agency?"

"Not at the moment. But I have a contact who might know someone there."

Ben inclined his head. "Got it. Thanks for your help."

"If you need someone to call my contact, let me know."

"I will and thanks again."

Chapter Twenty-Five

STEINS

Ben drove south toward Beth Ohr. He turned into the parking lot and found a space near the buildings. The lot was filling up and when Ben glanced at his watch, he realized that Shabbat services would soon begin.

He pulled out his phone, then searched his pockets for the scrap of paper that Kylee Dugan had given him with her phone number scrawled on it. After coming up empty, he realized that he had left that paper on his nightstand.

He had no more than ten minutes before services began and he wanted very much to be there for the opening prayers; most of the attendees would probably not attend the Saturday morning service—few Jews these days were so pious as to attend both.

His phone rang and the ID registered: Marcia Katz. He took the call.

"Hi Marcia," he said.

"Ben, how are you?" said Mrs. Katz.

"Fine but I only have a minute before Shabbat services."

"Of course. I found a woman who knows Leah Shevitz and her husband."

"Can you text me her contact info?"

"Right away. Shabbat Shalom."

"Shabbat Shalom," Ben replied. Peace to you on the Sabbath.

Chapter Twenty-six

Steins

Ben's Shabbat sermons on Friday night and Saturday morning were well received by the worshippers who nearly filled Beth Ohr's large sanctuary. Like most Orthodox synagogues, men and women sat in different sections, separated by a *mechitza* or curtain, a concept that originated during the Second Temple era (530 BCE to 70 CE). The idea was to prevent men from losing their concentration on prayer and being with God by looking at a woman. As Beth Ohr was a Modern Orthodox congregation, women participated in the service, although with many restrictions.

Ben's two sermons were similar but not identical and drew upon the writings of Nachman of Breslov, a revered Eighteenth-Century rabbi who lived and wrote in what is now Ukraine. Nachman was among the few of his era who praised the idea of women engaging in prayer and in synagogue life. Ben used that as his theme and suggested ways that the congregation could benefit from more participation by women.

Not everyone in the sanctuary was thrilled by Ben's ideas but it was clear from his reception after the event that most were.

On Saturday, following an excellent meal in the synagogue social hall, Ben retired to his tiny apartment for a few hours of reading Talmudic commentaries. He was very conscious of the fact that since his ordination, his life had rarely allowed for study and contemplation and he missed that. About 4:00, he laid his book aside and took a nap.

A little after 7:00 he awoke, bothered by the feeling that he had forgotten something. After a few minutes, he realized that he hadn't returned Kylee's call.

He found her number on the nightstand where he had emptied his pockets the previous day and punched the number into his cell phone.

The phone rang several times, then went to voice mail. Ben left his name and number and a brief message.

Then he read the text message from Marcie Katz and dialed the number of one Charmaine Hickenlooper, Certified Public Accountant. The number was her business and his call went straight to voice mail. Again, Ben left a message. Then he tried to find her home number. Only the business was listed.

There was something else nagging at his mind. He had searched Rubin's home but he had not been very thorough. He suspected that there might be more to find.

He brushed his teeth, then changed into dark jeans, a black pullover sweater, a warm navy jacket, and a dark watch cap. Ten minutes later, lights out, he pulled into Sunflower Road and parked around the corner from the cul de sac. There was only one parked car in the cul de sac, a late model Jaguar XF with Wisconsin plates.

Before he could get out of his car, a light went on in Rubin's house. A few minutes passed and the light went out. The glow of a flashlight, moving from room to room, tracked the movement of the invader.

The flashlight went out. After several seconds, a tall, well-built man in slacks and a windbreaker, a large black Stetson perched on his head, came down the sidewalk, climbed into the Jaguar and drove away.

By then Ben had memorized the license plate number.

He waited ten minutes, then got out of the Honda, went around to the back door and used his key to get in. Ben checked the front door: It was unlocked, suggesting that the tall man had entered that way. Ben left it unlocked and stood in the darkness, thinking.

Where would an older rabbi hide something that he didn't want to be found?

The basement door was also unlocked. Mindful of a recent

experience where he was locked into a house that was then set afire, Ben went into the kitchen, found a doorstop and wedged it under the basement door. He went down seven stairs and turned on the flashlight. The first thing he saw was a big freezer chest. Above it was a window. Ben hopped on the chest, pulled the window up a few inches and determined that there were no bars, only an insect screen.

He hopped down and searched the space, finding little but a workbench, a few tools, an empty filing cabinet, and a large wooden table.

He opened the freezer, half-afraid that he'd find the corpse of Deborah Rubin. Instead, it was filled with freezer bags with labels from Holzkopf's Kosher Meat Market in the Edgewater area. Reading the address on the label, Ben realized that the butcher shop was less than a mile from the high-rise where Rubin had installed Kylee Dugan.

He began to remove the meat from the freezer, stacking it on the table. There was a bit of everything: Beef, lamb, chicken, turkey, and fish. There were steaks, chops, roasts, ribs, sausage, several whole chickens, a small turkey, four swordfish steaks and two enormous salmon filets. When most of the meat was on the table, Ben used his flashlight to peer into the chest. On the bottom, between two large chickens, was a cardboard box wrapped in plastic and bubble wrap. He removed the chickens, then the box.

The bubble wrap was brittle from the cold and came apart in his hands. The plastic required the use of his penknife. Inside the box was an external hard drive with a 500-gigabyte capacity.

A strange place to keep a hard drive, Ben thought.

He put the drive in his jacket pocket, then was struck by a thought: He could put the meat back in the freezer and leave. But Rubin was never coming back and sooner or later his house would be cleaned out and sold, by an heir if he had one or by the local authorities.

He decided to load the meat into the trunk of his car and give it to a homeless shelter. It was a risk: The meat could be traced to the butcher shop and then to Rubin.

Ben decided it was worth the risk to perform this small *mitzvah* of feeding the poor.

Chapter Twenty-seven

Chicago

Ben parked in front of the Lincoln Park Community Shelter, went inside and found the night manager, who was visibly overjoyed to fill his almost empty freezer with high-quality kosher meat.

"You have no idea how much this will mean to our residents," he said. "Easter is just around the corner and we always try to put on a big feed."

"My pleasure," Ben said.

"Where did all this come from?"

"A man in our community, who was fairly wealthy, died recently. This meat was in his home freezer. I couldn't see it going to waste."

"Is there any ham? Our residents always ask for it on Easter Sunday."

Ben explained that it was all kosher, meaning meat from animals mentioned in the Torah and slaughtered and prepared in accordance with its law. Jews were not permitted to eat pork: Pigs have cloven hoofs but do not chew a cud; they were therefore not a kosher animal.

The manager seemed a little disappointed.

Ben shook his hand declined a receipt for the donation and made his way back to his car.

He checked the time: A little past 9:30.

He got his phone out and called Kylee. Again, the call went to voice mail.

An inner voice, more a feeling in Ben's viscera than an actual voice, told him that something was wrong. Her apartment was no more than ten minutes distant and he still had Rubin's keys and the garage door clicker.

§

Ben parked next to the red Miata, used the clicker to access the corridor and made his way soundlessly down the thick carpet. The building was utterly silent, except for faint music that grew louder as he approached 2006. He rang the bell and waited a full minute. Rang it again and waited two minutes. Then he used his key.

All the lights were on.

"Kylee?" called softly as he entered. "Kylee, are you here?"

He followed the music to the bedroom.

Kylee lay on her back, arms and legs akimbo, eyes staring at the ceiling. Something was wrapped tightly around her neck; she was otherwise nude.

Ben moved closer and flinched: Her arms, breasts and inner thighs were covered with angry red burns. She had been tortured.

What a terrible way to die, Ben thought.

Careful not to touch anything, Ben looked until he found Kylee's cell phone.

He thought for a long moment, then pocketed the phone, went back out to his car and sat behind the wheel.

The rented Honda had a Bluetooth setup to allow hands-free phone use. One of its features was that it could download and store a digital phone book from any linked phone. Ben had not linked his own phone to the car because he didn't spend much time in the car. Now he linked Kylee's phone to the car, then uploaded her contacts and call list. Thus he could learn who she called and how often, as well as who had called her.

That completed, Ben turned off the ignition and listened to

voicemails on her phone. There were seven. Three were from him, one was from Rubin, who had called two weeks earlier to say that he would be over later and three were from the same man, no name given, telling her to call him. The voice seemed to have a faint accent that Ben couldn't place but was possibly Spanish or Portuguese.

On the outgoing side, Kylee had twice called Beth Ohr, once to a number that looked like a business of some kind and had made seven calls over a week's time to the same number that had left the voice mails. The number was identified only as "A."

Ben deleted his voice mails to Kylee from her phone. Then he returned to the apartment, used Kylee's phone to call 911 and in a thick German accent, reported finding a dead woman in the apartment. Before leaving he wiped Kylee's phone down with a handkerchief and left it where he had first found it.

He left the door slightly ajar and returned to his car. He covered his front license with his handkerchief, pulled the sun visor down, put on sunglasses and drove out of the structure.

He parked two blocks away in a supermarket parking lot from where he could observe the entrance to the North Sheridan Road high-rise, removed his handkerchief from the plate, stowed the sunglasses and raised the visor.

A few minutes went by before he heard a siren. A Chicago patrol unit turned into the visitors' parking area.

Before he left the parking lot, he copied every phone number in Kylee's contacts list onto a page in Rubin's notebook and then deleted the phone data from the car.

Ben started the engine and headed back to Steins, feeling sad and powerless. Kylee had reached out to him and now she was dead. Maybe he could have saved her, he told himself.

Chapter Twenty-eight

Steins

Ben parked near the well-lit entrance to the sanctuary building. As he left the car, three large men stepped out of the darkness to bar his path.

"You're coming with us," said one of the men and grabbed Ben's left shoulder.

Lighting fast, Ben clamped his right hand atop the other man's paw, planted his left foot and kicked him in the groin with his right foot.

The man released him and stumbled away.

Ben whirled toward the second man, kicked his left kneecap hard and when the man bent forward, Ben clapped both fists on the man's ears, pulled his head down and brought his own right knee up to strike him under his chin.

The third man drew a gun and went around his writhing comrade.

Ben was waiting. His first kick knocked the gun away and the second struck his assailant's solar plexus.

Ben moved to each of the three fallen men and retrieved their guns.

"Who is in charge?" Ben said and one of the men groaned.

"Who sent you?"

The first man that Ben had fought struggled to his feet.

"You have something that belongs to our boss," he said, gasping for air.

"Who is your boss?"

"Jake. Jack"

"Jack what?" Ben said.

All three of the men, now on their feet, shrugged.

"We just call him Jake or Boss," said the man.

"What is it that I'm supposed to have that belongs to Jack?"

"A big aluminum case," said the first man.

"Okay," Ben said. "Tell Jack that I don't appreciate his bad manners. If he'd like to have his case back, I'll meet him at 11:00 tomorrow morning at Banners. We'll have coffee and discuss it. If he convinces me that the case is really his, I'll give it back."

"Just like that?" said the first man.

"That's how civilized people act," Ben said. "Do you know that this is a synagogue? A holy structure dedicated to God?"

"I guess," said the first man.

"Then can you see how inappropriate it was to just show up, manhandle me and demand something?"

All three men nodded, yes.

"You should be ashamed of yourselves," Ben said.

"Can we have our guns back?" said the last man that Ben had fought.

Ben removed the first gun's magazine, then racked the slide to eject a cartridge. He repeated this twice, then handed the guns but not the magazines, to each man in turn.

"I'll give your bullets back tomorrow when I see Jack," Ben said.

"Where'd you learn to fight like that?" said one of the men.

"At the 'Y' in New York," Ben said. "And in Israel."

The three men stared at Ben.

"Good night," Ben said and moved past the trio to the front door, which he unlocked. Behind him, he heard car doors slamming and an engine start.

In his apartment, Ben called Agent Gilmore and described what had happened in the parking lot, omitting any mention of fighting.

"What time is your meeting?" she said.

"Eleven."

"I'll have a team at your place by 9:00."

"Have them dress in dark suits and wear big black fedoras," Ben said.

As he undressed for bed, he found the hard drive in his jacket pocket. It was still very cold and Ben was unwilling to chance shattering its metal interior by plugging it in. He put in a dresser drawer under his underwear and socks.

Chapter Twenty-nine

Steins

Five men and one woman arrived at 8:30, just as Ben had left the shower. They wore dressy-casual attire.

"Sorry we're early," Pat said. "We've got a lot to do."

"I'll be downstairs getting some orange juice," Ben said.

When he returned a quarter of an hour had passed and most of the FBI crew was busy stamping invisible ink on every $50 and $100 bill in the case. One technician had carefully opened the case lining, inserted a tracking beacon and was sewing the lining shut with tiny, almost invisible stitches.

"You should wear a vest," Pat said as Ben came through the door.

"It won't go with my slacks and sports jacket," he said.

"I meant a Kevlar vest. In case you get shot."

Ben shook his head. "I'm sure they will pat me down. If they find Kevlar, they may well walk out.

Pat shrugged. "I'll have to have you sign a release."

"Then you'll have to run this op with someone else."

"Why are you being such a hard-ass?"

Ben cocked his head, considering. "Maybe I'm just a natural hard-ass. But I've always been able to trust my instincts and my instinct tells me that he'll have someone on the sidewalk or just inside the door to pat me down for weapons or a wire. I'm trying to pass myself off as an unworldly rabbi."

"A wire won't be a problem," said the technician working on the case. "There's a mic and a radio transmitter in the case's handle."

"And just to be sure, I've got a man over at Banners putting a mic on every table," Gilmore said.

§

The sky was gray and a frigid wind blew as Ben parked on the street and walked around the corner to Banners. A tall, graying, well-dressed man stopped him on the sidewalk.

"Rabbi Ben Maimon?" said the man.

"Guilty as charged," Ben replied. The man dropped an envelope at his feet.

"You're served," he said and walked away.

Ben grabbed the envelope off the sidewalk and stuffed it in his pocket.

Just inside Banner's door, he was stopped again, this time by one of the men from the previous evening.

"Sorry, Rabbi but I'm gonna have to pat you down. Understand it's nothing personal."

Ben dropped into a crouch and the taller man froze.

Ben laughed, straightened up, held his arms over his head and allowed himself to be searched.

Another well-dressed man waved from a table near the back of the room and Ben, hefting the big aluminum case above his shoulders to avoid hitting a table, made his way back to him.

"Jack Dworkin," said the man, rising. He was a little over six feet, solidly built, with dark, curly hair cut a little too long and a prominent nose. Ben guessed his age as early forties.

"I apologize for my men's actions last night," he said.

"And I apologize for roughing them up. But they were waving their guns around and I decided that letting them shoot me was not a good option."

Dworkin laughed, a deep, richly mellow sound. "And I

thought that I'd hired tough guys. Do you want a job?"

Ben shook his head. "No thanks, I've got one."

"What is it that you do?"

"I'm a rabbi," Ben said. "Right now, I'm filling in for the late Rabbi Rubin and I'm also filling in for Rabbi Shevitz, who is missing."

"Missing?"

"The folks at Beth Ohr think that Rabbi Shevitz and his wife were abducted."

Dworkin shook his curls. "And you?"

Ben shrugged. "They might have become alarmed when Rabbi Rubin was killed."

Dworkin started to reply when a waiter appeared.

"Good to see you, Rabbi," said the waiter, who was also an FBI agent named Price. "What would you like?"

"The usual," Ben said.

The waiter turned to Dworkin. "And you, sir?"

"Just coffee," he said.

The waiter left and Dworkin grinned. "Now I see how that process server knew you'd be here."

Ben shrugged. "Mr. Dworkin, can you give me some reason to believe that this Halliburton case belongs to you?"

"There's exactly $560,400 in it. Mostly twenties and tens."

"Anything else?"

"My initials are scratched into the back, lower right corner."

Ben hefted the case and looked.

"So they are. How did this case get into the trunk of Rabbi Rubin's Lincoln?"

"I put it there."

"May I ask why?"

"First, tell me about what you're doing here in Chicagoland. A week ago, you were in Israel. Before that, Buenos Aires for almost a month."

"You're unusually well informed."

"In my business, it's critical."

"May I ask your business?"

"I'm in personal entertainment."

"Personal entertainment. Do you mean video games, downloading movies, stuff like that?"

Dworkin tried to conceal his amusement but failed. "Something like that," he said. "So what are you doing here in Chicagoland? In Steins?"

"I was in Israel to get married," Ben said. "Before that, I was in Argentina to meet my fiancé's family. In Israel, a very important rabbi, a cousin to the late Rabbi Rubin, asked me, as a favor to his scholarship fund, to come to Chicago and wind up the charity that Rabbi Rubin ran."

"Wind it up as in shut it down?"

"Exactly. It's no longer accepting donations."

"I didn't know that Rubin was going to get hit by a car. I gave him that suitcase as a donation the day before."

"Then that explains it," Ben said. "Please, take your money."

"I could donate it to L'dor v'Dor, with the usual provisions."

Ben shook his head and just then the waiter returned with coffee. While Ben added sugar and stirred, Dworkin remained silent.

"You want the donation?"

Ben shook his head. "I told you, we're in the process of shutting things down."

"How long will that take?"

"We're just getting started," Ben said. "Maybe a month."

"Then why not take this as a final donation?"

Ben said, "I don't think so. But what are the "usual provisions" that you mentioned?"

Dworkin looked around the room, then leaned forward and lowered his voice.

"Rubin and I had this thing. I donate cash every month, he sends 18 percent to Israel, for his student rabbis and I get the balance back a week later in a wire transfer from Grand Cayman Island."

Ben nodded. "Now I understand. You've been doing this for some time?"

"A few years now."

"Is that even legal?"

"I don't see why not. So, do you want the donation?"

"I'd like to help you out, Mr. Dworkin but the fact is that I don't know how to send your 82 percent back via a wire transfer. I have no records of a bank account in Grand Cayman Island. Maybe all that's in the records that we haven't found yet."

Dworkin fished in his pocket and came out with a business card. "Look into that, Rabbi and give me a call if you can figure it out."

Ben nodded. "I'll do that. But you best keep your money. I don't have a safe place for it. Can't put it in the bank."

Dworkin nodded. He stood up, dropped a $20 bill on the table and hefted the aluminum case. Then he stopped and bent down to whisper in Ben's ear.

"I know what's in the subpoena, Rabbi. But how the hell could you be fooling around with Morgenstern's wife here while you were in Israel and Buenos Aires?"

Ben turned to Dworkin, deadpan, "The secrets of the Zohar are not for the uninitiated."

Dworkin cracked up, slapped Ben on the shoulder and walked out of the restaurant, still laughing.

When the waiter brought Ben his bagel with lox and cream cheese, he ate it, ordered a second cup of coffee and when he was finished, left the restaurant by a door leading to the parking structure.

He found Pat Gilmore in the elevator.

"That went very well," she said by way of greeting. "What did he whisper to you?"

"He told me, not in so many words, that he has someone in the Kishnef County State's Attorney's office."

Chapter Thirty

STEINS

It was a little past noon when Ben got back into his car. He headed for Skokie and the rental agency that owned the Honda.

Twenty minutes later he had returned the Honda, paid for the rental and then booked a year-old Toyota Rav 4, also black.

On his way back to Beth Ohr, Miryam called from Jerusalem.

"You didn't tell me that Yossi's secretary is a dish," she said, giggling.

"Mrs. Shapiro?"

"Aviva is a little too old for you but she's very attractive," she continued.

"You went to see Yossi?"

"Don't change the subject, Casanova Ben."

Ben laughed. "The first time I met Mrs. Shapiro and by the way, she's much more important than a secretary, she had four big IDF bodyguards with her and they searched me at gunpoint. So much for my charm."

"Yossi told me that you took the Codex gig because of the gorgeous woman you'd be working with."

"True. Chana Sara is her name. And I told you all about her on the day that you invited me to recite *Shacharis* [the morning prayer service] while standing in your tomato plants."

"What did she look like, Romeo Ben?"

"Tall and beautiful and a little distant. But you had the

womanly charms that I wanted and needed. So let us talk about Yossi."

"He's going to have his own people do a background check on Rabbi Abadi. If he comes up clean and he will, Yossi will ask the Israeli Consul General in Buenos Aires, who happens to be Yossi's nephew by marriage, to issue Abadi an Israeli diplomatic passport. That should solve the problem."

"You do good work, my sweet little Marita."

"Yossi would appreciate a wedding invitation."

"I guess we could squeeze in a couple more," Ben said.

"What about a place for our wedding?"

"How about the sanctuary of Beth Ohr? A Modern Orthodox *shul* that seats about 900?"

"And the reception?"

"I'm working on it. In a pinch, we could use the shul's social hall, which has a kosher kitchen and seats about 400?"

"Is there room to dance?"

"How many Moshons and how many Benkamals will attend?"

"About sixty of each. Maybe a few more. Better plan for a hundred and thirty."

"Then there will be plenty of room."

"If you can't find anything better, the Beth Ohr social hall is fine."

"I'll look around, consult a few experts."

"How have you been, Ben? Still no burning houses?"

"Not a one. I did have a little scuffle with some gun-toting goons but there were only three of them."

"Ben, you promised."

"I promised to stay safe. And I'm safe. As I said, just a scuffle."

"I've seen your scuffles, Bruce Lee Ben."

A soft tone sounded in Ben's ear."

"Can you hold on a minute? Another call."

"Surely you'd rather let it go to voicemail and tell me how much you miss me."

"I miss you more than David lusted after Bathsheba. More than Jacob wanted Rachel. More than life itself."

"Then call me tomorrow, dearest man."

"Before you go, how do you feel about cats?"

"We get along very well, as long as they know where to poop. Why?"

"I found a poor starving pussycat in Rabbi Rubin's house. It's in an animal hospital. I can keep it or try to find it a home."

"What's its name, Ben?"

"We'll have to give it a name."

"Then let's keep it. I love you, Ben. Stay safe."

"You are my one and only, Marita. Be well."

Ben broke the connection and looked at the call log—as he had suspected, it was the veterinarian's office that had just called.

On the way to the animal hospital, he stopped to buy cat food and water bowls, a giant litterbox, and a big bag of cat litter.

Later, after brushing his teeth, saying the evening prayer and getting ready for bed, he found the cat dozing on his pillow.

"In for a penny, in for a pound," said Ben to himself and got another pillow, then lay down beside the sleeping feline. She opened one eye, then closed it.

As Ben slid into sleep, he felt rather than heard the cat purring.

Chapter Thirty-one

Steins

Out of bed at 6:00 on Monday morning, Ben ran his five miles, choosing a somewhat different route than previously. Once he found his pace, he had time to think. His brief was to close down L'Dor v'Dor. That might be difficult without records, so finding those records was his first priority. Perhaps they were on the 500 GB hard drive that he'd taken from Rubin's freezer. Finding Rabbi Shevitz and his wife, however, might be a shortcut to records, so his first call would be to Charmaine Hickenlooper, CPA. Also, he would look through Shevitz's office and see what else he could find. The murder of Kylee Dugan was not his business, although Ben supposed that he had some information that might help find her killer. Likewise the death of Rabbi Rubin—he might have information that would be useful to find his killer. So after talking with Hickenlooper, he'd stop by the cop shop and see Captain Peters.

§

Charmaine was a bright, cheerful and heavy woman in her forties who offered him tea and a slice of her homemade crumb cake.

"Now, what can I do for you, Rabbi?" she said after Ben had taken a first bite of what turned out to be an excellent cake.

"Leah Shevitz," Ben said. "If she had some reason to hide, where might she go?"

"Hide from what?" Charmaine asked.

"Her husband's predecessor, a rabbi who had retired from the pulpit but still ran a nonprofit for which Leah kept the books, was killed. The next day Leah's husband disappeared. And then Leah disappeared."

"They were kidnapped?"

"It's possible. The FBI has the case. I'd like to explore the possibility that Rabbi and Leah Shevitz were in fear for their own lives and they went into hiding."

Charmaine thought for a long moment. "They have a cabin near Newville, on Lake Koshkonong."

"Have you been there?"

"Once, several years ago."

"Can you describe it?"

Charmain wrinkled her face. "White. One story pitched roof. Lots of windows. A chimney. Long gravel driveway and a front porch with a big swing and a couple of rocking chairs."

Ben told himself that this description probably fit half the cabins on the lake.

"Where on the lake, if you recall?"

"Well, not too far from Newville. East. On a street called... Oxblood or something like that."

"Anything else you can remember?"

"It was very close to the water and somewhere around there is a street called Pocahontas, I seem to recall."

"What kind of cars did they drive?"

"Leah had a new Malibu. Black. Her husband bought a Jag last year."

"What color?"

"Dark red or something. Maybe purple?"

"Four doors or two?"

"I'm not sure."

"You've been very helpful," Ben said. "One more question: Do you have their home address?"

§

Ben used the picks in his trouser cuffs and opened both of the locks on the Shevitz's back door in Steins.

It was a three-story home of brick, perhaps forty or fifty years old but with obvious upgrades to plumbing and electrical. Ben went from room to room, just looking. Downstairs was a kitchen, formal dining room, nicely appointed living room, a small study with an old roll-top desk.

The second floor was four bedrooms, including a nursery with two beds and dozens of toys in a box. There were two master bedrooms, each with its own bath, shower and toilet, all new. The closets in one were filled with women's clothing, while the other room's storage was almost evenly divided between male and female clothing. Ben decided that Mrs. Shevitz was a clothes horse.

The staircase door to the third floor was locked but not for long. The top floor was one long attic, with storage boxes, some older furniture, and filing cabinets with Leah's client files. The last folder in the back of the lower drawer was labeled L'Dor v'Dor. It was empty.

Ben went back downstairs and into the kitchen. He looked around. Near the refrigerator were a half-empty water dish and an empty dish with a few crumbs of dry dog food.

"Where is the dog?" Ben said and just then the front door opened and a teenaged boy with long, dirty blonde hair and orthodontic braces entered. A basset hound on a leash followed him. The dog ran over to Ben, who knelt, allowed the dog to sniff his hands, then gently scratched behind the hound's ears.

"Who are you?" said the boy. "How did you get in?"

Ben said, "I'm Rabbi Maimon. I came through the back door. How much do the Shevitz's owe you for walking…"

"Cleo is her name," the kid said. "Uh, I get $5 for a long walk."

"Did she poop today?"

"Oh yeah. Big time."

"How long since Rabbi Shevitz paid you?"

"Five days ago."

Ben reached in his wallet, found a twenty and five and gave it to the kid.

"Thanks," he said.

Ben said, "I forgot your name?"

"Harold. Harold Hoffman. Call me HH."

"Nice to meet you, Harold."

"I gotta take off," the kid said.

"Me too. Make sure you lock the doors, front and back."

"Sure."

Ben went out the front door, turned to wave at Harold and drove away very sure that neither of the Shevitzes had been kidnapped.

Chapter Thirty-two

Steins

Ben parked in the visitor's lot behind the police station. "Captain Peters," Ben told the sergeant at the desk. "I'm Rabbi Maimon."

"Expecting you, Rabbi?"

"He was going to find something for me and told me to stop by today."

"Have a seat."

Five minutes dragged by before Peters, beaming, appeared at the desk.

"Come on back, Ben," he said.

"Coffee?" Peters asked as they passed a Keurig coffeemaker on a table.

"I'm good," Ben said.

Ben waited until Peters was behind his desk before he sat down.

"Captain, the day before yesterday, a young woman named Kylee Dugan was murdered in Chicago. In an Edgewater Beach high-rise."

"A little out of my jurisdiction, Rabbi. How do you know this?"

"If you can keep this confidential, I found the body and called it in."

Peters shot Ben an appraising look. "You didn't give your name and you left the scene?"

Ben nodded agreement.

"How is it that you happened to find her?"

"I'll start at the beginning. The apartment belonged to Rabbi Rubin. I found his keys in his office at the synagogue. He had retired as the primary rabbi for Beth Ohr about three years ago. His pension was supposedly going to his sister, who lived at that address. I wanted to talk to the sister about the charity—she's listed as an officer. When I got to the apartment, I found Ms. Dugan living there. She was getting the rabbi's pension as a co-signer on the rabbi's sister's account."

"Where is the sister?"

"No idea. I'm guessing dead."

"How old was Ms. Dugan?"

Ben shrugged. "About twenty-four or so. Maybe a little younger."

"Old Rabbi Rubin was keeping a mistress in an expensive Edgewater apartment?"

"And having the synagogue send her his pension."

"Whoda thunk?" said Peters with a grim smile.

"Later, Dugan called me at the synagogue. By the time I got around to calling her back, the call went to voicemail, which I deleted from her phone."

Peters frowned. "Tampering with evidence?"

"The Chicago cops would have wasted a lot of time considering me a suspect and that would be routine. I didn't want to waste their time or mine."

"But now you're here. Are you wasting my time?"

"Maybe. But first and this is related, did you get anything on the Rubin hit-and-run paint from the FBI crime lab?"

"Turns out my crime-scene people didn't send it to the FBI. They sent the sample to Springfield, the State Police Forensic Lab."

Peters pawed through a pile of reports on his desk.

"Here we go. The car that killed Rabbi Rubin was a Subaru Forester, 2015 through 2017, "Ice Silver Metallic" paint.

Ben took out his notebook. Two things: "Dugan told me that she had another boyfriend—her arrangement with Rubin seems to have been purely business—whom she loved but was married. This boyfriend drove a silver Subaru. Second, there were only a few numbers in the phone's contact list. One of them called her several times and left a voice message: 'Call me.' No name. She called that number several times."

"You have that number?"

Ben wrote it out on a fresh sheet of paper, tore it out of the notebook and passed it across the desk.

"I don't know who killed Dugan. Or why she was tortured. I have a theory. But before I get to it, I'll suggest that with what you now know from the crime lab and that phone number, if it belongs to a man who owns or drives, a silver Subaru, 2015 through 2017, then he very likely ran down Rabbi Rubin."

"And his motive was what, jealousy?"

"I think so. Here's this rich old guy who's seeing his girlfriend. Does the boyfriend know that the old guy is paying her rent and then some? I'd guess not. Dugan told me that her boyfriend, the one she loved, was married and had no money. If he came by one night and saw Rubin's Lincoln parked next to Dugan's Miata, he could have gotten Rubin's home address off the Miata registration."

"It lines up. I'll have that phone number run and once we have the owner and address, we can cross-check Subaru registrations. Half an hour's work."

"One more thing. The man who repeatedly called Dugan had what sounded like a faint Latino accent. But not Spanish. I'll guess Portuguese. He might be from Brazil."

"Good work," Peters said. "You have a theory on who killed Dugan?"

"Two nights ago I was greeted by three tough guys in the synagogue parking lot. They wanted a big Halliburton case that I found in Rubin's car. In the trunk. The case was stuffed with cash."

"What did you do?"

"I convinced these guys to have their boss meet me at Banner's yesterday for coffee. Then I called the FBI. On their instructions, I handed the case to Jack Dworkin, who is some kind of thug. The FBI is tracking this."

"Why did Rubin have the case?"

"He was laundering money for Dworkin through the charity."

Peters sat back in his chair and seemed lost in thought for several seconds.

"And you think his minions might have known about Rubin's girlfriend and tried to find the missing money by torturing her?" Peters said.

"I have no proof. And I don't want to speak to the Chicago police because they will surely try to pin Kylee Dugan's murder on me. At best, I'm looking at a day or two of constant interrogation. Even if I say nothing and demand a lawyer, I have the feeling they'll just lock me up for a while."

"I'll handle the Chicago force. Tip from an unregistered informant."

"Then we're almost done. Who does Pete the Russkie work for?"

Again Peters riffled through the pile on his desk.

"Intelligence says he's a gun for hire. Mostly a con man,

small-time. Beyond that, we have nothing."

Chapter Thirty-Three

Steins

Ben found his way to the county courthouse using Google Maps. Inside he passed through the metal detector, consulted a wall directory and took an elevator to the fifth-floor offices of the States Attorney.

A stunning, perfectly formed young woman with natural blonde hair and a little too much mascara smiled professionally from behind her desk. "Can I help you?"

"Mr. Morgenstern is expecting me."

The woman glanced down and frowned. "He's in a meeting, Mister…?

"Rabbi. Rabbi Ben Maimon. I can wait."

"I don't see your name on his appointment calendar."

"He'll see me because he is so sure that I am diddling his wife that he sued me."

The woman smiled, a natural and quite lovely expression.

"And *are* you, um, diddling his wife?"

"Of course not. I've only known her for a few days. Our relationship is client-attorney."

The young woman positively beamed.

"Have a seat, Rabbi and I'll see if I can get him out of that meeting."

§

Fifteen minutes later, a very tall, exceedingly handsome and powerfully muscular man of about forty, wearing an expensive blue suit, appeared.

Ben got to his feet.

"You're Rabbi Maimon?" said the State's Attorney for Kishnef County.

"You were expecting someone better looking? And taller? Ben said, with a smile.

Morgenstern frowned, "Why are you here?"

"To tell you two things. One I'll say here, the other requires privacy."

"What's the first thing?"

"My relationship with your wife is entirely professional. I engaged her services to help shut down a nonprofit corporation—a charity—that I'm connected with via Congregation Beth Ohr. I'm the interim rabbi there. And until six days ago, I was in Israel, meeting my fiancé's family. I am told that you and your wife were legally separated several months ago. The idea that you might win a suit for alienation of affection against me is therefore ludicrous. I urge you to withdraw your suit because when it's thrown out of court, I will of course sue for filing a frivolous complaint."

Morgenstern looked Ben up and down. "I'll consider it," said. "The other matter?"

Ben shook his head. "Do you have a room that you are certain is secure?"

"Of course."

"Please take me there."

Ben followed Morgenstern down a long corridor to a locked door. The big man produced a key from his vest pocket and led Ben into a small, windowless room with two chairs and a small, scarred wooden table. He locked the door behind him, then gestured to a chair.

When they were both seated, Ben said, "Day before yesterday I had a brief meeting with one of your local hoodlums at Banner's."

"Which one?"

"Jack Dworkin."

"Why were you meeting him?"

Ben shook his head. "Special Agent Pat Gilmore, FBI, can tell you about it if she decides that you have a need to know."

Morgenstern did not try to hide his surprise.

"You were part of some FBI op?"

"Again and with great respect, Agent Gilmore can answer your questions."

"Then why are we sitting here?" Morgenstern growled.

"As it happened, as I headed for the entrance to Banner's, your process server stopped me to deliver your subpoena. Dworkin observed this. Later, seated in the restaurant, our business over, Dworkin confided that he knew what the subpoena was about. He then proved this by telling me in detail who was suing me and why."

Ben paused to let the words sink in.

"You're saying that he has someone in my office feeding him information?"

"Or that your office has a listening device installed. Or both."

Very slowly, Morgenstern nodded his head, then got to his feet. Ben stood up.

"Thank you, Rabbi. You didn't have to do this."

"My civic duty, Mr. Morgenstern."

"It would be better if we didn't leave this room together," Ben added.

"You go first," said Morgenstern and extended his hand to shake.

Ben took it and whispered, "You have a wonderful wife. You should do everything you can to persuade her to remain married. Now is the time to woo her with all your might. Whatever it takes."

Shocked, all the big man could do was nod his head.

Ben left the room, shut the door behind him and on his way out of the office basked in the warm smile of the beautiful young woman at the reception desk.

Chapter Thirty-four

STEINS

Ben had just slid behind the wheel of his car when his phone rang.

"I told you," Captain Peters said in Ben's ear. "You should have been a cop. Should *be* a cop."

Ben said, "And this is because...?"

"Because the guy who called Kylee Dugan all those times owns a 2015 Subaru Forester, painted 'Ice Silver Metallic,' with a bashed-in left fender showing traces of blood and dark wool clothing. Abel Gonçalves, US citizen born in Brazil. He lives in Albany Park with his wife and five kids, has a good job as a machinist and moonlights as a pizza deliveryman in the Edgewater area. Chicago cops just picked him up."

Ben said, "Thanks for getting back to me. The Chicago officers will try to get this guy to cop to murdering Dugan as well. Given that he had already eliminated his rival, I doubt seriously that he was involved with that. You can help protect him by getting him out of Chicago so he can be prosecuted in your jurisdiction."

"I'm on that. But Chicago homicide dicks don't always listen to suburban guys like me."

Ben said, "Then get my new buddy Mr. Morgenstern involved right away. You want Abel Gonçalves transferred to Steins immediately. At least, that's what I would do if I were in your shoes."

"Ben, I think I could get the City Council to cough up $60,000 a year or so for your services as an on-call consultant. What do you say?"

"I'm very flattered. I'll consider it and I'll even talk it over with my wife-to-be."

"And I'll sniff around City Hall to find a councilman to carry this."

"Don't push too hard. Right now I'm pretty busy with other stuff."

"Just going to take the water's temperature."

"Talk to you soon, Captain."

§

Ben drove back to Beth Ohr, his mind racing. If Rubin's murder was the work of a jealous lover, then it had nothing to do with the disappearances of Rabbi and Leah Shevitz, Josh Green's decision to go into hiding or the resignation of Beth Ohr's executive director. Green was back with his family and had resumed his independent scholar routine. If he were convinced that Rubin's death had nothing to do with his charity and its money laundering, would the Shevitzes return? And why did they leave? Were they involved in Rubin's scheme?

Ahead Ben saw the yellow bricks of the public library. He waited for traffic to abate and made a sharp turn across Finkelstein Boulevard into the library's parking structure.

Chapter Thirty-Five

Steins

Josh Green was in the library stacks when Ben found him.

"Got a few minutes?" Ben said.

"Got to finish this while I'm able to remember the publications," Green said.

"I'll meet you in the employee lounge."

§

When Green pushed the lounge door open, his face was flushed and his eyes sparkled.

"Is that a yellow feather on your chin?" Ben said, by way of greeting.

Green looked confused, then smiled and finally laughed. "I get it. Yes, I finally swallowed that canary—in a manner of speaking."

"Enlighten me, if you will?"

"It's an economics theory that I've been nibbling at for years and years and now, I think, I have found the missing pieces of the puzzle. Most of them, anyway."

"Sounds fascinating but I'll avoid displaying my ignorance. I bring news and some questions."

"Go ahead."

"In your learned opinion, did the resignation of our executive director, your decision to go into hiding and the disappearances of the Shevitzes have anything to do with Rabbi Rubin's money laundering?"

Green blanched. "Money laundering?"

Ben nodded, yes.

Green said, "That's a very serious allegation."

"I have plenty of proof."

"You must—*we* must go to the police immediately."

Ben said. "I've done that. Would you answer my question, please?"

Green said, "In my case, no. First, Rabbi Rubin is killed and then Mrs. Mather—the executive director—resigns and Rabbi Shevitz disappears. I thought that some anti-Semitic group was coming after Beth Ohr's leadership."

"Do you have an opinion about either Mrs. Mather or Rabbi Shevitz? About why they took off?"

"Surely Rabbi Shevitz and his wife were abducted?"

"I'm of the contrary opinion," Ben said. "I'm pretty sure I saw Rabbi Shevitz a few nights ago at Rabbi Rubin's house."

Green put his head in his hands. "They can't *all* be involved in money laundering?"

"I hope you're right. I ask you to keep all talk of money laundering under your kippah for now."

"Certainly, Rabbi."

"Today the police found the man who may have ran down Rabbi Rubin," Ben said. "He's in custody now."

"Why would he do such a thing?"

Ben shook his head. "I'm sure the police are pursuing that information."

§

Ben drove back to Beth Ohr and waved to Mr. Singh, who was spreading fertilizer on the synagogue's lawn.

BRIDE OF FINKELSTEIN

Back in his room, Ben cleaned the cat box, set out fresh food and water and watched the tiny cat eat.

Then he booted up his new MacBook Pro, then plugged the external hard drive retrieved from Rubin's freezer chest into it.

It crashed. The Mac Book attempted to reboot itself, got as far as the home screen, then crashed again. And again.

Ben unplugged the drive. The MacBook cycled through a reboot and came back to the home page.

Ben realized that something on that portable drive was toxic to his MacBook.

He thought about it for a while, then found the keys to Rabbi Rubin's office and went upstairs. He knocked to make sure that Julie wasn't in the room, then used his key. He booted up the desk computer and as before it whirred and came to a stop with a message asking for a boot disk to be inserted.

Ben shut the desktop computer down. He inspected the connections on the back panel and discovered that this computer was not connected to anything. At least, not with a wire. No Internet connection, no printer, no networking device. Perhaps, if he could find a way to boot the computer, there would be wifi or Bluetooth for connection to another device or the Internet.

He plugged the external drive's USB connector into the back of the computer. Then he turned it on and waited. After a few seconds, the tiny LED on the external drive began to flicker and the computer's screen showed a normal boot sequence. But when the computer reached what Ben expected to be a Windows home page he was instead greeted with an unfamiliar screen in a familiar language: Hebrew.

The screen offered six choices, all in Hebrew. Another hurdle for the uninitiated: each Hebrew "word" represented numbers that stood for years. But the years were according to the Hebrew calendar.

Ben clicked on the first and saw an ordinary spreadsheet for

5771

And there it was: Seven different sources of funds, each designated by a code word: Gideon, Daniel, Joshua, Samson, Manasseh/Ephraim, Jonah, and Ruth.

Ruth. Ben pondered that for a long moment. That had to be a woman.

Manasseh/Ephraim, the Biblical sons of Joseph, might be the Stern brothers, Jake and Mendel.

It was a start.

Looking at the numbers, which were standard Arabic numerals and doing some figuring in his head, Ben saw that, for example, "Joshua" had donated $860,000 in January of 2011. $154,800 of that had gone to a category marked "fund." The balance, $705,200, went to Jericho, Ltd., a Bahamas corporation. He did the math on his cellphone and yes, $154,800 was eighteen percent of $860,000.

Ben checked another entry. Daniel's contribution, less eighteen percent, went to Babylon Holdings, LLC, a Curaçao corporation.

He was looking at the lost books of L'Dor v'Dor. The real books.

Obviously, the cryptic form of the data was an attempt to confuse or mislead anyone looking into money laundering.

A tremendous blast shook the building, shattering windows.

Ben left the room, took the stairs two leaps to a flight and was in front of the building in seconds.

At the far end of the parking lot, Rubin's Lincoln had been turned into a smoldering scrap heap. Broken glass was everywhere. Mrs. Levy and a few other people who had been in the building came out through the main entrance. Mr. Singh left his fertilizing and rushed to the main entrance.

Ben said, "Is everyone in the building safe? Where's Tracey?"

Levy, obviously shaken, pointed toward the parking lot.

"Tracey left about ten minutes ago."

Ben turned and called for the six others who had been in the building to approach.

"Did any of you see anything?" Ben said

All but Singh shook their heads.

"I went inside to use the toilet and somebody had left the fire door open," he said. "In the back."

"When did you notice?" Ben said.

"Just a minute ago, when I left the men's room."

Ben turned to Mrs. Levy. "I'm sure that police and firefighters will be here soon. Keep all these people in the office, because the police will want to talk to them."

"But they just told you that they didn't see anything," she said.

Ben smiled. "I'm not the police. If anybody leaves, they will go to their homes and interview them. Let's save everyone a little time, okay?"

Levy nodded to show that she understood.

Ben moved a few feet away and called Pat Gilmore.

"Two things," he said. "I found L'Dor v'Dor's records and somebody detonated a bomb in Rabbi Rubin's Lincoln, in the synagogue parking lot."

"I heard the blast," she said. "I'll let the Steins police handle it but thanks for keeping me up to date. When can I see the records?"

Ben said, "As soon as I can find a way to copy them for you."

Gilmore said, "Make it soon, Rabbi," and broke the connection.

Ben hit the speed-dial key for Miryam.

"Ben!"

"Hello, my love. Did I wake you?"

"No, no. Just going over some notes. I'm interviewing candidates for a school administrator."

"Miryam, you'll hear on TV or read in the papers that a car bomb detonated in the synagogue parking lot. Here in Steins. At Beth Ohr."

"Oh my God! Are you hurt?"

"Nobody was hurt. I just wanted to let you know that I'm fine. It was in an empty car in the far corner of a very large lot."

"But you're fine?"

"Good as gold," Ben said. "Nothing to worry about."

"Why would somebody do that, Detective Ben? Blow up a car and not hurt anyone?"

"Don't know yet, Light of my Life. I love you and I miss you and we'll talk again soon, okay?"

"No more burning houses! You promised."

"From now on, I only go into a burning house if you go in first."

"I cannot lose you, Ben. There's nobody else in the whole world for me."

"I feel exactly the same, Marita. Be careful."

"Dream of me tonight and we will be together in our sleep."

Miryam ended the call, allowing Ben to picture her in bed.

Moments later, the first police car rolled in, followed by a fire truck.

Ben walked to the patrol car and waited for the officers to

dismount.

"I'm Rabbi Maimon," he said and briefly explained that all the witnesses from inside the synagogue were standing by the door.

"Got it," said the senior officer and turned to his partner.

"Better call for a couple more units. We're going to need to canvas every house and apartment with a view of the parking lot."

The officer turned to Ben. "What did you see, Rabbi?"

Ben shook his head. "I was upstairs in an office. First notice was the explosion."

"Okay. We'll wait for a detective but meanwhile, where can we interview your staff?"

Chapter Thirty-six

Steins

It was growing dark by the time the police had left and Ben was able to return to his rooms. He had decided to find a reliable computer specialist to copy the hard drive, as he had no tools or instruments.

Meanwhile, he was hungry.

Ben returned to his tiny apartment, turned on a light and put his own laptop away. He weighed the wisdom of raiding the synagogue refrigerator for leftovers versus driving to what he had heard was an excellent and strictly kosher restaurant a mile away.

He decided on the restaurant. In the stairwell, however, Ben realized that he had forgotten to lock Rabbi Rubin's office. He climbed back up to the third floor but when he entered the office through its half-open door, there was nothing on the desk where the computer had been.

Rubin's computer and the external drive were gone.

Pat Gilmore rapped on the open door and Ben looked up.

"Anybody hurt, Rabbi?" she said.

Ben shook his head.

"Can I get a peek at those records you found?" she said.

Ben shook his head.

"They're gone. They were on a computer on this desk. When the bomb went off I ran downstairs."

Pat's face arranged itself into what Ben had learned was its skeptical look.

"Our maintenance super said that someone left a fire door open," Ben added.

"So, the bomb was a diversion to allow someone to steal the computer?"

Ben nodded, yes. "Looks that way."

"You better not be lying," Pat said.

"What is it with you people? Why do you assume that everyone is lying to you?"

"Because usually, they are."

Ben shook his head. "You have my entire police record. Is there anything in that about me lying to a police officer or an FBI agent?"

"I haven't read it that closely."

"Go back to your office and do your homework before you come at me suspecting that I'm trying to dupe you, lie to you, mislead you."

"Wow. Look who's touchy."

"I meant it. Please leave."

"I'm going," she said. "By the way, we have the bomber in custody."

"Who is it?" Ben said, his mind reeling.

"The janitor. The Arab guy."

Ben shook his head. "You've got the wrong man. He's not an Arab. He's a Sikh."

"He was carrying a sword under his overalls. And when we field-tested him for explosives, his hands came up positive for nitrates.

Ben shook his head again. "He's *not* the bomber. I thought FBI agents were smart people. Ujjal Singh is a US citizen by birth. He carries a ceremonial sword called a Kirpan because he's a Sikh and his religion demands it. He tested positive for nitrates because he spent the day spreading fertilizer on our lawns and green belt."

Pat stared at Ben. Then she pulled out her phone and dialed a number.

Chapter Thirty-seven

Jerusalem

Miryam and her two cousins, Ronit and Noa, found a corner booth in a busy café on Ben Yehuda Street and ordered iced coffees. Ronit was the eldest, just thirty, while Noa and Miryam were five years younger and born only a few months apart.

A burly, bearded man wearing a kippah and a long black coat appeared at their table.

"You," he said, pointing at Miryam. "Tell your rabbi boyfriend in Chicago that he's got to learn teamwork!"

"Who are you?" Miryam said.

"Never mind. Just talk to your boyfriend, before something bad happens to you."

"Piss off!" yelled Ronit, hurling her coffee at him.

The man retreated but not before a second man, well behind him, snapped several photos of the three young women.

Chapter Thirty-eight

Steins

Ben spent the morning making notes on what he could recall from his brief exploration of Rubin's computer.

Then he booted up his MacBook Pro and began looking at Google Maps pictures of southern Wisconsin. He found Lake Koshkonong, one of the larger lakes in southern Wisconsin and only half an hour north of Steins. But there was no street or road named Pocahontas or Oxblood. He did find a street named Oxbow Bend and one named Pottawatomi Trail. He'd start there, Ben decided and began to study the roads and terrain around that area, which was on Stony Point, at Bingham's Bay.

His phone beeped and he found himself looking at a picture of Miryam. Her face was animated, as if the photo had been snapped while she was in conversation,

There was nothing else with the photo and Ben didn't recognize the number of the phone that sent it but it was obviously from Israel.

He sent a brief text to Miryam and resumed his work on the map.

An hour passed and his phone beeped again.

Miryam had sent a text message:

Go to 500 West Madison, Chicago. ASAP. Identify yourself and ask to speak to "Eliyahu Ben-Shaul"

Go now!

Ben pondered the instructions. Eliyahu Ben Shaul *Cohen* was a legendary Israeli spy who was hanged by the Syrian government in 1961.

So this was likely a codeword for something to do with clandestine services.

Ben took his computer, his phone, all his cash, walked two blocks to the corner of Finkelstein and Epstein and hailed a cab.

An hour later he stepped out in front of 500 West Madison, which turned out to be the Israeli Consulate.

Inside he showed his Israeli driver's license to a receptionist and said, "Eliyahu Ben Shaul, please," in Hebrew. The receptionist's face betrayed nothing. She dialed a number, touched a screen and looked up at Ben. "He'll be right out," she said.

A door behind the long counter in the reception area opened and a short, older man with a well-groomed white beard beckoned to him. A gap in the counter magically opened and in seconds Ben was sitting in the office of Mordecai Braun, the cultural attaché and also the case officer for Mossad agents, legal or otherwise, operating in the Midwest. He handed Ben a telephone, mumbled, "secure line," then left the room.

"This is Rabbi Ben Maimon," he said.

"It's so wonderful to hear your voice," Miryam said. "Are you good?"

"I'm great, my dearest. What's with all the cloak and dagger?"

Miryam giggled. "Your old girlfriend would like a word with you."

"Rabbi, this is Aviva Shapiro," said a voice in Ben's ear. "Miryam told me that she was threatened in a coffee shop yesterday evening. Yossi made a few calls and discovered that your life is in danger also."

"I'm overwhelmed. The President of Israel has nothing better to do than act as my personal protection agency?"

"He's the head of state but honestly, he doesn't have that

much to do. Just between us, he misses the IDF, where he had some crisis to solve every day. And he considers you a national asset, Ben."

"Who is after me now?"

"We don't know yet. There is an open kidnap contract on Miryam, subject to approval from whoever wants her. And you are also to be taken alive for some purpose. Do you have any idea what this is about?"

"This is a secure line?"

"Of course."

Ben described his assignment from Rabbi Farkas, omitting nothing. He spoke about his now-confirmed suspicion that the charity was heavily involved in money laundering.

"So my guess is that these guys—the ones that Rabbi Rubin was laundering money for—either want to silence me or they think that I can continue washing their dirty money."

"Can you? Wash their money?"

Ben said, "No and that's a problem. I don't have bank account codes, I don't even know which banks are involved."

"Yossi is having Shabak look into this. They will no doubt have to speak with Rabbi Farkas. Anything I should know?"

"Just that he asked me to close this charity, forward its records and any cash to him in Israel and threatened to expel my sister, a rabbinical student, from Israel if I didn't do as told. Also, he's listed as the charity's corporate secretary. Oh, and he told me that he was a first cousin to Rabbi Shmuel Rubin, who was killed here recently but I have proof that's not true."

"I'll pass that along to Yossi," Shapiro said.

"Thank him for that, please," Ben said. "And thank you, Mrs. Shapiro."

"Not at all," she said. "Two more things: Miryam is to have

bodyguards until further notice and we'll detail a couple of our guys to keep an eye on you. Chances are that you won't even notice them."

"Thank you," Ben said. "May I have Miryam back?"

Miryam said, "This is like a spy movie, except that it isn't fun."

Ben said, "Right on both counts. When are you coming to Chicago?"

"Do we have a place to live?"

"Would you like me to rent an apartment or a house, just until we can get something better?"

"That's good. Nothing special. Something like your Cambridge apartment, if you can find it."

"I'll get on that. We'll have to rent furniture or something."

"You can do that? I never heard of that."

"It's cheap furniture at a premium price."

"Then don't. We'll camp out and buy our own furniture. How long will that take?"

"Let's shoot for the first of next month. I'll start looking very soon. In fact, I'll find someone to do the hard part. Leave it to me."

"No burning houses, Ben. You promised."

"No burning houses, my love."

Chapter Thirty-Nine

Southern Wisconsin

Ben called an Uber car and returned to Beth Ohr. His first stop was his apartment, where he changed the cat box, fed the cat and made sure that the water bowl was full. On his way out, he stopped in the office and left Mrs. Levy a brief note explaining that he might be out of touch for a day or more and to please make sure the cat had food and water.

He got in his rented Toyota and headed north. An hour later he was south of the lake and driving east along Highway 26, looking for a street named Vogel. Miles past where he had supposed it was, Vogel appeared. He turned left and headed north, toward the lake.

After a time, without advance notice, Vogel changed its name to Pottawatomi Trail. The road angled eastward, paralleling the shoreline and he drove past the cutoff to Oxbow before he realized it. A half-mile down he found a place to turn around.

Oxbow Bend was a curved, narrow street on an island between a canal that led to the lake and the lake itself. There were perhaps twenty houses, none painted white and none with a plethora of windows.

Ben drove slowly, looking for the Jaguar but saw no cars that resembled either make. On his third pass down the street, a man with a shotgun on his shoulder waved him down. Ben stopped and rolled down his window.

"Lost?" said the man.

"Looking for an old friend. I don't have the address and I'm not sure that this is even the right street."

"Go back south to 26 and then go east and you'll come to a sheriff's station. They'll know all the property owners in these parts."

Ben thanked the man, returned to Pottawatomi and headed back toward 26. He pulled off the road and brought up Google Maps. The sheriff's station was nearly ten miles east.

Ben decided that a different approach was called for. He drove southwest and after half an hour found the road to Newville that he had taken earlier. He found a gas station and pulled in behind a pickup truck. A man came out of the bathroom, got into the pickup and drove off. Ben pulled up behind a plum-colored Jaguar XF with Wisconsin plates.

"Better lucky than smart," Ben said to himself.

He shut off the engine and got out. At that moment a tall, dark-haired man wearing a gray Stetson over a brown windbreaker and tan slacks left the station's office and headed toward the Jaguar.

Ben smiled, turned to his own pump and fiddled with it until the man was pumping gas into the Jaguar. Then he came up alongside the taller man.

"Please don't be alarmed, Rabbi, I mean you no harm," Ben said in a conversational tone of voice.

The tall man whirled and took a gun from his pocket, a Glock19 like the one Ben saw in Rabbi Rubin's office.

"Who are you? What do you want?" the man said and Ben heard the panic in his voice.

"I'm Rabbi Maimon. Ben Maimon. I have information that you will find useful and I mean you no harm."

"How do I know you're a rabbi?"

"I'm going to take my wallet out," Ben said. "It's just a wallet."

"I'm waiting," said Shevitz.

Ben took his wallet from his rear pants pocket, opened it and removed his Israeli driver's license and the photocopy of his ordainment certificate. He put both on the Jaguar's fender and stepped back.

Shevitz peered at each document in turn, then gestured for Ben to take them. He lowered the gun but did not put it away.

"You are related to Salomen Maimon? The one who taught Talmud at JTS?"

"My grandfather, of blessed memory. But you are too young to have studied under him."

"My father, Rabbi Daniel Shevitz, was his student. He took me to meet Rabbi Maimon when I was a boy. He said that it might be my only chance to meet a *tzadik*.

Ben's eyes filled and he wiped them with a handkerchief.

"My father abandoned my mother when I was born," Ben said. "She died when I was twelve. I was raised by my grandparents and your father had it right: He was the closest thing to a living saint that his generation produced. Certainly, there must have been others like Salomen, but they went to the ovens."

Shevitz put the gun back in his coat pocket.

"Either you are a fine actor or you are what you say. Do you have a pulpit?"

"At the moment, I'm filling in for you at Beth Ohr."

Shevitz frowned as that sank in.

"Listen," he said. "There's a little bakery a few miles west on 59. I need to gas up. When I'm done, why don't you follow me and we'll have coffee or something."

Ben smiled. "Sounds like a plan."

Chapter Forty

Wisconsin

To Ben's surprise and delight, the bakery offered cheese blintzes. Ben ordered coffee to go with them and Shevitz had mint tea with a cheese Danish. When both men had emptied their plates, each sat back in his chair and silently regarded the other.

Shevitz said, "At the gas station, you said that you had information for me."

Ben nodded his head. "Before I share that, I have two questions for you."

After a lengthy pause, Shevitz also nodded. "Go ahead."

"Why did you go into hiding?"

"Because I thought that whoever killed Rabbi Rubin might come after me next."

"And that was because?"

"Rabbi Rubin was involved with some very sketchy characters. Mostly Jewish but all hoodlums."

"You were not involved with those sketchy characters?"

"You said *two* questions."

"Humor me. I'm sure you'll like what I have to tell you."

Shevitz stared at Ben for a long moment.

"No. I was not involved with those characters."

"But you knew what Rubin was doing with them, didn't you?"

A long, pained silence ensued. After what seemed like several minutes, Shevitz nodded, yes. "I have a good idea that he was laundering money for criminals but I'm not familiar with the details."

Ben said. "Good. Yesterday, the police arrested a man named Abel Gonçalves. A US citizen, born in Brazil. He is probably the man who ran down Rabbi Rubin."

"He's a professional? A hitman?"

"Not likely. I don't think he had anything to do with Rabbi Rubin's 'sketchy characters.' Gonçalves is a machinist. He's married but he also had a girlfriend, a young woman named Kylee. Rabbi Rubin was keeping Kylee in an Edgewater Beach apartment. He saw her three times a week. Their relationship was primarily financial. I surmise that when Gonçalves became aware that Rubin was sleeping with his girlfriend, he decided to eliminate his rival."

Shevitz shook his head. "That doesn't sound like Rabbi Rubin. He is—was—a deeply spiritual man."

Ben said, "That may be so. He was nevertheless a widower who wanted female companionship and sex. He had Beth Ohr send his monthly pension to an account that Kylee drew upon."

"How do you know all this?"

Ben explained, leaving out unnecessary details.

Shevitz said, "So those hoodlums aren't after me?"

Ben said, "It's unlikely. Your wife, however, was involved with L'Dor v'Dor as their accountant. She may or may not have known about the money laundering. I suspect that she kept one set of books and Rabbi Rubin kept a different set. But at the moment, I can't prove it. I'd like to have a chat with Leah."

"Why?"

"Because I was asked by Rabbi Meir Kaplan of the Israeli Rabbinate to go to Steins, shut down L'Dor v'Dor and send all its records and assets to the Rabbinate's scholarship fund. I was also asked to sub for you at Beth Ohr until you returned. I think that you should return. You're not on the Mob's radar. You should have nothing to fear from them."

"Does Josh Green know about this?"

"I'm pretty sure that he didn't know about the money laundering. He's back at Beth Ohr, no longer in hiding."

"I'm going to need to call him before I drive back."

"By all means."

"Rabbi Maimon. If all this is true, then you've performed a great mitzvah. It's a big load off my mind and Leah will be overjoyed. Tell me, how did you find me?"

"Went to your house and observed a teenager walking your dog. That told me that you were in hiding. I found a colleague of your wife who recalled that you had a cabin near the lake."

"On Oxbow Bend," Shevitz said.

"Did it used to be painted white?"

"No, that was a cabin I rented for a few seasons. When one of the houses nearby—about half a mile east—came up for sale, I bought it."

"And while we're clearing up mysteries, why were you in Rabbi Rubin's house a few nights ago?"

Shevitz's face registered shock.

"How could you know that?"

"I was there. I saw you leave. But at the time, I didn't know who you were."

"I went there to feed Rabbi Rubin's cat. Earlier that afternoon, Leah asked me if anybody was looking after it. I couldn't let it starve, so I went there to feed it. But the cat was gone."

"She was probably hiding. I have her now. I went to Rubin's house—he left keys in his office—to see if there were any clues to his murder. The cat was dehydrated and starving, so I fed it, let it drink water and took her to an animal hospital."

"Another mitzvah, Rabbi."

"Did you go back to the house to get Rabbi Rubin's gun? His Glock 19?"

Shevitz blushed. "I thought I might need it."

"I thoroughly understand. Rabbi Rubin no longer needs it, so you might as well hang on to it. Register it or whatever the local law requires. Also, you should learn how to use it."

"That's an excellent suggestion, Rabbi."

"You can call me Ben."

"I'm Manny."

"Manny? Manny Shevitz? What were your parents thinking?"

Shevitz colored. "My father had an odd sense of humor. He said it would make it easier for people to remember my name."

"He was right. I'm pleased to meet you, although I wish the circumstances were different."

"So now what?" Shevitz said.

"I'm going back to Beth Ohr. Could you call your wife and ask her for me, if she knows, the name of the bank or banks where L'Dor v'Dor has accounts and who has signatory authority. And then text that to me at your early convenience."

"Sure."

Ben wrote his cell phone number down on a page from his notebook, tore it out and gave it to Shevitz.

"You need this information for what reason?"

"I hired Mrs. Morgenstern—she's an attorney, if you've forgotten—to do the paperwork required to shut L'Dor v'Dor down and liquidate its assets. Those include bank accounts. If you prefer, send the information directly to Morgenstern."

"Got it. Thanks again, Ben."

"See you soon Manny."

Chapter Forty-one

Chicago

Ben parked near the entrance to Beth Ohr and got out of the Toyota. Two large men in wrinkled, off-the-rack suits stepped from the shadows. Behind them were two uniformed Chicago patrolmen.

"Mark Glass?" said the smaller of the two men.

Ben said, "I'm Rabbi Mark Glass. What can I do for you, Detective?"

"Do you know a young woman named Nadia Roldugin?" said the second man.

Ben shook his head. "No, I don't think so?"

"How about Kylee Dugan, which is her uh, professional name?"

"We've met," Ben said.

"Turn around," said the first detective."

"You're outside your jurisdiction. Do the Steins police know you're here?"

"Shut the hell up," said one of the uniformed cops.

"You're under arrest for the murder of Nadia Roldugin, aka Kylee Dugan," said the bigger detective. "You have the right to remain silent. Anything that you say may be used against you in a court of law. You have the right to an attorney. If you cannot afford an attorney, one will be provided for you. Do you understand your rights?"

Ben remained mute.

The detective who was shackling Ben's hands behind his back paused to slap the back of his head, hard.

"He said, do you understand these rights?"

"He also said that I have the right to remain silent."

The big detective shoved Ben hard and he let his body go limp and twisted to the left to allow his right hip and shoulder to take the majority of the impact when he hit the pavement.

"Don't think you can play games with us, you murderer. You tortured that girl for hours before you killed her," said the smaller detective.

Awkwardly, Ben got to his feet. "I deny killing anyone at any time. I want a lawyer. I have nothing further to say," Ben said and the smaller detective slapped his face, hard.

§

The space seemed like a prototype for all police interrogation rooms: Small, poorly lit, with a scarred table, old, beat-up chairs and a large mirror which hid a window through which others could observe activities.

Ben sat handcuffed in a chair for more than an hour before a tall, rotund, olive-skinned man in an expensive suit entered carrying a black Bosca briefcase that Ben knew cost almost $1,000.

"James Dalessandro," said the man. "Your attorney."

He sat down across the table from Ben.

Ben shook his head. "You may be an attorney but I didn't call you. Why are you here?"

"I can make all this go away in ten minutes," Dalessandro said, in a low voice. "All charges will be dropped."

Ben shook his head. "Who sent you?"

"It doesn't matter. Ten minutes and you're out of here."

"In exchange for what?"

"A conversation."

"With whom?"

The man smiled. "Someone who admires your style and can help you."

Ben shook his head. "I'll be represented by someone of my own choosing," he said. "No offense intended but I am nobody's pigeon."

"Don't be hasty," Dalessandro said. "If I leave, I won't be back."

Ben looked at the mirror. "I would like my phone call. This man does not represent me."

Shaking his head, Dalessandro got up, collected his briefcase and left the room.

A few minutes later a uniformed police officer brought a wireless telephone into the room, wordlessly set it down on the table and removed Ben's cuffs before departing.

Ben called Mitch Katz, told him in a sentence what had happened and asked him to send an attorney versed in criminal law to his location.

"Where are you?" Katz asked.

"Not sure," Ben said. He looked at the window. "Please tell me where I'm at so I can get my attorney here."

There was no response.

Ben said, "It's a game the police like to play. The attorney will have to find me. All I know is that I'm in police custody. Chicago police."

Katz said, "I'm calling my brother-in-law, Mel Cohen. He'll figure it out."

Ben shut the phone down. Half a minute later the uniformed officer returned, handcuffed Ben and took him out of the room and down the hall to a cell with four other men. Ben's cuffs were removed and he was pushed into the cell. He found a seat on a bench and sat back, trying to clear his mind, trying to sleep for as long as he could. He closed his eyes.

A moment later, someone poked him in the chest. Ben opened his eyes to see a tall, burly, unkempt and unshaven man of perhaps forty standing before him.

"Whatcha in for?" the man said.

"Not your business," Ben said.

The man's right hand came flying toward Ben's head.

Leaping to his feet, Ben intercepted the punch, snatched the man's wrist with his own left hand pivoted to his right as he jerked the extended arm. The man flew forward to hit the wall above the bench with his face.

He fell to the floor, his nose gushing blood.

The others on the bench moved as far from Ben as they could get.

A uniformed officer appeared outside the cage.

"What happened?" he said.

Slowly, the burly prisoner climbed to his feet. "Nothing. I tripped is all. I need a doctor," he said.

The door opened, the bleeding prisoner was handcuffed and taken away.

Ben sat back on the bench and closed his eyes.

§

"Glass! Wake up!"

Ben opened his eyes.

"Your lawyer's here," said the cop standing outside the cage.

Ben got to his feet, stepped through the open door and was again cuffed. He was herded down a long hallway and into a tiny, windowless room with two chairs, a small table, and the usual one-way mirror. A tall, slim, man with thick, well-coifed salt-and-pepper hair was in one chair. He rose to his feet as Ben entered and once the cuffs were removed, shook hands with Ben.

"Mel Cohen," he said, displaying a deep, mellifluous voice.

"What time is it?" Ben said. "They took my watch."

Cohen glanced at his thin gold Piaget. "Just about seven a.m.," he said.

"Sorry for getting you up in the middle of the night, counselor," Ben said.

"Comes with the territory. We can speak openly in here. As we have not met previously, I will say that I have practiced criminal defense law for the last twenty-two years, that for five years before that I was an Assistant State's Attorney. I have defended more than twenty people charged with capital murder. None was executed."

"What is your fee?"

"For now, one dollar. My sister Marcia assures me that you could not possibly have killed anyone. Her husband has known you since rabbinical school and he vouches for your good character and even temperament."

"Good. I was arrested for murdering a woman. I didn't kill her or anyone else."

"I've reviewed the evidence," Cohen said. "It's not much. The police say that the security video from Ms. Rodugin's apartment parking structure shows that you've been seeing Ms. Roldugin three times a week for at least the last year. They have your fingerprint on the registration of her car. They say you've been paying her a sum every month from the coffers of Congregation Beth Ohr. They claim that you found out that she was seeing another man, Abel Gonçalves and that you tortured and murdered her in a jealous rage."

Ben nodded. "None of that is true. First, I've met this woman, whom I knew only as Kylee Dugan, only once. Second, I've only been back in the Chicago area for about a week. Before that, I was in Jerusalem for about ten days, Buenos Aires for close to a month and in Pittsburgh for several months.

Ben then briefly described how and when he had met the murder victim.

"You can prove that you were out of the country for some time before this?"

"The police have my passport. As for Pittsburgh, I was in a medical trial there for several months at the University of Pittsburgh."

"They have no case. Might take an hour or so to get you released," Cohen said.

"One thing more," Ben said. "About an hour after I got here last night, an attorney named James Dalessandro arrived. He offered to get the charges dropped in exchange for a conversation with an unnamed person. I declined his services."

Cohen frowned. "Dalessandro is a Mob attorney. Represents about fifty known mobsters in Chicago and the suburbs."

"Is one of them Jack Dworkin?"

"I believe so but I'm not sure. Excuse me, I'll get started on your release."

Chapter Forty-two

Steins

Back at Beth Ohr, Ben took a quick shower, fed the cat and fell into bed, exhausted.

A relentless pounding on the door of his tiny apartment woke him.

"I'm coming," he yelled and got out of bed. He pulled on a bathrobe and cracked the door.

"Sleeping beauty," said Agent Gilmore. "You decent?"

"Five minutes," Ben said and closed the door.

When he opened it again he was fully dressed.

"Welcome to my hovel. What's up?" Ben said as he stood aside to let Gilmore in.

"I heard about your little tête-à-tête with Chicago's finest," she began. "Condolences and sympathies. The way they treated you is inexcusable."

"Could have been worse. I could have let James Dalessandro represent me."

Gilmore frowned. "What do you know about Dalessandro?"

"He showed up out of nowhere and offered to spring me, in exchange for meeting someone, he said, 'who liked my style.' Whatever that means. My attorney told me, later, that he represents local mobsters."

"That he does. And what might be a perfectly reputable bank? Or not."

"A Mob bank?"

"Omicron Bank in Cicero. A one-location bank capitalized at about $8.5 million. Dalessandro is a director of the bank and has an office there. I don't have any reliable information that it's anything but a small, state-chartered bank."

Ben said, "There's one thing that's been bothering me about this murder. Recall that Rabbi Rubin, who was almost seventy years old, was keeping this young woman, Kylee Dugan, in a swanky Edgewater Beach high-rise. That was interesting but not all that surprising. He had plenty of money, his wife was dead and Dugan was willing to sell her services. But—and this is very strange—last night the police said that her real name was Nadia Roldugin. I think she might be Russian. Some of the thugs that Rubin was washing money for are Russian. At least they have Russian names."

Gilmore nodded to show she was following.

"This suggests that Nadia Roldugin was not merely a prostitute. That she had been introduced to Rubin for reasons other than sexual commerce."

Again Gilmore nodded. "It could look that way."

"So then I have to ask why?" Ben finished. "To keep an eye on Rubin? To compromise him and open him to blackmail?"

"Plenty of wealthy older men, single or married, keep a mistress."

"But not many are respected elder rabbis who are laundering money for the Russian Mafia," Ben said. "Was Roldugin their insurance policy? If Rubin decided to close his laundry, she could stop him with the threat of exposing his secret life."

Gilmore said, "Very possible. But murder is not usually a Federal crime. If there's evidence that Roldugin's murder was related to our money-laundering investigation, we would look into it. But so far, there's no link."

Ben said, "Why are you here?"

"Mostly to keep in touch. See how you were doing after your meeting with Chicago cops."

"Mostly?"

"Well. It has occurred to me that you are ideally suited to go undercover and penetrate the whole money washing scheme and bring down the heads of the six or seven OC families operating in the northern suburbs."

"No, thank you," Ben said.

Someone knocked on the door.

"Come in," said Ben and Julie Morgenstern pushed the door open. She carried a thick manila folder.

"Am I interrupting?" she said, glancing back and forth between, Ben and Gilmore.

"Not at all," Ben said. "This is Detective Gilchrist. She's following up on the bombing."

"Actually, I'm done," Gilmore said. "If I have more questions, I'll call."

"Of course," Ben said.

Gilmore smiled at Julie and left, closing the door behind her.

Julie said, "I have a big problem and I have news."

"Good or bad news?"

"Just news, Rabbi—are you dating that detective?"

Ben guffawed. "No, of course not. What gave you such an idea?"

"The way she smiled at me and the way she looked at you."

Ben shook his head. "This must be something, a sixth sense, that women have. I have no inkling of anything untoward in the look she gave either of us. And as I told you, I am about to marry the love of my life."

Julie shrugged. "Maybe I'm mistaken. It's just that—I thought that she seemed very possessive of you and her smile seemed like a warning."

"You mentioned a problem?"

Julie opened the manila folder. "These are the by-laws. I've circled the section that you need to see."

Ben took a thick sheaf of paper and carefully read a long paragraph that spanned two pages.

Julie said, "Now read the second paragraph,"

Ben read the short paragraph and nodded.

"Is there any way around this?"

"Involuntary dissolution. I can get the State of Delaware to take it over."

"I don't think Rabbi Farkas is going to be happy about that."

Julie shrugged.

"Okay then. What's your news, Julie?"

"Oh, yes. Mrs. Shevitz called. She's coming back to town and she gave me the account numbers of the L'Dor v'Dor accounts. There are two. One has more than $500,000 in it and the other one about $28,000.

"But before she called, I did a careful search of Rabbi Rubin's office and I found a metal box with a stack of CD-ROMS labeled as tax returns for every year since 1998, the year that L'Dor v'Dor was chartered.

"Does your office computer have a CD player?

"I think so. But for safety's sake, I think I should get a copy of the discs made."

"You can probably do that on your own computer. I can show you how if need be."

"You seem to know a lot about computers, Rabbi."

"My bachelor's degree is in electrical engineering. Anything else I should know about?"

"I also found bank statements for two accounts in a bank that I'm not familiar with—Omicron Bank. One of them has more than $2 million in it and the other about $350,000. According to the paperwork, the smaller account is L'Dor v'Dor and the $2 million account was jointly held by Rabbi Rubin and someone named Meir Farkas. Is that the rabbi who sent you here?"

Ben nodded. "It is. Can you tell if either Farkas or Rubin had accessed the account recently?"

Julie shook her head. "The last statement was December of last year."

Ben said, "Is there a way to find out if both accounts are active?"

"I think the bank would tell me that much. The executor of Rabbi Rubin's estate could access the account. Did he leave a will?"

Ben shook his head. "Haven't seen a will and I don't know if there's an executor."

"Can you get in touch with this Farkas gentleman?"

"I'll do that," Ben said. "May I ask a favor of you?"

"Anything, Rabbi."

"Actually, two favors."

"Of course."

"If your husband tries to reconcile with you, would you at least hear him out? Give him a chance to show why you should stay married?"

"Did he put you up to this? Offer you something?"

Ben shook his head. "Not at all. You deserve to have a husband that you can love and respect. And Leonard might not be that man. But if you still care anything about him and if he asks for another chance, can you just hear him out? I'm not asking you to go back to him. Just give him a chance to make his case."

Julie shrugged. "I don't know if I can do that. But I'll think about it."

"That's all I ask."

"What's the other one?"

"Do you know someone in Chicago that might assist me in finding a place to live within easy commuting of the University of Chicago?"

"Why?"

"My fiancé will start her doctoral program there in June. We should be married by then and I want to find a place to live."

"Will you remain here, at Beth Ohr?"

Ben shook his head. "Not much longer. I expect Rabbi Shevitz back soon."

Julie said, "I'd be glad to help. I know a few people in Chicago real estate. I'll ask around."

"Thank you, Julie. I very much appreciate your help."

Chapter Forty-three

STEINS

Ben needed to think about what he had just learned from Julie. But he also had another urgent task that he had postponed for too long. Ben spent more than an hour calling around the Chicago area, looking for a suitable place for a large Jewish wedding. Banquet managers at one venue after another told Ben that they were booked through the spring and summer. Finally, a helpful manager suggested that he call a place only a few miles from Steins that she'd heard had a recent cancellation.

A surprised woman at the Skokie Banquet and Conference Center told Ben that someone had canceled their wedding only an hour earlier due to a tragedy: The groom had died in an auto accident.

The Village of Skokie, best known for a 1980 march by neo-Nazis, is a largely Jewish community and home to the Hebrew Theological College, the Jewish University of America and the Illinois Holocaust Museum. The woman who accepted Ben's reservation for the second Sunday in May assured Ben that their caterer's food was prepared under the supervision of Rabbi Yitzchak Blum, the culinary supervisor of a well-known Kosher restaurant.

Ben was about to call Miryam with the good news when Hilly Lippman called.

"I have a report for you," Lippman said. "I'll email it to you but I thought you'd like to hear the highlights."

"Of course and thank you," Ben said.

"Deborah L. Rubin has no car, boat, motorcycle, aircraft or real estate registered in her name. She has no current credit cards. Her driver's license expired several years ago.

"She has one bank account and for the past thirty-five months, it has received a monthly deposit for $4123.08 and a quarterly deposit of $11,250. An accountant in Delaware has filed a tax return with her electronic signature each year."

Ben said, "You got this from the IRS?"

"No comment."

"Go on."

"She has not earned any other money in the last twelve years. She is not a hospital patient, the resident of a hospice or a licensed board and care, nor is she a state or federal prisoner. There is no death certificate. There is no fugitive warrant. She has not married anyone or given birth to a child."

"So she might be dead but not officially?"

"Rabbi, this is the strangest missing person's case I've ever worked."

"Any theories?"

"A couple. One, she was murdered and her body never found. Hard to pull off but not impossible. And yet no one, including her brother, reported her missing."

Ben said, "What else?"

"She might have snuck out of the country. Driven across the border into Canada or Mexico and taken up residence. Bought or contrived identification papers. That has happened in the past, though rarely. Both borders have been much harder to cross for US citizens in recent years but ten or twelve years ago, it was easy to go into Mexico or Canada, especially if you were driving a US licensed car or were part of a group. She might even have caught a bus from San Diego to Tijuana. They didn't use to check IDs going south, only coming back. Same with a bus from Boston to Montreal. They only checked papers coming back to the US."

Ben said, "What if she went to a foreign consulate in the United States and persuaded someone there to issue her a passport from that country?"

"Possible, I guess. But why would, say, England France, Germany or Russia—whatever—want to do that? She'd need to give them a pretty good reason."

"Thanks, Hilly. Send me your bill."

"You've got a refund from your retainer. My check is with your report."

"You're a prince," Ben said.

"Glad to be of service."

Chapter Forty-four

Chicago

Ben decided that it was time to hash things out with Rabbi Farkas. He drove toward Chicago on surface streets, thinking. Was his cell phone tapped by the FBI? Probably. He could buy a cheap phone and a lot of minutes and use it to call Israel. Or he could get Gilmore to help him.

An hour later he parked on the second level of the Federal building off Roosevelt Road. A young, clean-cut man in a tight, dark suit materialized as Ben got out of the car. "Rabbi Maimon?" he said.

"Yes."

"Come with me, please."

An elevator whisked them to a middle floor and Ben was led to a windowless room where agents Gilmore and Roberts waited. Aside from a framed picture of the previous President of the United States, the room was barren of decoration.

Roberts gestured toward a comfortable chair. A telephone sat on a nearby table.

Ben sat down and took out his notebook.

"Ready?" said Roberts and Ben nodded in the affirmative.

"Pick up the phone, say the number, including the country code and we'll place the call."

"What incoming number will show on Farkas' cellphone?"

"That number will be your cell phone."

Ben nodded, picked up the receiver and recited a number

from memory.

On the distant end, Ben heard the phone rang three times.

"Ben!" said Farkas in English, sounding pleased.

"Rabbi Farkas," Ben said. "You are well?"

"Very well indeed. And you?"

"I'm fine," Ben said and waited.

"Damn you!" Farkas said. "I don't like this game. Just give me a progress report."

"Very well. The police have discovered that Rabbi Rubin was killed by a car driven by a jealous man who learned that Shmuel was seeing his girlfriend. This man was arrested."

"Shmuel had a girlfriend?"

"I believe it was mostly a…financial arrangement."

"Ah. That makes much more sense. What else?"

"I learned that you are one of the officers of L'Dor v'Dor."

"Of course. So what?"

"I hired an attorney to help wind up the corporation. According to the corporate bylaws, winding up the corporation requires at least one officer to introduce a motion to do that and two-thirds of the directors and officers to approve it. You're the only officer and there are presently no directors."

"What about Shmuel's sister Deborah? She's the treasurer."

"I can't locate her. She seems to have vanished."

"How can that be?"

"Rabbi, I hired a private investigator. I'll send you his report. Deborah Rubin is not to be found."

"Convene a meeting and I'll attend by telephone."

"What about directors? All the previous directors served one-year terms. No board meetings have been held since last year."

"Find five or six people and pay them the standard fee—a thousand dollars each. Explain what they must do."

"Rabbi, that won't work. The corporate bylaws say that any new board member has to be approved by a majority of voting members at a meeting with a quorum of two-thirds of all members, plus one."

"If I could have solved this from here, I wouldn't have sent you. Isn't there any other way to do this?"

"There is but you won't like it."

"What?"

"I can have the lawyer declare that the corporation is no longer viable. The State of Delaware will go to court and get an order for involuntary dissolution and take over and close the corporation."

"What's so bad about that?"

"They will seize all corporate assets."

Farkas was silent for a long moment.

Then he exploded into rapid-fire Hebrew. "What kind of idiot did I send to Chicago? Create the damn board minutes. Invent the directors if you have to. Or round up some homeless people, pay them and tell them to shut up. Get the paperwork together, fold it up in Delaware and send me the money."

Ben replied in Hebrew. "You're asking me to commit at least two felonies."

"I'll have your apostate sister on a plane to New York before dinner."

"I'm telling you, these are serious matters. You can't expect me to risk prison just so you get rich."

"All right. There's an account with about $350,000 in it. You can have it—if you wind this up and get me the rest of the money."

"I understand," Ben said. "There's another issue. Rabbi Rubin has a considerable estate. I don't know if he has a will or a lawyer or someone to dispose of his assets. I can just ignore this and let the State of Illinois handle it. But if you're his cousin, you may have a claim on his estate."

"Look into it. If you can get the money out, I'll split it with you."

Ben said. "Last item. The principal donors are at present unknown. Rabbi Rubin had his books encoded, so these people are not mentioned. Then someone stole the computer with the data."

"Do you know even one donor?"

"One, yes."

"See if he can help name the others. If not, get me his contact information."

"Okay."

"Is that all?

"Yes."

Farkas said, "Call me when you have something to report," and broke the connection.

"It was very nice talking to you, too," Ben said to the dead line.

Chapter Forty-five

Chicago

Ben said, "Was there someone listening on this end who speaks Hebrew?"

Gilmore shook her head, no. "We recorded it and we have Hebrew linguists available. What was the gist?"

"He as much as admitted that he knew what Rabbi Rubin was doing. He told me to forge minutes of fictitious board meetings to meet legal requirements for folding up the corporation and then send him the money. He offered me a bribe and threatened to deport my sister. He pretends to be Rabbi Rubin's first cousin but that isn't so. So I told him that Rubin didn't leave a will but as his cousin, Farkas might have a claim on the estate. He offered me half if I could get him the inheritance."

Roberts said, "And what did you say to that?"

"I was careful not to agree to anything."

Gilmore said, "That was wise."

Ben said, "Now I have a question. When Rabbi Farkas sent me here, right after Leah Shevitz disappeared, he gave me your name. How did he get it and why was he working with the FBI."

Gilmore shook her head. "Leah's disappearance and apparent kidnapping were reported to the Steins police. They contacted us, as the FBI has jurisdiction over kidnappings. We contacted her employers, who told us that she also did work for L'Dor v'Dor. That charity has been on our radar for several months. The only L'Dor v'Dor corporate officer we could find was Farkas. So we called him, about Leah's kidnapping and he told us that you were coming here."

Ben nodded. "He seems to be unaware that you are investigating money laundering by L'Dor v'Dor."

"Let's keep it that way," Roberts said.

Gilmore said, "If you can get Farkas to come to the States, we'll arrest him for racketeering and money laundering."

Ben said, "He's an officer of a US corporation. Why not get an indictment and extradite him?"

Gilmore shook her head. "That would tip off all his clients. We don't have enough evidence to arrest his so-called donors and those are the people who we really want behind bars."

Roberts said, "If you can at least identify those people, the mobsters washing their money through Rubin's charity, that would help us get court orders for wiretaps and surveillance."

"I'll see what I can do about that," Ben said.

Chapter Forty-six

Chicago

Ben returned to his tiny apartment. He fired up his Mac Book and discovered several large scrap-metal businesses in the Chicago area. He called the nearest one, asked for the manager and was connected to a soft-spoken woman. After a little coaxing, she said that the Stern brothers, Jake and Mendel, owned a gigantic scrap yard south of Chicago in Calumet City. Google Maps yielded an address for South Lake Recycling and two hours later, Ben parked his rented Toyota on the shoulder of Wentworth Avenue and carefully picked his way through the mud and piles of dog feces to a ramshackle office.

A huge Alsatian, chained to the wall, issued a low growl as Ben carefully stepped through the door.

"Hep ya?" said an enormous black man, close to seven feet tall, with hair like a rusty Brillo pad, from behind a massive desk. He smiled, revealing corroded stainless steel teeth that had been filed to sharp points.

"I'm looking for Jake or Mendel," Ben said.

The black man regarded him with suspicion.

"What fer?"

"I'm the rabbi of the synagogue they go to. It's about a charity called L'Dor v'Dor."

The man shook his head. "They ain't gonna write no check to no Jew charity," he said.

Ben smiled. "That's not it. Both the brothers have donated in the past. I just want to tell them that it's under new management."

"Youse could leave me a number, maybe they gonna call, maybe not," he said.

Ben smiled again. He took out Rabbi Rubin's notebook, wrote his own name, his cell number, and L'Dor v'Dor on a sheet, tore it out and put it on the desk in front of the man.

"Thank you very much," Ben said. "Appreciate your help."

The man grunted and as Ben turned to go, the dog lunged at him—and was stopped by the length of a chain attached to its collar.

The giant behind the desk snickered.

§

Ben climbed back into the Toyota and before he could start the engine, his phone chimed.

He started the engine, put on his seat belt and as he drove away listened to the message that the caller left.

"This is Loraine Silverman," she said. "Your friend Julie Morgenstern told me that you're looking for a place to live near the University."

Ben touched the screen to call Ms. Silverman and after a brief exchange, he pulled off the road and typed an address into his phone's GPS.

Forty minutes later he turned off 54th Street into Greensward Avenue and parked halfway down the block. As he got out of the car, he saw a short, slender woman of uncertain age with carefully coifed blonde hair waving at him from the curb across the street in front of a two-story house of gray brick. Ben crossed the street and extended his hand toward the woman.

"Rabbi Maimon?" she said, with doubt in her voice.

"You were expecting someone taller?"

Silverman laughed. "Someone dressed more like an Orthodox rabbi. Someone who would never shake hands with a woman."

"I'm sorry to disappoint you. I'm a Conservative rabbi and we fetch, sit up, roll over *and* shake hands."

Silverman giggled.

For the next twenty minutes, they moved through the house, which had three bedrooms upstairs, two smaller ones downstairs, central air and heating, a finished basement, a new roof, and many other goodies.

"You haven't seen the best part," Silverman said.

Ben smiled "What's that?"

"Come with me," Silverman said and led Ben through the kitchen and out into the back yard. At the end of the spacious yard sat a small house.

"It's called a 'mother-in-law,"' she said. "And it has central air and heat."

Inside, the small house seemed bigger: Two bedrooms, a full bath, a smaller bath with just a sink and toilet, a small but well-equipped kitchen and a spacious living/dining room.

Ben smiled. "Miryam will love this. What's in the attic?"

Silverman led the way to a small but well-ventilated space that looked out on the back yard. "You could make this into another bedroom," she said.

"Or an office," Ben replied, thinking.

"Would you like to make an offer?"

"What are they asking?" Ben said.

"$520,000," Silverman replied.

"My fiancé is in Israel. I'll connect her on Zillow and we'll see her reaction."

"Do you have financing in place?" said Silverman.

"I think we'll probably pay cash," Ben said. "But we'll see. About how far is it to the university?"

"A five-minute walk. And by the way, this is one of Chicago's safer neighborhoods."

"Just how safe is that?"

"Not much street violence for the last few years. Almost none. But frankly, all of Chicago is somewhat more dangerous than the northern suburbs."

"I'll keep that in mind," Ben said.

"You should also know that this neighborhood is mostly black," Silverman said.

"So there's no synagogue around the corner?"

Again Silverman giggled. "I have several other homes that I could show you. But frankly, this is the best in the neighborhood."

"I'll get back to you once Miryam sees it. I'm hoping she'll be here in a week or so."

"I'm not trying to pressure you but this one will go fast."

"Understood."

Chapter Forty-seven

Chicago

From Greensward, Ben headed east and then took Lakeshore Drive north. As he made the left turn onto the drive, he glanced out over the lake.

And looked again. It was sunny on Lakeshore Drive and the sky overhead was blue. But over the lake, the sky was dark and threatening. Gusts of wind off the water buffeted his car. Glancing around, he saw little traffic. People with more sense and experience were heading for shelter.

Ben picked up his pace to the speed limit, periodically eyeing the sky above the lake.

The blizzard hit just as Lakeshore Drive ended in the Edgewater neighborhood.

In half a minute, wind-driven snow covered the Toyota's windows, blinding him except for the space cleared by his wipers. As Ben picked his way north along Ridge Avenue toward the suburb of Evanston, he saw a black Cadillac Escalade start to turn into Ridge but instead slide across four lanes and smack into the curb and the huge tree just beyond it.

The car's hood flew up.

Steam and what Ben thought might be smoke boiled from the front of the car.

As Ben pulled in behind the SUV, he saw the driver struggling to open the door.

Ben got out of the Toyota, then dodged several broken tree limbs propelled by hurricane-force gusts. Wind-driven snowflakes stung his face as he ran to the Escalade and the cold was a bitter knife through his jacket. In seconds he was chilled to the bone. He signaled the driver, a woman, to roll the window down. It jammed two inches down.

Flames six feet high shot from the front of the car.

Ben ran to his car, grabbed a lug wrench from the back and ran back. Peeling off his jacket, he shoved it through the two-inch gap in the window.

"Cover your face!" he yelled.

When she had, Ben shattered the window with one blow from the wrench. Then he used it to clear away shards of broken glass.

Ben was now almost covered in snow.

He stuck both arms through the window and under the woman's arms and pulled her out, backing slowly until she could put her feet on the street. Ben was shocked to find that she towered over him. For a long moment, her soft, overlarge breasts engulfed Ben's face.

He stepped back and craned his neck to see a face that might have graced a Botticelli masterpiece. She was a stunning, Junoesque woman in her middle years. It was Mrs. Finkelstein, Ben was sure.

"Get in my car!" Ben said, pointing.

He followed her, opened the passenger door for her, then ran around to the driver's side and got in. He backed the Toyota away from the flaming wreck.

The woman pointed at Ben and laughed.

He looked down and saw that he was blanketed in snow.

Ben said, "You're Mrs. Finkelstein? Are you okay?"

"How do you know my name?

"I'm Rabbi Ben Maimon and I saw you singing in the Beth

Ohr choir. Igor gave me your name. Are you okay?

"Nothing broken. Nothing is torn. It was just so sudden—I'm a little shook up.

Its siren blaring, a fire truck skidded around the corner. The driver tried to correct the skid but spun out on the icy street and ran up on a curb. A minute later a police car crept around the corner and stopped.

"Stay here," he said.

Ben got out, found the police and told him what he had seen.

A sudden gust of wind staggered both men.

As if on cue, the SUV's gas tank went off like a bomb.

A pair of firemen appeared from the direction of their truck, each carrying a large extinguisher. They began to spray the base of the blaze, getting close so that the wind didn't blow their chemical spray wide of its mark.

A police officer climbed into the backseat of Ben's car.

"Are you okay?" the officer said. "I've got an ambulance coming."

"I'll be fine," Mrs. Finkelstein said in a throaty voice.

"Driver's license?" said the cop.

The woman gestured toward the still burning car. "In my purse."

"What's your name?"

"Lillian Golden," she said. "The car belongs to my husband Randolph Finkelstein."

Something clicked in Ben's head. And then another thing.

"Let me take your contact information," the officer said. "Address?"

The woman gave him a street number along Finkelstein

Boulevard and added her phone number.

The cop looked at Ben. "Did you witness the accident, sir?"

Ben said, "She was heading south at about ten miles an hour, turned into this street and the car skidded across all four lanes and into the curb."

The cop looked at the woman. "Does that sound about right?"

"It was closer to twenty," she said. "When the blizzard hit, I couldn't see much. I started to make a wide turn around the corner and the car just got away from me."

"Are you sure that you don't want an ambulance, Ma'am?"

The woman shook her head. "I'm fine, thanks to this young man. He left out the part about him pulling me out of the car just before it exploded.

"If I call the Evanston police, will I be able to get a copy of the accident report?"

"Yes, Ma'am." He handed her a business card. "Call that number after 2:00 pm tomorrow and we'll have a copy for you."

The cop got out of the car and headed for his own vehicle.

While all this happened, Ben closed his eyes and pictured the driver's license he had seen in Shmuel Rubin's home. His sister was named Deborah Lillian Rubin. She had married Richard Golden, then divorced him. Now she was Lillian Golden, using her middle name and her former husband's family name. And maybe a new Social Security number.

Ben looked again. He saw a mature woman, a little heavier, her long dark hair piled into a bun fashionably streaked through with gray but unmistakably the stunning bride in the wedding picture. He was all but certain that she was Deborah Rubin.

Ben said, "I'm sure the police will be happy to take you home."

The woman turned and examined Ben with her eyes, a searching look that went past the melting snow on his clothes.

"Would it be too much to ask *you* to take me home?"

"If you'll answer two questions."

"Go ahead."

"Where is Igor, your chauffeur and why do you need a bodyguard?"

"Mr. Falkenberg has the day off. And my husband's daughter, Naomi, seems to think that someone might want to kidnap me."

Chapter Forty-eight

Steins

Ben's phone rang as he unlocked his apartment at Beth Ohr. He closed the door behind him, stripped off his wet clothes, then glanced at Caller ID—Captain Peters of Steins PD.

"Rabbi?" said Peters.

"What's up, Fin?"

"Abel Gonçalves. Chicago PD transferred him to us. They liked him for the Roldugin murder but he was at Disneyworld with his wife and kids the week she was killed."

Ben said, "Interesting. Is that why you called?"

"Only partly. He's got a story to tell, according to his public defender and you might want to be here to hear him tell it."

"Give me a hint?"

"He claims that he loaned his car keys to a guy who gave him money to leave town for a month."

Chapter Forty-Nine

Steins

A uniformed cop led Ben to where Peters waited in a room with a two-way mirror.

In the interview room were Detective Gray and a tall, handsome, olive-skinned man of perhaps thirty. His lip was split and the beginnings of a dark purple bruise surrounded his bloodshot left eye.

Peters tapped the mirror and Gray left the interview room and entered the observation room, where he was again introduced to Ben.

Ben said, "Have you asked who hired him?"

Gray nodded. "He doesn't have a name. Said he had some kind of accent that he couldn't ID."

"Showed him a photo of Pete the Russkie?

Peters said, "Good idea, Ben."

"We'll put him in as part of a six-pack."

Ten minutes later Gray returned to the interview room.

"I'm going to show you more pictures," he said.

Gonçalves shrugged. "Okay."

Gray showed him an 8x10 sheet with six mug shots. Gonçalves shook his head.

"Nope."

Gray showed him a second sheet and Gonçalves shook his head. "Nope. He's not there."

Peters said, "Ben, you want to take a crack at this?"

"Sure. But I'm confident that Detective Gray will do a professional job."

"Give it a whirl anyway," Peters said.

Two minutes later, Ben sat down at the table across from Gonçalves.

"My name is Ben," he said. "I'm not a cop. Just helping out. I have a couple of more questions but first, is there anything that you need?"

"Can I get something to eat?" Gonçalves said.

Ben looked at the window.

"What would you like?" Ben said.

"A burger is okay. And a coke."

"You want fries with that?"

Gonçalves smiled. "Sure. Thanks."

§

Ben waited while Gonçalves wolfed down the food. When he finished, Ben said.

"Do you need the bathroom?"

"No, not yet. Thanks for asking."

Ben said, "When that guy gave you money to leave town, did you know that he was going to kill someone with your car?"

Gonçalves looked shocked, then fearful.

"No! Hell no! Who did he kill?"

"An older man, a rabbi."

Gonçalves shook his head. "What's a rabbi?"

"Do you know what a minister is?"

"Like a priest but a different kind of church, right?"

"He's also the spiritual leader of all those who go to that church."

"So a rabbi is kind of like a priest? Except, what?"

"A rabbi is a Jewish teacher and spiritual leader."

"Jewish is what? We don't have those in Brazil."

"*Judaico*. The man who died was *Rabbo Judaico*."

"Oh, yeah. Sure. Judaico."

"Why did you run that old man down?"

"I told you, I didn't run anyone down. Dude gave me $5,000 and told me to take my wife and kids to Disneyland or something."

"You didn't think that was pretty strange? Do you know anyone else who would give you that kind of money to borrow your car? He could have rented a car for less than that."

"I told the other guys what went down."

"Please tell me, again."

"I came back from delivering a pizza, I mean back to my car and there was this guy standing next to it. His car was blocking mine in, so I asked him to move it."

"What kind of car was it?"

"One of them big SUVs," Gonçalves said.

"An Escalade?"

"Something like that, maybe. And there's a girl or woman, I think, in the car, behind the wheel, see and I tapped on the window and then this guy came up behind me. A little taller than me, lots of muscles—kinda scary. His voice was kinda on the high side, sorta raspy but he has a gun. And he says, 'You Abel?'"

"I said, who's asking."

"He says, 'Never mind. You want to make five thousand dollars?'"

"I say, what I got to do?

"He says, 'Let me borrow your car for a few days.'

"I told him, I don't know you. Why I gonna let you have my car? And he shows me a picture of my little girl, Juliana, she's five. And he says, 'You wanna go to her funeral?'

"So I say, 'When do you want to borrow it?'"

"He say, 'Next Saturday, for three or four days.'

"I say, Show me the money," and he gives me an envelope. Twenties and fifties."

Ben said, "And that's it? You took the money?"

"No, no. Not yet. He said I should leave my car in front of my house, unlocked and put the keys under the floor mat. And he says, 'Tell anyone about this and I kill both your kids. Do what I tell you and there's another grand in it when I come back.'"

"You believed him?" Ben said."

"Don't matter if I believe him. He's got a gun and a picture of my little girl. So I said okay, I do it. But I never see this guy again, he don't pay me the rest."

Ben said, "You reported your car stolen. Why?"

"Because when I got home and find my car, I see that he hit someone with it."

"How do you know that?"

"Dried blood on the front of my car, in the grill. Headlight smashed. The fender is bent. So then I know why he wants my car. I drive to the South Side and leave the car, take a bus home. Then I call the police and say my car was stolen."

Ben said, "That's quite a story. Why didn't you tell the Chicago police?"

"Chicago cops, all they want is to beat on me, tell me I'm going to get the needle 'cause I killed my girlfriend and before that, I put cigarettes on her, burn her. But that's bullshit, an' they know it. So now they send me here and I get a lawyer, he tell me to say everything, tell the truth, things won't be so bad if I just tell the truth."

Ben said, "What did the woman in the car look like?"

"It was pretty dark. She turn her head away, I try to look at her. All I know is a woman, for sure. Dark hair, that's all I see."

"Was she tall?"

Gonçalves shook his head. "Kind of average. Like I said, was dark."

"Long hair or short?"

"Kinda short, I think."

"Would you recognize her if you saw her again?"

"I just tole you it was dark and I didn't see her face.

Ben said, "After you took the money, where did the guy go?"

"Got in the car. Next to the gal. Then they drive away."

"Did you get a look at the license plate?"

"Kinda. Indiana, I think. Not Illinois."

"What color was the car?"

"Black. Or maybe dark blue."

"What did you do then?"

"I finished my shift, deliver the pizzas and I go home."

"Did you tell your wife about this?"

"You think I crazy? I told her I won $5,000 in the lottery and we were going to Disney World with the kids on Friday. Next day is Thursday. I go to work, I tell my boss that my avó, my grandma, died in Sao Paolo and I need to go down there, take care of things. He says okay and gives me $1,000, an advance on my pay. We fly to Orlando, spend all the money. Two weeks and we come home."

"Senhor Gonçalves, do you know a man named Sam Rubin?"

Gonçalves smiled, then shook his head. "No."

"Did anyone tell you that he had a business relationship with Kylee Dugan?"

"*What* kind of relationship?"

"He did business with her."

"Kylee wasn't in business. She was going to college at Navy Pier to be a lawyer."

Ben sat back in his chair. "Is there anything else you can remember about the man and the woman who paid you to borrow your car"

"Maybe," Gonçalves said. "The woman was boss. The man worked for her."

Ben said, "Why do you think that?"

"Because she gave him the money to give to me."

"One more thing," Ben said. "You said the money was in an envelope. What did you do with the envelope?"

Gonçalves scratched the bridge of his nose, thinking.

"Threw it away, I guess."

"Where? At home? On your job?"

Gonçalves shook his head. "Right there in the parking lot. I watched their car leave and then I counted the money again and threw the envelope away and put the cash in my pants pocket."

"Why? Why did you throw the envelope away?"

Gonçalves shrugged. "Didn't need it, I guess."

Chapter Fifty

Steins

Ben left Gonçalves at the table and found Gray and Peters.

"What do you think?" said Peters.

"I think Detective Gray would have gotten the same information that I did."

Gray said, "But it didn't occur to me that he might be hungry. Chicago PD sent him up here about 2:00, so I assumed they fed him."

Peters shook his head but was silent.

Ben said, "I think he's telling the truth. And it puts a different spin on this case."

"Who would want to kill Rabbi Rubin?" Peters said. "And who would know that Gonçalves was her lover and could set him up to make it look like a jealous lover had avenged himself on the rabbi?"

"That *is* the question," Ben said.

"What do you think we should do with young Gonçalves?"

"I think he might make an excellent goat."

"Goat?"

"When villagers in India were troubled by a marauding tiger, instead of trying to track it and kill it, they would stake a goat in a forest clearing and hide downwind of the goat. When the tiger pounced on the goat, they would kill it with spears and clubs."

"Interesting," Peters said. "But I don't have the manpower for that and his home is outside my jurisdiction."

Ben nodded. "Surely you must know someone on the Chicago force that you can trust, someone with enough clout to organize an operation?"

"I might," Peters said. "I'll look into it."

"Let me know," Ben said. "I want to observe."

"I don't think my friendship goes that far, that he'd let a civilian—a clergyman—get involved."

"Tell them that Gonçalves trusts me and he sure doesn't like the Chicago cops."

"I'll give it a shot," Peters said.

Chapter Fifty-one

Steins

Back in his room, Ben called Agent Gilmore and updated her on what Gonçalves had told him.

Gilmore said, "Who would have a reason to kill Rubin? Who might want him dead?"

Ben said, "One thing comes to mind: He seems to have gotten rich over the years, far more so than seems likely on a rabbi's salary. If he was skimming money from the washing scheme, whose money was he taking?"

"If he was charging them all a straight eighteen percent, then he was taking the charity's money," Gilmore said.

"If he was skimming some of that, who would know?"

"The bookkeeper?"

"Maybe, maybe not. He kept another set of books on an external hard drive. I don't know if Mrs. Shevitz was aware of them. I doubt that she was."

"So anyone could have ordered the hit."

"Anyone who had reason to profit by removing Rubin from the scene. I learned from the mobster who kidnapped Mrs. Morgenstern that he had access to someone charging fifteen percent to launder their money."

"So why kill Rubin, when he was charging eighteen percent?"

"Maybe he had announced that he would take fifteen. Or less."

"So, if we can find that money launderer, we might also find Gonçalves' killer?"

"That's my take."

"Stay in touch, Ben."

Gilmore hung up.

Immediately, his phone rang again.

"Ben!" said Miryam and his heart beat faster.

"How are you, my love?" Ben said.

"Tired and hungry. Will you pick me up in two hours?"

Ben grinned. She was coming to Chicago!

"Where will you be in two hours?"

"Just off the Southwest flight from LaGuardia to Midway Airport."

"Not O'Hare?"

"There was a blizzard or something and according to the El Al people, O'Hare is a madhouse. Nothing coming or going. But Midway is open. I had to take a taxi from JFK to LaGuardia

"You're in New York?"

"I had some business with the museum. I'll tell you later. I'm on the plane now and by the time we take off and fly and land and I pick up my bags, it will be two hours. Meet me by baggage pickup? I mean on the street. I'll call when we land and you should give me fifteen or twenty minutes to get my suitcases."

"I'll be there," Ben said. "I can hardly wait."

Chapter Fifty-two

Steins

Ben changed into his warmest clothes and headed downstairs. As he passed the temple office, someone called out to him.

Rabbi Shevitz came out of the office to shake Ben's hand.

"Good to see you, Rabbi," Ben said.

"Good to be back. Can we talk for a minute about the Shabbat service?"

"Sure. Shall we go to your office?"

"This is fine. Two things: I'd like us both on the *bimah* during the service."

"Both Friday night and Saturday morning?"

"Yes, if possible."

"Sure. I'm not leaving the area any time soon but this will be my swan song as the acting rabbi. What's the second thing?"

"Mrs. Finkelstein just returned from Israel and learned that her brother died."

Ben nodded. "Yes, I ran into her the other day."

Shevitz laughed. "You mean you pulled her out of a burning car."

"That, too."

"Well, she'd like to talk about a memorial service for her brother on Saturday morning and she'd like to meet with you first to discuss that."

"How about tomorrow afternoon in Rabbi Rubin's office?"

"I'll call her. By the way, I wasn't aware that Randy Finkelstein had remarried."

"I just heard. Does that make her the Bride of Finkelstein?"

Shevitz laughed, a deep, contagious sound.

"That's a good one," he said. "I'm going to tell my wife that one."

Ben said, "Did you know the brother who died?"

Shevitz shook his head. "I don't think so. But I don't know her very well. She's a new member. I saw her during the High Holy Days—she's big enough to play center for the Bears, sings like an angel and is quite striking—but that's pretty much all I know about her."

Chapter Fifty-three

Midway Airport

By the time Ben got to Midway Airport, on Chicago's South Side near the lake, the skies were clear, but the roads were packed with snow and slush.

Ben pulled away from the curb, finding it hard to keep his eyes on the road when he really wanted to look at Miryam.

"You said you were hungry," Ben said.

"Starving. But I also need to sleep, so I don't want a lot of food."

"How 'bout a couple of nice cheese blintzes or a latke with sour cream?"

"You know a place?"

"I used to come to Chicago a lot."

"Wake me when we get there," Miryam said and closed her eyes.

By the time Ben reached Kaufman's in Skokie, Miryam was fast asleep. He turned north and headed to Steins.

Ben made two trips from the Beth Ohr parking lot. On the first, he carried Miryam and gently settled her into his bed. Then he brought her luggage upstairs.

Ben wrote a brief note, locked the door behind him and drove to Wolfie's, the best truly kosher deli in Steins. When he returned with sandwiches, Miryam was still asleep.

§

Ben sat watching Miryam sleep until his cell phone vibrated against his hip.

He took the call in the suite's small bathroom.

"Rabbi, this is Leonard Morgenstern," said a low voice in Ben's ear.

"What can I do for you?" Ben said.

"It's Julie—my wife. She's been kidnapped."

"When did this happen and have you notified the FBI?"

"No FBI. No police—they'll kill her. It looks like she was taken from the parking structure of the building where she works. This morning."

"Mr. Morgenstern. You of all people should know that every kidnapper warns that if the police are involved they'll kill the hostage. Almost every time. And yet only the police and the FBI have any realistic chance of getting your wife back in one piece."

"I know all that. But they want *you* to negotiate her release."

"Me?"

"You are to come alone and unarmed to an address that I'll send you."

The bathroom door opened and Miryam, clad only in one of Ben's T-shirts and holding half of a partly eaten corned beef sandwich, came in.

"Who's been kidnapped," she whispered and wrapped Ben in her arms.

Ben smiled at Miryam, squeezed her tight with his free arm.

"Mr. Morgenstern, send me the address and any other information that you have. You can text it to this number."

"Thank you, Rabbi. Please, get my wife back. She means the world to me."

"Send the information," Ben said and hung up.

Ben put the phone down and hugged Miryam with both arms.

"What's going on?" she said.

Ben explained about the Morgensterns and the kidnapping.

"There was another kidnapping attempt," Ben said. "Last week, we were having coffee in the restaurant downstairs from her office and one guy distracted me and the other grabbed her."

"So you kicked his butt, Bruce Lee Ben?"

"Not exactly. But I got Julie back and he went to jail."

"Julie? Another member of your harem, Sultan Ben?"

Ben couldn't help laughing. "She's president of the Sisterhood and a lawyer. I hired her to help shut down this so-called-charity."

"So-called?"

"Rabbi Rubin was laundering Mob money and I think, skimming some for himself."

Miryam's beautiful face twisted into a fearful scowl. "This is beginning to sound dangerous."

"Miryam. Remember what I told you on the day that I first said that I loved you?"

"That your job is dangerous sometimes and you would have to try to find another way to make a living."

"Right. And I'm trying. But I'm not there yet. I do have some news on that front."

"Tell me."

"A captain in the Steins police department wants to hire me as a consultant."

"What would that mean?"

"I'm not sure, exactly. But no burning houses and no gunplay."

"Is it for sure?"

"No. I said I'd think about it and he said he'd try to get the city council to give him a $60,000 a year budget."

"That doesn't sound like very much."

"It's part-time. On-call. And Steins is not very big—about 55,000 people."

"What would you do with the rest of your time?"

Ben shrugged. "Maybe I can find a part-time rabbi gig. There are about 300,000 Jews in Chicagoland."

"And if you can't?"

"I could be a stay-at-home dad?"

"This sounds better and better."

"And don't forget, I'll be getting $105,000 every year from the Sanoker endowment. We could live on that very nicely."

"Ben, you're forgetting that I still have millions in the bank."

"That would be for rainy days."

"You never stop surprising me, Moshe Binyamin."

"Why don't you finish your sandwich and go back to sleep. I'll be back before you know it."

"Hurry."

Chapter Fifty-four

Calumet City

Ben started the Toyota and headed south. The address that Morgenstern sent was in Calumet City, very near the Stern brother's scrapyard. A couple of times on the long ride over slushy roads through the suburbs and Chicago, he had the feeling that he was being followed but he couldn't identify any particular car that might be tracking him.

It was almost dark as Ben approached the house on Torrence Avenue. He switched off his lights, put the transmission in neutral and coasted to a stop across a long, narrow lot of oily, slush-covered dirt. The house was little more than a shack, its white paint peeling from weathered boards, a flat, tarpaper roof over a single story with two windows and a sagging porch.

Ben remained in his car and looked all around.

The streetlight nearest the shack was out. Half a block away a small neon sign for a tax preparer provided faint illumination.

Near the tax preparer, an old Cadillac was parked at the curb.

In the other direction, the lights of a service station, at least a half-mile distant, did little to dispel the darkness.

In the twilight gloom, Ben eased out of his Toyota and walked confidently to the shack. The front door was ajar. He knocked, listened, waited, knocked again.

A car approached from the north but sped by without stopping.

Ben took out his phone and brought up a flashlight app. Holding it high above his head, he stepped across the threshold.

Arms like steel bands pinned his hands to his sides.

Before he could launch a kick, someone grabbed his ankles and raised them.

A cloth reeking of ether was placed over his head.

As he descended into darkness, Ben heard the door shut behind him.

Chapter Fifty-Five

STEINS

Pounding on the door awakened Miryam. "I'm coming," she yelled and swung her legs off the bed and onto the carpeted floor.

At the door, she grabbed the knob, then stopped. "Who's there?" she said.

"FBI," came a woman's voice. "Are you Miryam Benkamal?"

"What if I am?"

"Then I have news for you about Ben."

"Slide your credentials under the door."

"This isn't a movie, Ms. Benkamal."

"I'm not opening this door until I know who you are."

"I could break it down."

"You have a warrant?"

"I'm trying to help you. Ben is a friend."

"Warrant, credentials or go away."

"You're just like Ben. Stubborn to a fault."

"Go ahead and break the door down. This is a synagogue. We'll see who the law decides is right. Or how the network news decides to play the story."

A sigh came through the door. A moment later an FBI credential was pushed through the crack beneath the door. Miryam stooped for it, looked at it carefully.

"What's your name?"

"Special Agent Patton Gilmore."

"What kind of a name is Patton?"

"Open the damn door!"

Miryam slid the deadbolt back, unlocked the door and opened it.

"Patton was my great-grandmother's family name," Gilmore said as she stepped past Miryam and looked around.

"Where's your partner?" Miryam said."

"Downstairs flirting with a pregnant black woman."

"Why are you here?"

"Get dressed and I'll tell you on the way."

"Tell me now."

"Is this a Jewish thing? Questioning everything?"

"How do you think that we survived 2,000 years of oppression?"

A sigh of exasperation escaped Gilmore's lips.

"How old are you, anyway? Fifteen?"

"Old enough to have earned a master's degree from the University of California, to serve as president of a non-profit foundation with a $25 million endowment and to marry the best man you'll ever know."

Gilmore sighed again.

"Ben is helping us find Mrs. Shulamit Morgenstern, wife of the state's attorney for Kishnef County, who was kidnapped."

"Tell me something that I don't know," Miryam said, as she slid into a pair of skinny jeans.

"When he completes his mission, Ben will want to see friendly faces. You're coming with us to make that happen."

"Five minutes," Miryam said, as she grabbed a shirt from her suitcase and headed for the bathroom."

Chapter Fifty-six

Calumet City

Ben awoke in the cold night air, his eyes covered by a blindfold. He felt thick rope being wrapped around his chest and he inhaled deeply, then flexed his chest and arm muscles until the wrapping was completed. When he relaxed his muscles, the binding felt looser.

Someone picked him up and carried him, then none-too-gently deposited him into a space lined with some kind of thick fabric—a rug, Ben realized. He felt the air around him compress as a door or hatch was slammed shut. An engine started nearby and he felt himself moving.

He was in the trunk of a car.

Ben rolled and scooted until he could stretch out diagonally in the large trunk. Then he willed himself to think only about his present situation.

Alternately flexing his muscles and rubbing the ropes against the floor, in twenty-odd minutes he freed his right hand. Then, with great difficulty, his left.

He rolled over on his stomach and laboriously untied the knots behind his back.

Then he remembered that since 2002, all cars sold in the US have been required to have an emergency trunk latch which glowed in the dark.

Ben had no idea what kind of a car he was in but there was no emergency trunk latch. He felt around in the dark, discovering with his hands objects that might be useful.

The car slowed and Ben felt it turning, slowing, then stopping. Three doors opened, then closed.

Ben kept feeling around the margins of his prison.

Then he heard a faint noise.

Someone was trying to open the trunk.

Chapter Fifty-Seven

Interior Car Trunk-Night

The trunk lid slowly rose, exposing a hunched figure silhouetted against the neon of a convenience store window.

Ben sprang to his knees, a lug wrench his left hand and a highway flare in his right. He raised the flare to scratch it against the trunk roof.

A hand of steel grabbed each wrist.

"No, Rabbi," said a man's low voice in Hebrew.

Ben relaxed.

"Come with us," said the same voice, again in Hebrew.

"Who are you?" Ben said.

"Call me Gideon," said the man.

"Mossad?"

"A friend, that's all you need to know."

"You have a gun?"

"Two," he said in English with a thick Israeli accent.

"Then get in here with me," Ben said.

§

The car doors slammed, the engine started and in seconds the car was accelerating. Within a few minutes, Ben heard the sound of the tires change. The car seemed to be on an expressway.

Ben and his new pal whispered to each other in Hebrew. Gideon said that his partner was following, tracking them with an app that Gideon had somehow covertly placed in Ben's cell phone.

"I don't have my phone. The guys in the car must have taken it."

"Either way, we found you."

"You hacked my phone?"

Gideon whispered, "No, no, it's not one of ours. FBI or CIA, I think."

Ben remembered that he had foolishly left his phone in his room while half a dozen FBI agents were marking money and supposedly putting tracking bugs into Jake's big aluminum case.

Ben said, "Show me the app. It should tell you where we are."

"Smart thinking," said Gideon.

In seconds he showed Ben the glowing face of his own phone. They were on Interstate 90, heading east.

After about fifteen minutes the car slowed, then seemed to change directions. The phone showed them leaving the Interstate and heading north toward the Lake.

In minutes the road grew rough and the car slowed.

Then it turned again and bumped down what felt like an unpaved road.

The car slowed to a halt, then lurched forward across the rough ground before it swerved to the left and slowed to a crawl.

Gideon put the phone away, rolled until he was facing the back of the car and then both men rested their backs against the rug and brought their feet under them.

The car stopped. Doors slammed. Indistinct voices came from all around.

The trunk was lifted and Ben catapulted himself head-first at a dark silhouette.

The man went down with a groan as Gideon leaped from the trunk, a 9mm Barak in his left hand.

The stutter of a heavy-caliber automatic weapon split the night and stopped both men. The car was flooded with bright light.

"Put your gun away," said a deep voice in a pleasant tone.

A tall, burly man with curly blond hair and dressed in stylish khaki slacks and a crew-neck sweater stepped out of the darkness. An ancient but serviceable Thompson submachine gun was cradled in the crook of his right arm, the butt of its stock resting on his hip. Two dozen men armed with shotguns and pistols surrounded the car.

"You're among friends," said the big blond. "Put your gun away."

Gideon holstered his pistol.

"Rabbi, I apologize for the method of your transport," continued the blond. "It seemed to be the simplest way of bringing you here."

Climbing to his feet, Ben shook his head. "Ever heard of the telephone?" he said.

The blond laughed. "Where's the fun in that?"

"You might have sent someone with an engraved invitation."

"I considered that and then I realized that even three or

four men might have had a tough time handing it to you. So, now that you're here, who's your friend?"

Ben smiled. "This is Gideon, my rabbi."

The blond guffawed. "A rabbi's rabbi?"

"A rabbi is a teacher. Gideon taught me how to use my body as a weapon, which is why I don't usually carry a gun."

"But *he* carries a gun."

"Gideon has many other skills as well."

The blond turned to the man that Ben had decked, an enormous black man with hair like a used Brillo pad—the man from the Calumet City junkyard.

"Simon—how many men did you put in the trunk?"

The big man beamed a corroded stainless-steel smile. "Jest the one. The little one."

The blond cocked his head. "Rabbi, how did your friend get into that trunk."

Again Ben smiled. "Have you heard of the Zohar, Mr. Stern?"

"You can call me Joe, Rabbi. The Zohar is a book about Jewish magic?"

Ben nodded. "It is that and much more. It describes, among many things, how to be in more than one place at once and how to travel to and from the Heavenly Realms, in order to instantly move hundreds or thousands of miles."

All the men laughed but Stern frowned. "That's total bullshit, right?"

Ben shook his head. "In the Seventeenth Century, several reliable witnesses placed Rabbi Eliezar ben Yehuda at two different places hundreds of miles apart on the afternoon of a particular Shabbat. It is said that Rabbi Eliezar had many powers, including teleportation, which he learned from his study of Torah, in the manner taught by Rabbi Isaac Luria of Safed."

Simon said, "He musta got in the trunk when we stopped for a case of beer."

Ben laughed. "That was my next guess, except I didn't know that it was beer."

Stern laughed, hard, and his men joined in.

"You had me going, Rabbi."

"Why am I here?"

"Come inside and we'll talk."

Ben turned to see the dimly-lit open door of an expansive two-story building.

"What is this place?"

"My lair," Stern said. "Used to be a steel mill. This was the fire station."

Ben shrugged. "But why am I here?'

"Let's go inside. Hey, could your guy teach my guys some of those moves?"

Ben turned to Gideon and spoke in Hebrew.

Gideon made a face and then shrugged.

"Sure, okay," he said in an accent from Brooklyn.

Stern led Ben to a well-appointed office inside the station, flipped on the lights and pointed to the wet bar in a corner. "Fix yourself a drink, if you like."

Ben went to the bar, filled a cocktail glass with ice and tonic water, then splashed a few drops of Angostura bitters in and mixed it with a spoon.

He took a sip and smiled.

"Never saw that before," Stern said. "No alcohol?"

"On the contrary. Bitters is almost half alcohol."

"Let me taste it."

Ben handed him the glass and Stern took a cautious sip.

"Very refreshing," he said. "This has a name?"

"Partch. After the cartoonist, Virgil Partch. After a career cartooning for magazines, he spent his last years drawing Angostura Bitters ads. He was an alcoholic and when he went on the wagon, this was his drink. Shall I build one for you?"

"Don't bother," he said and poured three fingers of The Glenlivet into a glass.

He gestured toward a circle of chairs and Ben chose one.

Through the door's window, he could see Gideon demonstrating the way to disarm an opponent with a knife.

"So?" said Ben.

"Two things, Rabbi. The State's Attorney can have his wife back if he knocks the charges against Pete the Russkie—Pyotr Sapozhnik—knocks them down to misdemeanors, gets a judge to sentence him to 30 days—it's gonna take that long before he can walk, anyway—and slips his lawyer fifty thousand, cash."

"Fifty?"

"Fifty. The lawyer has to take his cut and Pete needs enough to take a vacation for a few months. I'd ask for more but I happen to know it would take him too long to raise it. But fifty—he can turn that over in a day."

Ben said, "I think he might go for that but I need to see

Mrs. Morgenstern before I tell him anything."

"It'll be a minute," Stern said and sipped his drink. "Until then, let's talk about the currency sanitation business."

Ben shrugged. "What would you like to know?"

Stern sat down and took another sip. "I'm now able to get a full wash for fifteen percent."

"Minimum load?"

"Half a million."

"Who's offering fifteen?"

Stern shook his head. "Not important. I'm assured that it's a guaranteed service."

Ben said, "Then you should take it. I can't beat that."

"What's the best you can do?"

"The truth is, Joe, that the guy who sent me here from Israel is feeling the heat. From who, he hasn't said but I can guess. I'm here to wrap this end of the business up, at least for a time. He might get back to you in a year or so with a better offer than fifteen but I'm just a messenger."

"I kinda thought you were running things?"

"Not really my bag, Joe. I'm into different things."

"Such as?"

"Teaching Torah and Talmud. Counseling families. Presiding over *B'nai mitzvot* services. Leading services. Visiting the sick. Comforting families in times of distress."

"So you're actually a rabbi?"

"I am. And I don't much like doing this for Rabbi Meir but he has me over a barrel."

"Too bad," Joe said. "I think you'd make a helluva villain."

Ben shrugged. "Tell the truth, it's exciting and kind of interesting. But then I'd likely wind up dead or behind bars and that's just not a good way to spend my time."

Stern guffawed. "Funny guy. We should go out on the town sometime. Hit the bars on Rush Street, all like that."

"Maybe after my fiancée gets here and we finally tie the knot."

The office door opened and two men brought Julie Morgenstern in.

Something wasn't quite right with Julie. She was glassy-eyed, had trouble moving her feet, didn't seem to know where she was.

Ben looked at Stern.

"We gave her something to ease her anxieties."

"Something like heroin?"

"Like that, yeah."

Ben put an arm around Julie and led her to a chair, helped her to sit.

The lights went out.

Several loud explosions were heard in the space outside.

Three men in dark green camouflage fatigues, body armor, night-vision goggles and carrying assault rifles burst through the door. The lights came back on and the trio pushed their goggles aside.

One pointed his rifle at Stern. "Federal agents. You're under arrest for kidnapping."

The agent looked at Ben. "Both of you, on your feet and turn around. Move it."

§

Their hands cuffed behind their backs, Ben and Stern were herded into the next room, where several agents were pushing Stern's men into a wide rank—Gideon was nowhere in sight.

After what seemed like a long time, the door to Stern's office opened and Julie, escorted by two paramedics, was rolled out on a gurney, then out of the building and into the night. Seconds later, the sound of a helicopter landing nearby came through the open door. After a few minutes, Ben heard it taking off.

Agents went down the rank of handcuffed men on both sides, checking identification papers. One stopped at Ben, spun him around none too gently and went through his pockets.

He took Ben's wallet from his pocket, found his Israeli driver's license, his Massachusetts license and then a business card. He left Ben and took the papers to a somewhat smaller figure in dark green camouflage fatigues, body armor and a helmet with a face guard. Ben thought that there was something different about the way that this agent moved. It might be a woman, he thought.

And then he knew: Agent Gilmore.

He waited for her to send an agent back, to offer some glimmer of recognition.

She ignored him.

§

"Glass!" shouted a detention officer.

"Here," Ben said, raising his right arm in the large cell that he shared with six men from the Stern gang.

"Step to the bars, turn around, hands behind your back."

Ben did as he was told. The officer reached through the bars and put cuffs on Ben's hands.

The cell door slid open. "Come," said the officer.

The officer grabbed his left arm and led Ben down a corridor, then turned right and down a much longer passageway, through a series of barred gates that opened to his shouted commands and then into yet another corridor, this one carpeted and then through a final barred gate.

"Stop," said the officer, spun him around, removed his cuffs and pointed to a door with a frosted window.

"Inside," he said and watched Ben push the door open to find three women and a very tall man, all beaming.

"Thank you," said Assistant State's Attorney Leonard Morgenstern as Miryam flew halfway across the room and wrapped herself around Ben.

"I missed you," she whispered in his ear.

They kissed, briefly, then Miryam gently pulled away and turned to Julie.

"Your turn—but no kissing," she said with a grim smile.

Julie hugged Ben, kissed his cheek, then kissed the other one.

"That's twice you've saved me," she said and broke away.

"You don't get a hug from me but thanks and good work," said Gilmore and they shook hands.

"I had to leave you in custody because I didn't want to blow your cover," she said.

Ben shrugged. "Not hard to figure that out. And thanks for not telling me that you bugged my phone."

Gilmore laughed. "Safety precaution."

Chapter Fifty-Eight

STEINS

"Wake up," Miryam said.

Ben opened one eye.

"What's going on?"

"You promised to show me a house. And I have to buy a dress."

"I've never seen you in a dress," Ben said. "except for a sundress on the day that we met."

"I have to buy a wedding dress."

"I'll call the real estate lady."

§

Mrs. Silverman eyed Miryam uncertainly. "Who are you again?"

"Miryam. Rabbi Ben's fiancé."

"You can't be more than eighteen!"

Miryam frowned. It was as if the sun had gone behind a cloud.

"My age is not your concern. Ben is looking for a place to park and will join us in a few minutes. In the meanwhile, would you please show me this house?"

With a sigh that spoke volumes, Silverman led Miryam up the steps to the porch.

"This is all new construction," the Realtor said, indicating the timbers and planking of the expansive porch. She pointed to the lower part of the gray brick. "There's a natural gas connection and two electrical outlets, in case you want a gas barbeque."

"Very nice," Miryam said. "In back, too? I mean the gas and electric."

"I think so."

They had reached the second floor before Ben arrived.

"Ben, Mrs. Silverman thinks I'm too young to be a *rebbetzin* (wife of a rabbi).

Silverman blushed. "I said no such thing!"

Ben said, "It's a normal reaction. Miryam is indeed very youthful in appearance and of course, many movie stars would like to be that beautiful."

It was Miryam's turn to blush.

"But, as it happens, Miryam is very much my equal. Aside from her looks, she had gifts that I can only envy. But, more to the point, if Miryam is not an ordinary rebbetzin, I am not exactly your *bubbe's rebbe* either."

Silverman said, "I didn't mean to imply—"

Ben held up his hand. "Let us not quarrel. The truth is that I'm only temporary at Beth Ohr. I am a consultant and a problem-solver and I go from place to place to render help, as it's needed."

Silverman said, "How do you like the house so far, Miryam?"

"It seems like it will do, at least for the next two years, while I study for my doctorate."

Ben said, "Have you seen the mother-in-law?"

Miryam frowned. "Excuse me? Who?"

"This way," Ben said and led Miryam into the back yard.

As he had anticipated, Miryam was delighted.

"Ben, do you know what we could do with that little house?"

"Start a university for very small students?"

Miryam punched him, not very hard, in the shoulder.

"We'd need to offer football to be a university. But this could be a little neighborhood preschool! Maybe ten or twelve children."

Silverman said, "The rabbi knew you'd love this. Do you want to make an offer?"

Miryam and Ben exchanged glances.

Miryam said, "Subject to inspection and with a 45-day escrow, we will pay $495,000, cash and not a shekel more."

Silverman said, "I'll write it up."

Ben said, "Mrs. Silverman, do you happen to know a good place to buy a wedding dress?"

"Something ready-made or…?"

Miryam said, "Anything that I might select off the rack will require a lot of sewing to fit me. I'm open to that but I could also see something custom made."

"Then you should start with Mignonette, on Belmont Avenue."

"Expensive?" Miryam said.

"I'd say so."

Chapter Fifty-Nine

Steins

As Ben and Miryam walked arm-in-arm toward Beth Ohr's front door, it opened and Rabbi Shevitz came out, smiling.

"So *this* is the famous Miryam!" he said.

"In the flesh," Miryam said.

Ben said, "Miryam, my colleague, Rabbi Shevitz."

Shevitz said, "Manny. Just Manny, Miryam. I see that Ben is a very fortunate man."

Miryam laughed, a cacophony of tiny silver bells. "*I* am the lucky one, Rabbi. From the moment he jumped over the wall into my tomato patch, dressed, mind you, as a Roman Catholic priest, I knew that he was my *Beshert*."

"Dressed as a priest?" Shevitz said.

"It's a long story," Ben said.

"Mrs. Finkelstein is in our office and she insists on talking to you."

Miryam said, "Who is Mrs. Finkelstein?"

"A member. Her brother died," Rabbi Shevitz explained.

"She's a beauty," Ben said. "six feet tall, a face to make men swoon, a figure to match."

"And only fifty," Rabbi Shevitz added. "At the height of her sexual powers."

Miryam elbowed Ben. "You're trying to make me jealous!"

Both men laughed.

Ben turned to Shevitz and said, "Ten minutes and I'll see Mrs. Finkelstein."

Chapter Sixty

Jerusalem

Marcia Bender left Rabbi Danziger's office, careful to suppress her anger. She left the small, shabby synagogue, one of many on Jerusalem's Mea Shearim Street and walked as quickly as her ugly, low-heeled shoes and ankle-length skirt would permit.

Leaving the ultra-orthodox Mea Shearim district, she removed her knee-length coat and carried it in her arms until she could hail a taxi.

The taxi took her to the bright, spacious apartment that she rented for herself and her six-year-old brother. Marcia changed into her normal garb, slacks and a loose blouse, washed her hands and still fuming, began preparing lunch for Mort and herself. It was too early to call Chicago but later, before she went to bed, she vowed to call Ben and tell him what Rabbi Danziger had demanded of her in exchange for a certificate of conversion that would meet Rabbi Farkas's approval.

Chapter Sixty-one

Steins

Ben opened the door to the rabbi's office and Lillian Golden beamed at him.

"So good to see you again, Rabbi," she said.

Ben smiled. "Thank you. Did you know that I was looking for you?"

"Looking for *me?* "Why on earth would you look for me?"

"When your brother died about two weeks ago, I was asked to wind up his affairs. You seem to be his sole heir."

Lillian blanched. "You knew that I'm Rabbi's Rubin's sister?"

"From the moment that I laid eyes on you, I knew that you were Deborah Rubin."

"Why didn't you say something then?"

"Because it would have been very awkward. You'd just had an accident, you might have died, you were very shaken. That didn't seem like a very good time to speak about your brother."

'Who else knows that Shmuel was my brother?"

Ben shook his head. "I've told no one. I recognized you from a wedding picture among your brother's papers."

"Rabbi, I haven't spoken to Shmuel in more than fifteen years."

"Where have you been?"

"Israel. The Negev. I paint. When Shmuel died, I was there making sketches and taking photos and I didn't learn that he had been killed until a few days ago."

"You now call yourself Lillian Golden. Why?"

"Who are you, really?"

"As I told you. I'm a rabbi. I was asked to wind up your brother's charity and forward the books and so forth to Rabbi Farkas, secretary to Rabbi Wein of the Israeli Rabbinate."

"Rabbi *Meir* Farkas?"

"The same. Do you know him?"

"He's a devil in a holy man's clothes."

"I have to agree with you."

"But you're working for him!"

"I didn't know much about him when I took the job, except that he promised to deport my sister, a rabbinical student in Jerusalem, if I didn't help him."

"What does want you to do?"

"Shut L'Dor v'Dor down and send its remaining funds to the Rabbinate."

"That doesn't sound very hard."

Ben shook his head. "It has turned out to be far more complicated and dangerous than I expected," Ben said. "How do you know Rabbi Farkas?"

"He corrupted my brother. And he raped me."

Ben said, "Farkas convinced Shmuel to turn L'Dor v'Dor into a money-laundering machine?"

"Yes," she whispered, blinking back tears. "He told

Shmuel that if he didn't take donations from criminals, they would simply find another way to clean their money, so he might as well get some of it to educate rabbinical students. I told my brother that it was money milked from human misery, from addicts, from women forced into prostitution, from men who gambled their family's grocery money away. He didn't listen. And then I learned that there was so much dirty money flowing through that charity that he regularly siphoned some of it off for himself."

"What did you do about it?"

"I went back to Israel to beg Meir Farkas to leave Shmuel alone. Instead, he put something in my coffee. When I woke up, he was on top of me. Inside me.

"He told me how beautiful I was, how much he could do for me and he offered me an apartment in Jerusalem and an allowance if he could see me three or four afternoons a week.

"While he was putting his pants back on, I grabbed a feather quill from his desk and tried to put out his eye. Maybe I even did—there was a lot of blood.

Ben said, "He now wears a patch over his left eye."

"It serves him right, And by the way, as I left his presence, he said that if I got in his way, Shmuel would be killed."

"Then what? Did you report it?"

"The authorities said that it was nonsense that a man like Farkas would rape a visitor, especially a Jew. His wife—Meir's wife—threatened to sue me for slander."

"But you stayed in Israel?"

"There are men like Meir Farkas in every country. I had made *aliya* [went to live in Israel] more than twenty years ago, after my divorce. I came back to the States a few years later, just for a visit. That was when I found out about the money laundering. Shmuel was like a father to me. He raised me after *abba* died. I couldn't bear to see what he had become. So, I returned to Israel. I had an apartment in Beersheba and I felt at home there."

"Then what?"

"What Farkas did almost destroyed me. After a while, a year or so of self-loathing, I began seeing a psychiatrist. With her support, I reinvented myself. I changed my name. I got a part-time job in an upscale restaurant and spent most of my days painting scenes from the Negev. After a few years of struggle, I was making a decent living that way. Then a gallery in Tel Aviv offered to represent me. Now my work is also in a London gallery and one in New York. I'm selling canvases almost as fast as I can paint them—eighteen or twenty a year."

Ben said, "I admired your work in a gallery in Chelsea last year. In Hebrew, Golden is Muzhav. Your professional name is Lillian Muzhav?"

"Yes. Please call me Lilly."

"But you came back to the States again?" Ben said.

"About a year ago but I didn't look up any of my old friends. I didn't even see my brother, although now I wish that I had."

"Then why did you come back?"

"I grew up with Randy Finkelstein. As children, we were outcasts together. Me because I was very tall, because I developed early and because we were poor. I never had good clothes—we dressed almost in rags. Randy was singled out because his parents were very wealthy and because he was very shy and had no social skills. We were each other's best friends. But only friends."

"And he asked you to come back?"

"His daughter Naomi called. Randy has early-onset

Alzheimer's. His wife left him a couple of years ago. Somehow, in Randy's mind, *I* was his wife. He began asking Naomi where I was and became very agitated. So, I came back and as a kindness to him, we got married. A civil ceremony, very quiet, nobody but a judge, his clerk, and Naomi."

"You were heading south when I saw you crash."

"Every few days I must get away for a little while—he can be very intense. He's impotent but he can't fall asleep unless I'm holding him. When I can steal a few hours, I do."

"It sounds like a hellish life for you."

"It's not so bad. He's getting worse and his doctors give him only a few more months. I definitely make him calmer when we're together. He sometimes likes to watch me paint and that's a relief for both of us."

"Let's talk about your brother."

"I know that he was buried."

"The congregation did that. He was rabbi emeritus."

"He should have some kind of a memorial service but I dread having to tell anyone about his secret life. And I'm not sure if I want anyone to know that I was Deborah Rubin and that now I'm Lillian Golden. I'm not ashamed but I fear that my identity would get back to Rabbi Farkas. I wouldn't feel safe. So. It's a dilemma and I'm hoping you can help me with this."

Ben shut his eyes for a moment, then opened them. "Ifffff you tell people that Shmuel was your brother, members who were around fifteen years ago will know that you are Deborah Rubin. And you're right, that could get back to Farkas. But Ifffff you don't mention that you are sister and brother…"

"Rabbi, there is no one in this *shul* that resembles me in the slightest way. I'm six-feet, two inches tall. I'm surprised that no one has recognized me yet."

Ben nodded his understanding. "According to Mrs. Levy, when your brother retired and Rabbi Shevitz took his place, some of the older members, more than fifty families, joined another Orthodox *shul*, Anshe Yakov. Then, after your brother was killed and Rabbi Shevitz and his wife went into hiding, even more members left the congregation.

"I think there's a good chance that very few members will remember you.

"Here's my suggestion. With your help, I'll prepare a eulogy that mentions your brother's accomplishments. If you wish to participate, you can talk about how Shmuel raised you after your parents died. You don't need to mention that you shared a father. Let people assume whatever they will. If you want to speak, keep it short.

"But if you don't want to speak, that's fine. Tell me what you would have said and I'll say it in my words."

Lillian beamed. "Thank you, rabbi. I think I'll let you speak and I'll just listen."

Ben nodded his agreement.

"There is something that you could do for me if you care to. I emphasize that I'm not asking for a *quid pro quo*. You can decline my invitation and I'll do as I've already explained and I won't think less of you."

"Tell me what you want me to do," Lillian said.

Chapter Sixty-two

STEINS

Ben felt the phone vibrating against his leg.

"What are you doing day after tomorrow," Peters said.

"I'm not sure. What am I doing?"

"You could join Deputy Chief Johnson on a tiger hunt."

"Who is Johnson, exactly?"

"We went to grad school together. Chicago PD has a whole basket of chiefs, including a Chief of Organized Crime and two deputy chiefs. Phil Johnson is the OC division's junior deputy chief. You are invited to wait in the jungle with him for a tiger to come after the goat."

"Gonçalves agreed to cooperate?"

"Gray explained that when we turned him loose, whoever it was who borrowed his car would find out pretty quick. His family would not be safe."

"You dropped all charges?"

"We had him plead to a misdemeanor—making a false police report—no jail, three years unsupervised probation."

Ben said, "When does this little soirée kick off?"

"We're going to turn him loose the day after tomorrow. A Chicago patrol unit will take him home around 10:00 am. Chief Johnson will send an unmarked car for you about 9:00."

"I'm in," Ben said.

"I'll let him know," Peters said and rang off.

Chapter Sixty-three

Steins

Miryam was changing for dinner when there was a soft knock at the door.

"In a minute," she called and pulled on a red cashmere sweater above her skinny jeans.

At the door, she said, "Who is it?"

A man's deep voice said "Gideon."

Miryam switched to Hebrew. "The Gideon of the horns, pitchers, and torches?"

"The Gideon of the trunk of the Cadillac."

Miryam opened the door to find a man of about forty years, of average height and ordinary appearance and dressed in a nicely tailored blue business suit.

"Where is the red-headed rabbi?" he said.

"Downstairs, counseling a lady in mourning."

Gideon nodded. "Are there any more like you at home? A sister or cousin?"

Miryam blushed deep red from the roots of her dark hair to her toes.

"My cousin Noa Benkamal looks something like me but she's taller."

"Is she here?"

Miryam shook her head, sending her curls shivering. "Tel

Aviv."

"Married?"

"Not yet. She has a boyfriend but I don't know how serious they are."

Gideon said, "I am a very serious man but if Noa is your age, she's probably too young for me."

Miryam smiled. "My cousin Ronit Amon is thirty, single, beautiful and very feisty. She is also in Tel Aviv. Her mother is a Benkamal."

"I think your rabbi and I will be good friends. When it's time for me to go home, we will speak of this Ronit again."

Miryam said, "What brings you here today?"

"I thought that Ben might be worried about me. I want to tell him what happened when the lights went out at the steel mill."

"Then come in and sit down. He'll be back soon."

A moment later the door opened and Ben started to come inside, then stopped. His face lit up when he saw Gideon.

"What happened to you?" Ben said. "Last I saw, you were teaching those bozos how to fight a man with a knife."

"My partner was on a motorcycle. Big, fast BMW. He followed us, found a place to hide in a rail yard and after about twenty minutes, saw the FBI task force assembling, getting ready to storm the fire station. He sent an emergency signal, then a text message. I excused myself to use the restroom, went out the window and ran about a kilometer east to where he was waiting. We were on the Interstate about the time the helicopter took off with, I assume, Mrs. Morgenstern."

Miryam said, "You never told me that you had help, Ben."

Gideon said, "As it turned out, I wasn't needed."

Ben said, "Nevertheless, it was a comfort having you there."

Gideon stuck his hand out and Ben shook it. "I came by just to let you know that I was fine," he said.

Miryam said, "But why are you here? In America—in Chicago?"

Gideon frowned. "Chicago has a container port. The gigantic ships that come from Europe, West Africa, and the Mideast can't get through the St. Lawrence Seaway from the Atlantic. So they offload containers at Quebec and load them on smaller ships. My unit is interested in containers from certain parts of the world. We work with your Coast Guard and Homeland Security to screen those containers."

Ben said, "That doesn't sound very exciting."

Gideon shook his head. "No, it's not. So, thank you for an entertaining week. We got to see a lot more of the city than before."

Ben said, "Thanks for being there."

Gideon turned to leave, then turned back to Miryam. "Ronit Amon, Tel Aviv?"

Miryam smiled. "I'll tell her to expect your call," she said.

"It will be a few months," he said, then waved and left through the door.

Ben said, "What was that about?"

Miryam smiled again. "He's looking for a girlfriend. Ronit might like him."

Ben shook his head. "He's probably Mossad."

Now it was Miryam's turn to frown. "Maybe I shouldn't say anything to her."

Ben shrugged. "All I'm saying is that field operatives are often away from home for months and years. Not the sort of career that lends itself to marriage."

Miryam shrugged. "Not really our problem. I'm starved.

Where are we going for dinner?"

Before Ben could answer, Miryam's phone rang.

"Nobody in Chicago has my number," she said.

"Answer it and find out."

"Loraine Silverman," said the voice in Miryam's ear.

"Hello, Lorraine. Did they accept our offer?"

"I'm afraid I have some bad news," she said.

"Tell me," Miryam said.

"The owner has received another offer. Unless you care to raise your offer, I'm afraid you're out of luck."

"Hold on a minute while I discuss this with my rabbi," Miryam said and looked at Ben.

"The house? Somebody beat our offer?"

"Yes. And I want that house," Miryam said.

"Mrs. Silverman, what's it going to take?" Miryam said.

"I'm afraid that I am not allowed to tell you what someone else bid," she said. "But I can tell you that it was significantly more than yours."

Miryam covered the mouthpiece and looked at Ben. "How much should we offer?"

Ben shrugged. "If you really want that house, go big. Otherwise, we will be in a bidding war for a week."

"Mrs. Silverman, we offer $521,000. That's more than the asking price," she added,

"I will tell the owner," she said.

Chapter Sixty-four

Steins

Arm-in-arm, Miryam and Ben walked down to the lobby. Just as they reached the lower level, the door to Rabbi Shevitz's office opened and he stepped out, followed by a tall, thin, fashionably dressed woman of perhaps thirty-five. Her makeup was perfect and her short blonde hair was artfully streaked and arranged.

Manny's face lit up. "Ben, Miryam, this is Leah, my wife."

The four cordially shook hands.

Ben said, "We're just off to dinner at my best friend's house, so as much as I'd like to visit, that will have to wait until next time."

Leah took Miryam's hand and smiled. "We'll have you over soon," she said in a surprisingly low register. "Miryam, you are the most gorgeous woman I've ever laid eyes on."

Miryam blushed. "Thanks. You are also very beautiful. Who does your hair?"

"I'll get you his card," Leah said and with a chorus of goodbyes, Ben and Miryam went out the door.

Chapter Sixty-Five

Steins

Ben closed the Toyota's door, put on his seat belt and started the engine.

"So where are you taking me?" Miryam said.

"To see a shrink," Ben said.

"What?"

"Mitch Katz, MD. One of my best friends. He's also a rabbi. His wife is a CPA and they are both excellent cooks. Miriam—Mrs. Katz—said she was making something special for us."

"So, the shrink is for you and the chef is for me?"

Ben laughed and guided the car out of the parking lot.

"What did you think of Mrs. Shevitz?" Miryam said.

"Very charming—a fashion plate."

"Anything else?"

"Not really. She seemed nice enough."

"Ben, I'm almost certain that Leah is a lesbian."

"What?" Ben turned in his seat, craning his head to see Miryam's face.

"No joke," Miryam said. "Didn't you see the way she looked at me? She was undressing me with her eyes."

Ben shook his head. "This is something that all women can do? Unravel sexual interest from a quick look at someone?"

"Don't know about everyone. But my sixth sense or whatever it is, has always been right on. Leah is a lesbian—I'd bet my eyeteeth on that."

"Then why is she married to a very masculine rabbi?"

Miryam smiled. "What better camouflage for a gay rabbi than a beautiful wife? And who will suspect that the wife prefers ladies to gentlemen?"

Ben said, "So their marriage is a fraud?"

"Not necessarily. I'm inclined to think that they care for each other greatly but each gets sexual satisfaction outside of the home."

Ben scratched his jaw. "I just remembered something. While the Shevitzes were missing and presumed kidnapped, I gave myself a tour of their home. On the second floor are two small bedrooms, one of which is a nursery for their two toddlers and two master suites, each with their own bath."

"Ah-ha!"

"Wait. There's more. The closets of one were filled with women's dresses and such. The closets of the other were split about fifty-fifty between his and hers."

Miryam said, "Where does she keep her underwear? That's where she sleeps."

Ben shrugged. "I'm not that big a creep. I didn't open any bedroom drawers."

Ben's phone rang and the applications screen on the dashboard showed "M. Bender" as the caller.

Ben punched the "accept call" button.

"Hi Sis," he said, "I'm in the car with Miryam."

"Hi Marcia," Miryam said.

"Hello, hello. I have much to tell you."

Ben pulled to the side of the road and parked behind a pickup truck on Finkelstein Boulevard.

"Go ahead," he said,

"I met with Rabbi Danziger, who claims to be the Crasna Rebbe but I looked it up and the last of the Crasna Rebbes died in the Holocaust."

Ben said. "Some of those dynasties have been reestablished, with people who trace their ancestors to the town or province where the rabbinic dynasty flourished."

Marcia said, "Anyway, he's a creep. First, he told me that I was to see him every Thursday at 2:00 pm for the next year and then he'd give me an exam. I got the impression that he wasn't much interested in using those afternoons for study, so I offered to take his final exam on the spot. He asked me seven questions and I could see that he was surprised. Then he asked if I was married. I said that I was a widow and he lit into me for being immodest—I don't shave my head. He said that the Talmud teaches that for a married woman to display her hair is the equivalent of physical nudity."

Miryam said, "Nonsense. Sephardic women are as observant as any Jews and we have never, ever, shaved our heads. Nor do the *Mizrahi*."

Marcia said, "Exactly. But I didn't say that. I told him that Jewish law forbids a woman to shave her head because we are forbidden to imitate the practices of a man. And I said that in the Talmud, in Nazir 28b, forcing a husband to see his wife without hair is repulsive."

Ben said, "So then what? He tried to browbeat you with another Talmud citation?"

"No. He said that it was apparent that I was very learned but how could an American woman be permitted to study Talmud? That is the province of men and I should not distract men in a study hall.

"I responded with a quotation from Nachman of Breslov and that shut him down on that front. He said that if I was actually planning to become a rabbi, it would deprive a man with a family of a job rightfully his.

"I said, 'Enough of this nonsense. How much do you want?'

"'In dollars?'

"In American dollars, how much?

"Then he goes on and on about how poor his synagogue is, about how much he will have to give to Rabbi Farkas and so on and so forth. And he asks for $100,000.

"I got up, put on my coat and started to leave. 'Fifty thousand' he said. 'Cash—hundred dollar bills.'

"We settled for $35,000 and he told me Rabbi Farkas would be furious."

Miryam said, "He is a disgrace. It's a *shanda* that rabbis are permitted to do such things."

Marcia chuckled. "I have every word in a digital sound file on my phone. Every word. And I marked each hundred-dollar bill with my signature in lemon juice, just as Ben told me. Thanks, big brother."

Marcia said, "What do I do with the file?"

Ben said, "Copy it onto a flash drive and take it to Aviva Shapiro."

"Who is she?"

Miryam said, "One of Ben's old girlfriends. Now Yossi's chief of staff."

"Yossi is who?"

"Yossi Bar Tzvi."

Marcia shrieked, "My brother knows the President of Israel?"

Miryam said. "And Yossi owes Ben a favor."

Ben said, "Not really. Ask Aviva to pass this recording on to Shabak, the Shin Bet, Israel's version of the FBI. Tell her what's on the file and let me know what Aviva says about it."

Marcia said, "My brother is pals with the President of Israel and he never told me!"

Ben said, "I love you, little sister. Kiss Mort for me."

Marcia said, "Bye Ben. Bye Miryam. Love you."

After the connection was broken, Miryam turned to Ben.

"What are you up to, love of my life?"

Ben smiled. "I'll let you know after I speak to Pat Gilmore. And the day after tomorrow, I'm going on a tiger hunt."

Chapter Sixty-six

Skokie

Dinner at the Katzes began with a hummus appetizer, then a roast chicken stuffed with *kasha* [buckwheat groats], caramelized onions and walnuts and a huge salad of baby spinach, mandarin orange segments, snap peas, chopped celery, and candied pecans.

Before dessert was served, Miryam insisted on helping Marcia with the dishes, which left Mitch and Ben regarding each other across the empty table. They sat in silence for almost a minute before the psychiatrist frowned. "Ben, you are my brother, my best friend but I have to ask: Do you know what you're doing?"

Ben sighed. He had half expected this. "Last year you encouraged me to push past Rachel's death, to move beyond mourning her, to get out and date a few women. I dated a couple of women. I thought that I had found the one who might fill the hole in my life that was the loss of Rachel. Then, two days later, I met Miryam and I knew that dating wasn't going to be enough for me."

Mitch smiled. "She is gorgeous, no doubt. But she's so young."

"Miryam is 25, almost 26. She does appear younger but that is merely packaging.

"She has a master's in early childhood education and just enrolled in a doctoral program here. Miryam is an only child, as am I. Her parents disappeared when she was about eight. She was raised in a big old house by her great uncle and his housekeeper. By the way, we are now pretty sure that her actual great uncle was murdered by a man who appropriated his identity and later murdered her parents. Miryam has been through some of life's most agonizing traumas and has emerged as a bright, happy, curious woman. She is mature far beyond her years. And her devotion to me is absolute."

"Ben, I wonder if she'd be willing to have a session or two with me—or someone I could refer her to."

"To what end?"

"You just told me that she's been traumatized. She may have any number of issues lurking below the surface of her personality, problems that will emerge later in life and whose cause may then be difficult to pin down."

Ben shrugged. "I can't tell her that she has to see a shrink before I'll marry her."

Mitch paled and shook his head. "That isn't what I'm suggesting. Have your wedding. Enjoy your honeymoon. She will then, as you just told me, return to her studies. That might be an appropriate time for her to establish a professional relationship with a therapist. Once every month, perhaps."

Ben nodded his understanding. "I take your point. I'll raise the issue and see how she responds. She may embrace the idea and she may think I'm testing her or trying to take over her life."

"Why don't you just invite her to join one of our sessions, yours and mine and she will then, I hope, understand your life and your issues a little more completely."

Ben smiled. "I've been meaning to ask her just that."

"At your convenience," Mitch said, as the door to the kitchen opened.

"Ben, Marcia made the most amazing dessert," Miryam said. "It tastes like ice cream but it's tofu!"

Chapter Sixty-seven

Chicago

At nine in the morning, Ben entered the Israeli Consulate, stood in line until he reached a pleasant, middle-aged woman behind the counter.

"Eliyahu Ben Shaul," he said, watching the woman's eyes widen.

A gap appeared in the counter and the same short man with a white beard beckoned him through and into a private office.

"We were not expecting you," said the man.

"I apologize but you will understand the concept of operational necessity."

"Of course. What can I do for you?"

"I need a secure line to Aviva Shapiro."

"Is she expecting to hear from you?"

"I feel confident that she is, although we do not have an appointment."

"Sit there," said the man, pointing to a chair next to a telephone and left the room.

Half an hour dragged by until the phone rang. Ben answered it.

"This is Rabbi Moshe Benyamin Maimon," he said in Hebrew.

"Ben, I think we should give you a code name," said Mrs. Shapiro.

"That might raise issues of foreign agency," he replied.

"I'll look into that. What can I do for you today?"

Ben asked her if she had met Marcia and if she had listened to the recording.

"I have and I did. The digital file went to a friend of my husband's at Shabak."

"I would like Shabak to take a certain action if it is justified by the evidence and within their authority."

"Spell it out," said Aviva and listened carefully.

"I think that will work. From now on, you are known as *Colev* (Caleb). We're not paying you or controlling you. But once that name gets in the system, it will expedite communications."

"Thanks," Ben said. "My best to Yossi."

Chapter Sixty-eight

Chicago

At noon Ben climbed into the back seat of a dark blue SUV parked in a crowded lot across from Ridgelawn Cemetery in the Edgewater neighborhood.

From behind the wheel, Agent Ed Robertson nodded a greeting. Pat Gilmore took Ben's hand in hers and gave it a perfunctory squeeze.

"And the lovely Miryam?" she said.

"First fitting of her wedding dress. No grooms allowed."

"Surely Jews don't have that superstition too?"

Ben shrugged. "It's not a Jewish thing but it's part of American culture. And the seamstress was pretty clear that I wasn't welcome."

Roberts said, "So, what do you have?"

Ben said, "My sister Marcia is a rabbinical student in Jerusalem. You may recall that it was that fact that gave Rabbi Farkas a way to get me to come here and wind up his charity?"

Gilmore nodded her head in agreement. "So now what?"

"My sister's mother was a convert to Judaism. In her tween years, Marcia also converted. Farkas demanded that Marcia undergo a second conversion on the ground that the rabbi who performed her first conversion was not sufficiently Jewish and not recognizably a rabbi—Rabbi Elizabeth Mendelsohn doesn't have a penis.

"Farkas told Marcia to see a particular rabbi in Jerusalem—

Nehemiah Danziger—for instruction and eventual conversion.

"As I suspected, this was little more than a shakedown. Danziger first put a move on Marcia, suggesting without saying so that she ought to sleep with him in addition to receiving unnecessary religious instruction. She shrugged it off, so he demanded that Marcia pay him $100,000. He settled for $35,000, all the while complaining that Farkas would be angry because his, Farkas's, share would be a disappointment.

"Marcia recorded all this, the solicitation, the bargaining, the acceptance, on her cell phone. The hundred-dollar notes that she gave him were marked with her name in invisible ink."

Gilmore said, "What is this to us, to the FBI?"

Ben said, "You told me that you had enough evidence to convict Farkas on racketeering and money laundering but he would have to be arrested in the US."

"And?"

"My sister took her evidence to the Shin Bet. The Israeli authorities will likely try to arrest Farkas and if my source has it right, freeze all his bank accounts. He's very well connected in the government, so they will probably release him on bail until his trial."

Roberts said, "And that might send him here, to collect his money, wire it someplace safe and then either disappear or go back to Israel and see what happens."

"I'm hoping so."

Gilmore said, "What do you need from us?"

Chapter Sixty-nine

Chicago

Ben parked at a meter on Belmont and texted Miryam.

A moment later, his phone rang: Julie Morgenstern.

"Shalom, Rabbi," she said. "I have good news."

Ben said, "I can always use good news."

Julie said, "But first, I want to thank you, again, for all that you've done for us."

Ben noted the "us."

"Go on. "Yesterday, I moved back in with Leonard. We're going to find a new house and try to start over."

"Congratulations."

"We have been talking, at length and now, I think, I hope, I pray, he's ready to be the husband that I always wanted."

Ben smiled. "I'm very happy for both of you."

"That isn't the good news!"

"But it *is* very good news. What else?"

"With Leah's help, I have assembled almost all the L'Dor v'Dor records. We went through the minutes of all board meetings and in March 1992, the board approved a policy that will be a big help to us in winding up the charity."

"Go on," Ben said.

"It said that under unusual circumstances, including the death or incapacity of an officer, a temporary board member may be appointed to the board of directors by any officer. These appointees must be members in good standing of Beth Ohr and they will be paid $1,000 for each meeting they attend. They cannot attend more than two consecutive meetings without approval as provided in the by-laws."

"So we could have enough voting members if either Rabbi Farkas or Deborah Rubin approve?"

"Exactly."

"Great. By the way, I've located Deborah. She'll be at the meeting."

"Really? How?"

At that moment Miryam came out of the bridal shop, looked both ways, then hurried toward the Toyota.

"Tell you later," Ben said. "Gotta go."

Ben broke the connection as Miryam slid in beside him. Before strapping herself in, she wrapped Ben in her arms and held him for a long minute.

"I have good news and I have bad news," she said.

"Start with the bad."

"I have made a big mistake," Miryam said.

"Tell me."

"It's about the wedding. I asked you to plan for the Moshons and the Benkamals, sixty guests each but I forgot to mention my friends in Berkeley and all my friends in Brooklyn."

Ben said, "I added fifty to the dinner order to cover both. Will that be enough?"

Miryam beamed and Ben felt light and warmth embrace him.

"You think of everything!"

Ben shook his head. "I was married before, remember. We were adding and subtracting guests to the reception until almost the last day."

"Fifty will be enough. There are about twenty people in Brooklyn that I really must invite and about eight in California but I know I'll think of others. And I didn't ask you how many guests you were inviting."

"I added twenty for that. Ten couples, if they all make it."

"So we're good?"

"We're good. And I'd rather pay for a dozen extra than be one dinner short."

Miryam beamed again.

"What's your good news, Light of my Life?"

"I bought a dress. Oh, and we got the house. They accepted our bid and we can start escrow as soon as we do the paperwork and give her a small deposit—$1,000."

Ben said, "Wonderful. What are you doing this afternoon?"

"Shall we go look at furniture?"

"Maybe. By the way, do you have a gift registry?"

"At Saks and Bloomingdale's in New York and Barney's here. What are *you* doing this afternoon?"

"I have an appointment with Mitch at 4:00, in his office."

"But we saw him yesterday?"

Ben said, "This is a therapy session. For my PTSD and other issues."

Miryam touched Ben's arm. "I didn't know this was a regular thing."

Ben said, "It isn't. Instead of tranquilizers, my prescription is lots of exercise. That's why I run every morning if I can. But whenever I'm in Chicago for a few days, I like to have a session with Mitch. I'd like you to come along—we should have no secrets between us."

Miryam reached up and kissed Ben. "You are the most amazing man."

Ben said, "Then I guess I should also tell you that as of today, I have an Israeli code name, courtesy of Aviva Shapiro."

"Shall I guess what it is?"

"It's better that you don't know. But next time I speak to Aviva, I'll ask her if it's okay."

Chapter Seventy

Chicago

Ben and Miryam sat next to each other on a small couch across from Mitch Katz, who slouched in a comfortable armchair.

Miryam said, "I've never done this before."

Mitch said, "Never had a therapy session?"

Miryam shook her head. "As a child, after my parents died, I had about a year of weekly sessions with Doctor Milgram. But I've never observed someone else's therapy."

Ben said, "We're all friends. It's just a conversation."

Miryam said, "Mitch, I have a question for you: Ben told me that you are a rabbi. Why did you give that up?"

Mitch smiled. "An excellent question, Miryam. As a rookie rabbi in a big temple with another rabbi and a cantor, I spent most of my time working with the younger members of the congregation—bar- and bat-mitzvah students, our youth group for teens and the younger unmarried members. It was the usual sort of work—teaching, holding services, writing sermons. Sometimes, someone needed counseling. Usually, they were referred to the senior rabbi, then a man in his fifties with a Master's degree in psychology. But on the relatively few occasions when I could sit down with someone and try to help them sort out their problems or cope with a long-term issue, I experienced a lot of satisfaction. It came to me, gradually, that counseling was what I really wanted to do. I quit and went back to school. And thank you for asking."

Miryam said, "Thank *you* for being so forthcoming."

Mitch said, "Do you still have flashbacks, Ben?'

"After moments of high stress or when I'm very tired."

Miryam said, "I know about this. Once, I think, we were together when they happened. I'd like to understand what that's like for you."

Ben said, "Sometimes, I'm back in the café, right after the bomb went off. Dead and dying all around me. I can taste and smell smoke and explosives and blood. I experience waking from unconsciousness. I'm desperate to find Rachel. I'm overcome with fear and horror. I often faint or pass out."

Mitch said, "Still on a running regimen?"

"Usually five miles before breakfast."

Miryam took Ben's hand. "I should go with you," she said.

Ben nodded. "I'd like that."

Mitch said, "Losing a spouse can sometimes trigger effects long after the event. Are you having any anxiety about that now, as your marriage date approaches?"

Ben said, "I'm in a line of work that creates enemies. I worry about reprisals against Miryam."

"What are you doing about that?"

"I'm trying—so far unsuccessfully—to get out of the paladin business. I want to be a pulpit rabbi—it's why I became a rabbi. If I can't find a pulpit, there are other jobs for rabbis. Maybe I'll teach or run a community center, something like that."

Mitch said, "Miryam, how do you feel about this?"

"I worry that Ben's luck will run out. I know that he

worries a lot about something happening to me. But at the same time, Ben is the strongest, most fearless man that I know. Just in the few months that we've been together, he's handled all sorts of emergencies and confrontations and somehow always comes out fine. Yet, when we have children, I'm sure that I'll worry even more."

Ben said, "And yet you still want to marry me?"

"More than ever. I feel very safe with you. I can't picture myself with anyone but you."

Mitch said, "Have you talked about children? How many and when?"

Ben said, "A little. I think we want to wait for Miryam to get her doctorate first and then we'll figure out where we're going to live—here, New England, New York or someplace else."

Miryam said, "At first I wanted to have lots of children. Eight, at least. But now I'm thinking that two or three would be ideal."

Ben said, "I didn't know that."

Miryam smiled. "Now you do. Do you have any thoughts on the subject?"

Ben shook his head. "I've always thought that one was not enough—we were both only children and yet four would be a stretch. Two or three sounds just right."

Mitch said, "What was it like being an only child, Miryam?"

Miryam's eyes filled and tears streaked her cheeks. "Horrible. I dream about being alone—it's terrifying."

"Tell me more," Mitch said.

"Well, a few days ago I dreamt I was wandering around Bloomingdale's in a blouse, barefoot, with nothing under my blouse. I was trying to find the changing room, where I'd left my purse and the rest of my clothes but every floor was the wrong floor. And nobody spoke to me. I asked a sales clerk and she looked right through me to speak to the woman behind me."

Mitch said, "Have you had that dream more than once?"

Miryam ducked her head, yes. "Every so often. And I have other dreams, where I'm naked or half-dressed and I'm wandering the streets, trying to find where I left my car. Or I'm looking for my home but I can't remember what it looks like."

"When did these dreams begin?" Mitch asked.

"Junior high. I hadn't had one for a long time, until a couple of days ago."

"What happened just before that?"

Ben said, "I was kidnapped but rescued."

Mitch said, "Do you see the connection, Miryam?"

She nodded, yes. "When I was a little girl, my parents died. I was raised by a man whom I thought was my great uncle and his housekeeper. They were both in their seventies then. I always felt that I was alone, that no one understood me."

"Did you have friends?"

Miryam smiled. "Lots of friends. I liked going to their homes, meeting their parents and sisters and brothers. But they never came to my house."

Ben said, "Your uncle prohibited it?"

Miryam shook her head. "No. But he was *very* strange—and thanks to Ben, I learned why he was that way. I was ashamed to invite friends over because I knew they'd see how weird he was."

Mitch said, "We have to stop soon. Miryam, would you care to come back sometime and talk some more?"

She cocked her head, considering.

"Yes, I'd like that. I feel a little better now, unburdened. A little, anyway."

Chapter Seventy-one

Chicago

After breakfast, Miryam took the Toyota and went shopping for furniture.

Around 9:00, an unmarked car with two plainclothes officers picked Ben up and delivered him to a Trader Joe's parking lot in suburban Park Ridge, just northwest of Chicago. "In the freezer truck," said the cop behind the wheel. Ben got out and walked to a corner of the lot to a huge truck with a "Pioneer Wholesale Meat" logo on its side.

On tiptoe, he knocked on the side of the truck. A door in the back opened and a cloud of white crystals rose from the opening. "What?" said a man in soiled butcher's whites. "We don't sell retail."

"Chief Johnson?" Ben replied.

"Make it fast," said the butcher.

A set of stairs unfolded below the door and the butcher extended a hand to pull Ben up them and through the door. The door shut behind him and Ben found himself in a narrow compartment full of blocks of dry ice. He went through it to an almost invisible door and then into a large, dimly lit space where several men and women sat behind color monitors.

A tall African-American in CPD uniform with a five-pointed silver star on each collar approached. "Rabbi Ben Maimon?" he said, smiling. He extended his hand and they shook. "Peters tells me you're some kind of Jewish Sherlock Holmes," Chief Johnson said.

"Holmes couldn't write computer code," Ben said, deadpan. Johnson laughed.

"Touché," Johnson said.

"That's our goat's front yard and porch," the chief said, pointing at a screen where Gonçalves and a chubby, dark-haired woman worked at trimming a hedge.

"We have a female officer inside with their two kids and a man in the alley. There's an unmarked car at either end of the street with a pair of officers in each. There's a man in plain clothes patrolling the block And around the corner, in an unmarked SUV, is a SWAT squad."

"On the way here. I noticed a church with a tall belfry," Ben said.

"St. Paul of the Cross," Johnson said. The belfry atop the steeple is no longer in use and the inside and outside doors are locked. In any case, I've got two plainclothes on the grounds."

"So you've got all the bases covered?"

"I think so."

"We passed a nine-story apartment building and a hospital on the way here," Ben said. From the roof—"

"Too far for anyone but a military sniper with a large-caliber weapon. Besides, we have a drone circling at 8,000 feet. That should take care of anything I haven't thought of."

"Got it," Ben said.

"There's coffee in the corner. Make yourself at home but don't converse with the screen operators. They've got enough to do."

"Thanks, Chief," Ben said.

Ben stood behind a man at a screen that showed the sidewalk and street in front of the Gonçalves home. On another screen with a view down the street, he saw a short, dark-skinned, possibly Latino man in a straw hat and wearing a front-and-back canvas vest stuffed with advertising materials slowly making his way down the block tossing a small bundle of brochures up each driveway as he passed it.

As he approached the Gonçalves's house, two men in casual clothing stopped the man in the straw hat. One flashed a badge. The other snatched a bundle of brochures from the man's right hand opened it, then said something to the other officer, who wrestled the shorter man to the pavement and handcuffed him. The first officer held up a bundle of advertising. From it, he pulled a large white envelope, which he tore open to reveal a cell phone pressed into what looked like a block of clay. The officer jerked the phone out of the clay and threw it to the pavement, then stomped on it.

"We got him," announced the officer at the console. He wore a headset and as the cop on the street spoke, the man at the console repeated his words.

"Officer Kent says the phone is a cheap burner. The explosive smells like tar, so maybe its C-4."

On the screen, the other officer pulled the smaller man to his feet and questioned him for a few seconds. The console operator said, "The suspect says a girl gave him $50 to deliver the envelope. She was about seventeen, Caucasian, blonde, skinny, with lots of acne on her face.

Chief Johnson tapped the operator on the shoulder.

"Tell him to take the suspect into custody for questioning," he said, loud enough for Ben to hear.

Johnson turned to a uniformed officer with the double silver bars of a captain on his collars. "Leave the officer in the house and the officer in the alley and shut the rest of it down," he said.

Ben approached Johnson, concern on his face. "May I

have a word in private?" he said and Johnson led him to a corner alcove.

"What is it?" he said.

Ben said, "I understand that I'm only an observer and I respect that you are a very experienced officer but think it's a mistake to shut down your operation now."

"And why is that, Rabbi?"

"I suspect that the people who killed Rabbi Rubin and Nadia Roldugin have just offered you a distraction. When you remove the majority of your officers, they will strike again."

"What makes you think that?"

"It's a pattern. They blew up a car in the synagogue parking lot as a distraction, then stole a crucial piece of evidence from my room while I was in the parking lot. They bribed Abel Gonçalves to leave town so they could use his car to kill Rabbi Rubin, knowing that police would suspect him of killing both Rubin and Nadia Roldugin because he was Nadia's boyfriend and his car was used to kill Rubin. I'm fairly sure they'll find a way to get Gonçalves as soon as your men leave."

"Thanks for sharing your thoughts, Rabbi but you're postulating a criminal mastermind."

"Or a few very smart people."

"Most murderers are not smart. Dumb as dirt, in my experience. But I appreciate you sharing your thoughts and your discretion for doing it in private, Rabbi."

"So you don't believe me?"

"Frankly, no. But I do respect your trying to help. I'll have an officer take you home."

"Actually, I'm meeting my fiancé in Chicago. I'll call an Uber."

"Whatever. Nice meeting you, Rabbi."

They shook hands and Ben left the van and walked south, toward a major intersection.

He ducked into a convenience store on the corner and browsed for five minutes until he saw the "Pioneer Wholesale Meat" truck rumble by. Then he bought a bottle of water and crossed the street, heading for the Gonçalves home.

He stopped at the corner, three houses from his destination, and noted that the front porch was narrow and elevated to the height of four steps. Then he went down the intersecting street until he could see the top of the high-rise apartment building. He checked his watch: A little after 2:00 p.m. It would be another two hours before someone on that building's roof had the sun behind him and could then, with the help of a telescopic sight, peer into the Gonçalves' living room. Walking slowly, Ben made his way to the tall building at 3232 Belmonde. On one side was a row of retail stores. On the other, a small parking lot for deliveries. Tenants and visitors entered from the street, went through the lot and then down separate ramps to underground parking on that side of the structure.

Ben reversed course, went back along the street past a row of stores, then ducked around the corner and went down the block to the alley. He turned into the alley and carefully approached the high rise. As he had expected, there was a loading dock in the rear, a place for trash and recycling trucks to pick up, and maintenance supplies to be delivered.

He climbed a set of stairs to a locked fire door, then knelt to remove his picks from his right trouser cuff. The door yielded in a little over half a minute and Ben went in, closing the door quietly behind him. To his right he found a service elevator waiting. The sound of a radio or television set came from the corridor to his right. Hoping that it was loud enough to cover the noise of the elevator, he got on, pulled the door shut and punched the top button, which took him to a service porch where a small dumpster sat. An unlocked door opened on a very long corridor of apartment doors.

Stealthily, Ben eased into the corridor. He crouched against the wall, listening. Hearing not even a murmur coming through the thick doors, he edged down the corridor past an elevator to a fire door. Inside was a set of stairs going down and a ladder against the wall leading to a square door in the ceiling.

He checked his watch again: In an hour, the light would be good and getting better until darkness fell.

Acting on a sudden thought, Ben went back through the fire door and glided almost silently down the very long corridor until he came to a second fire door. Inside he found the layout a mirror image of the other fire escape: A descending stairway and a ladder to a square door.

What if the shooter was already on the roof? Which door would be closest to the sniper's position. After a few minutes' thought, Ben realized that the other door was directly below a spot that had a perfect sightline to the Gonçalves living room.

Because he didn't want to encounter the shooter or anyone else in the ladder or the space above it, Ben went up the ladder in front of him, but when he reached the top he saw that the door was secured by eight large Phillips-head screws—and he had no screwdriver.

Ben fished in his pocket for a coin, and then put a dime in the slot of the first screw and tried to twist it. In vain—the coin did not provide enough leverage to turn the screw.

He tried two other screws with the dime before he gave up.

He had a Phillips screwdriver in his car, but that was miles away.

Maybe there was a nearby store that had one. Or maybe the building's maintenance team had left one laying around.

Ben retreated down the ladder, then went down the hallway, hugging the wall.

The sharp DING! of an arriving elevator startled him and he backed into a doorway, flattened himself against the door and watched as less than fifty feet ahead a man carrying two bags of groceries stepped out of the elevator.

He turned toward Ben and came down the hall. He stopped at a door on the other side of the hall. Ben heard the jingle of keys as the man opened the door and went inside, closing the door behind him with his heel.

Ben let out his breath and then hurried down the hall until he came to the stairs and ducked inside.

His blood froze.

The door atop the ladder was open. In the corner, on the floor, was a screwdriver and eight large screws.

Chapter Seventy-two

Chicago

Ben mounted the ladder and peered upward. Slowly he began to climb until his head and shoulders were above the door. To his left, he saw light bleeding through the crack of a full-size door.

He pulled himself up into the tiny room and found the square door on the floor next to the entryway from the ladder.

Cautiously he pulled the big door open an inch or so. Directly ahead of him, perhaps thirty feet distant, was a man in dark clothes assembling a black rifle with a box magazine and a large telescopic sight.

Ben eased the door open. In a crouch, he crept toward the rifleman.

He heard and felt steps approaching and out of the corner of his right eye saw movement. Ben whirled to confront this threat and saw a man about his size with Asian features and hooded eyelids. The man assumed a Taekwondo fighting stance and danced forward on his toes.

Ben mirrored his stance and danced toward his foe.

The man, who appeared to be in his late forties, stopped and bowed.

Ben bowed and said "Glass, sixth dan."

"Paek, Dan jegu."

Ben flinched and felt a chill running down his spine. He was to fight a ninth Dan or Grand Master. He had never had a match with anyone above the seventh dan. And such was the power of an adult taekwondo fighter—a kick could fracture a skull or a breastbone—that in all sanctioned tournaments, contestants are required to wear light but super-strong carbon fiber chest pads, and helmets of the same material.

Lacking these, he was in a fight to the death.

With his left leg forward, Paek danced toward Ben.

Ben went to his toes and in an instant, Paek surged forward throwing first one leg and then the other at Ben's head and chest.

He jumped back, he ducked, he leaped sideways, then back.

Then Paek stopped and switched legs, putting his right leg forward behind his left. He renewed his attack, driving Ben back. Hopping rearward and to either side to escape the blows.

When Paek paused, Ben went on the attack, grazing Paek's chest with his first kick and landing a glancing blow to his head with his third.

Then the sniper came up behind Ben to pull a burlap bag over his head and shoulders pinning his arms to his sides. The sniper tripped him and Ben fell backward.

"*Joesonghabnida. dangsin-eun habdanghan sangdaeibnida,*" said Paek. From his dojo instruction Ben understood that this was Korean and meant "I am sorry. You are a worthy opponent."

The sniper produced a two-inch roll of gaffer's tape and wound several lengths around Ben's waist to keep Ben's arms to his sides, and then taped Ben's ankles together.

§

Laying on the warm roof, Ben heard Paek and the sniper conversing in low voices, but couldn't make out what was said.

Then all was quiet for what seemed like a long time. Ben dozed off.

He was awakened by a shot.

Then he heard the sounds of the sniper breaking down his rifle. The two men separately went to the door and down the ladder.

Ben silently prayed that in their haste to leave, they would leave the door above the ladder open. Or that there was another route to the roof.

He could see light through the loosely woven burlap, and when he awoke sometime later it was dark and he was cold and stiff.

After what seemed like a long time. Someone kicked him, not hard, and Ben said "Hey, cut it out."

He felt rather than heard someone with a sharp blade cutting the tape on his ankles and around the bag at his waist. The bag was pulled off and a flashlight shined in his face.

"Who are you? Whadda doing up here?" said a man with an eastern European accent.

"I'm a rabbi," Ben said. "I was trying to stop a murder."

"So you stole my screwdriver and took the screws out of the door?"

Ben shook his head. "There were two men on the roof. One had a rifle, and he used that to kill someone three blocks from here. The other one was a martial-arts expert."

"They put you in the bag?"

"Yes."

The man dropped the flashlight to his side and pulled

Ben to his feet.

"Are you the police?" Ben said to the burly man standing before him."

"Hell no, I ain't the police. Name's Wasnewski. I'm the maintenance supervisor. "

"Thanks for coming up and cutting me loose," Ben said.

"Do I gotta call the police?"

"It would be a good idea. Take your light and see what you can find over *there*," Ben said, pointing to where the sniper had set up.

Followed by Ben, Chavez walked to the edge of the roof and a low wall. He played the light beam back and forth near the base of the wall until both men saw a faint gleam. Chavez bent and came up with a tiny stainless-steel screw.

"When you call the police, show them where that came from?"

"What do you think it came off? Chavez said.

"I think it's a mounting bracket screw for a telescopic rifle sight," Ben said.

"Could be."

"Did you hear a shot? About a half hour before sunset?"

"I thought it sounded like a car backfiring. There's a garage down the street."

'You gonna stay and talk to the police?"

Ben shrugged. "No. Just tell them what you saw, the way you found me, and give them my card," Ben said, taking out a business card and giving it to Chavez.

"Need help getting down the ladder?"

"I think I'm okay, Ben said.

Chapter Seventy-three

Steins

It was almost nine when Ben returned to Beth Ohr. As he mounted the steps, his phone vibrated. Pulling it out he glanced at the caller's name: Peters.

"Shalom," Ben said.

"Bad news," Peters said. "Gonçalves was killed a few hours ago."

"It was a sniper on the roof of 3232 Belmonde."

"How did you know?"

"I was there. Got into a taekwondo match with an international grandmaster, a middle- aged Korean man who was the sniper's backup. I'm pretty sure his name is Paek Chung Ho. The sniper grabbed me from behind, stuck a potato sack over my head and trussed me up with tape. I was still there when the building maintenance super found me about an hour ago.

"The police never came to the roof."

Peters said. "That's because Mrs. Gonçalvez needed to go grocery shopping. She took the kids with her and the policewoman in the e house went with them. They got home half an hour ago and found her husband dead with a bullet in his head. A small hole in the living room window. Chief Johnson told me it was almost a quarter-mile from that building and Gonçalves was in his living room. Amazing."

Ben shook his head. "Not really. Laser and telescopic sights are available in most sporting goods stores. So are laser rangefinders. A quarter-mile is 1320 feet or 440 yards. Army and Marine snipers in Afghanistan have killed targets from more than five times that distance. Any marksman with a good rifle could have made that shot."

"Rabbi, do you have any idea what all these killings are about?"

"Only a glimmer and I might be wrong."

"Tell me."

"Not until I'm sure. But thanks for letting me observe the tiger hunt."

"The tiger got the goat."

"Sometimes the tiger is smarter than the villagers," Ben said.

But Ben felt that although he had done his best to save the machinist, he was at least partly responsible for Gonçalves's death.

"Chief Johnson will want to talk to you," Peters said.

"He has my number.

Chapter Seventy-Four

Steins

At midmorning the next day, Ben found Julie Morgenstern, Leah Shevitz and four men of various ages seated around a circular table in the synagogue's ground-floor conference room.

Julie said, "Rabbi, this is Ezra Cohen, (a skinny man in his early twenties), Stuart Woodman (a balding, heavy-set man with shirtsleeves rolled to reveal massive forearms), Larry Mintz, (a handsome, well-groomed man of perhaps fifty) and Brett Baum, (an elderly man with a scraggly white beard.)"

"All are synagogue members in good standing," continued Julie.

Ben said, "Do you understand why you are here?"

All four nodded in agreement.

"Mr. Cohen, why don't you tell us what we are supposed to do today."

Cohen scratched his nose "We are to vote to shut this charity down. And then we are to vote a second time to confirm that vote. We each get $2,000," he said.

"Wait, hold on," said Woodman. "He's getting $2,000? I was promised $1,000."

Ben smiled. "You will each get a check for $1,000 per meeting. We're going to hold two short meetings today, one after another. At the first, we will vote to close down L'Dor v'Dor and remit the records and all assets to the Israeli Rabbinate in Jerusalem. Mrs. Shevitz will act as our recording secretary and take notes on all items. One of our officers, Rabbi Farkas, will be present by telephone from Israel. When the meeting is concluded, we will adjourn and you will each get a check for $1,000. Then we will convene a second meeting and the sole purpose of that meeting is to approve the minutes of the earlier meeting. When we adjourn, you will each get a second check for $1,000. Any questions?"

Frail and wizened, Brett Baum raised his hand and Ben nodded in his direction.

"Why are you shutting down?"

Ben said, "In recent years, I am told, we've been unable to find enough young men who wish to spend five years in Israel studying to be an Orthodox rabbi. Rabbi Ruben, the director, is gone. And our list of reliable donors has dwindled to just a few. The beneficiary of our fundraising decided to shut us down and try a different approach."

"Then why do we need to vote?" said Woodman.

"Good question," Ben said. "We are incorporated in the State of Delaware. To shut down any corporation, we have to follow the rules of the state where it is registered."

Woodman grunted to show that he understood but maybe didn't like it.

Larry Mintz raised his hand. "Rabbi, why is the corporation ruled by the State of Delaware, not Illinois?"

Julie said, "Another good question. Some states have very strict laws about corporations, some are very loose. Delaware has only minimal reporting requirements, for example. Under the Constitution, every state must give full faith and credit to the laws of all other states. You'll find that many of the country's largest corporations are chartered in one state but have branch offices or other facilities in several other states. For example, banking laws are very liberal in South Dakota and North Carolina, so many of our biggest banks are chartered in one or the other."

Ben said, "Ladies, may I have a word with you outside?"

In the hallway, Ben spoke in a low voice. "What I am about to tell you must remain a secret between us. Do you all agree?"

Both women nodded their agreement.

"Lillian Golden has authorized me to tell you that she was born Deborah Rubin. She is the treasurer of L'Dor v'Dor and although divorced and remarried, she uses her married name professionally. She would like this to remain confidential because she doesn't want anyone to know she was Rabbi Rubin's sister."

Leah said, "Of course. She's down in the office. Shall I go get her?"

Ben nodded and accompanied Julie back into the conference room.

The speakerphone at the head of the table rang. Julie answered it.

"This is Rabbi Farkas," a voice from the speaker said.

Ben said, "Shalom Rabbi and may I introduce our new directors. They will each say their name:

"Julie Morgenstern, director."

"Brett Bauer, director."

"Ezra Cohen, director."

"Larry Mintz, director.

"Stuart Woodman, director."

The conference room door opened and Leah and Lillian Golden entered.

"Deborah Rubin, Treasurer," she said and sat down near the phone.

Farkas said, "Deborah, is that really you?"

Lillian/Deborah said, "It is. I understand that you've been keeping an eye out for me?"

Ben almost choked while stifling a laugh.

Farkas said, "Don't go there! I was very sorry to learn that Rabbi Ruben died. How are you doing?" Farkas replied.

Lilly/Deborah said, "Let's stick to business."

Ben said, "Also present are Leah Shevitz, who will act as our recording secretary and Rabbi Moshe ben Maimon, advisor. Be advised, everyone, that Mrs. Morgenstern is also an attorney retained by the organization."

Farkas said, "The meeting will come to order. Will someone call the roll?"

Leah went around the room, writing each name on her pad a second time, as each of the directors gave his name and position.

Farkas said, "Is there any old business?"

The room went silent.

"New business?"

Lillian Golden said, "In view of our dwindling number of student applicants, our shrinking list of reliable contributors, the untimely death of Rabbi Ruben and in response to a request by the Rabbinate of the State of Israel, I move that L'Dor v'Dor cease operations, dissolve its corporation in accordance with our by-laws and the statutes of the State of Delaware and forward all documents and funds to the Rabbinate, in the custody or Rabbi Meir Farkas, Rabbinate Secretary."

Julie said, "I second the motion."

After a suitable pause, Farkas said, "Is there any discussion?"

Ezra raised his hand.

"Mr. Cohen wishes to speak," said Lillian.

"Proceed, Mr. Cohen," said Farkas.

"Uh, there's something wrong here," he mumbled, barely loud enough for anyone to hear. "I bet I could find you ten Jewish guys who would love to have a five-year scholarship in Israel to become a rabbi. So why are you really folding this up?"

Ben looked at Julie, who shrugged and made a face.

Farkas said, "I hope you are right. Have them apply directly to me."

Woodman raised his hand.

Lilliam said, "Mr. Woodman?"

Woodman said, "Why are we sending the money to Rabbi Farkas? Shouldn't we return it to the donors?"

Julie said, "L'Dor v'Dor was set up to remit all donations, less a reserve for operating costs, to the Rabbinate, on an annual basis. It's in the by-laws. Those funds underwrite the education of rabbis. Now that we are closing the charity down, the remaining funds are the property of the Rabbinate. Every donor knew this when they made their contribution."

Lillian Golden said, "All those in favor of the motion to dissolve L'Dor v'Dor, please raise your hands."

Everyone except Cohen and Woodman raised their hands.

"All those against the motion, raise their hands."

No one raised their hands.

Lillian said, "The motion passes. Is there more new business?"

No one moved.

Julie said, "I move we adjourn."

Lillian said, "All those in favor?"

Everyone except Cohen and Woodman raised their hands.

"The meeting is adjourned," Lillian said.

Woodman said, "This is a scam. I won't be a party to it."

Lillian said, "Then you may leave."

"Me, too," Cohen said. "Something's going on here."

Leah handed each of the five directors a check for $1,000.

Cohen said, "You said $2,000!"

Leah said, "We said $1,000 for each meeting. The second meeting will begin in a moment."

Lillian said, "The meeting will come to order."

Cohen and Woodman remained in their seats.

Again, Leah named all present.

The first order of business was to approve the minutes of the previous meeting. The vote was five for, none against, two abstaining.

There was no new business and no more old business.

The meeting was adjourned.

Each of the directors was given a second check for $1,000.

Everyone left except Ben and Lillian.

On the speakerphone, Farkas said, "How long will it take before the funds can be transferred?"

Ben said, "I'm told about a month before the paperwork is approved by Delaware."

"A month! That's too long," Farkas said.

Ben said, "I'll do my best to expedite the process but these things take as long as they take."

Farkas said, "Put Deborah on and take us off the speaker."

Lillian picked up the phone. Ben remained in the room.

"What it is it, Rabbi?"

"Deborah, it's so good to hear your voice. I might be in town for a few days soon. I'd love to get together. Perhaps we could have dinner?"

Lillian blanched. "Rabbi, hear me well. If I ever see you again, I'll kill you."

Chapter Seventy-five

STEINS

After the meeting, Ben went to his rooms and changed clothes into what he thought of as his rabbi outfit: the same suit, shirt and tie as he had worn to meet Rabbi Farkas, along with custom made shoes of shiny but flexible cordovan leather with hidden steel toes and soles much like those on running shoes, along with a Stetson fedora in dark gray wool.

On his way out of the building, Ben stopped in the office and found Mrs. Levy. "I've hired a couple of repairmen to do some work on what used to be Rabbi Rubin's office. I'm paying for this. They should be here soon, so please show them to his office."

"Always glad to help, Rabbi," Levy said. "Where are you going, all dressed up?"

"Job interview," Ben said. "My work here is almost done."

§

Ben found an open space in the visitor's lot behind City Hall, then got directions at the information desk. Captain Peters was waiting outside the City Manager's office.

"Good to see you, Ben."

Ben smiled. "Something's going on that you didn't tell me about."

Peters' grin widened. "I think you're going to like what Gilbert Rodenstock has to say."

"A hint?"

"Not a chance."

Rodenstock was a tall, bulky man with a receding hairline,

sporty blond goatee, and a contagious smile. After a hearty handshake, the city manager waved Ben to a comfortable corner chair and plopped himself down across the table from him.

He said, "I'll get right to the point, Rabbi. I want to offer you two jobs and one salary."

Ben smiled. "What's the first job?"

"Chaplain of the Steins Township Police Department. About a third of our force, including sworn officers and civilian support staff, are Jewish. There are four Muslim officers, two Buddhists, a Sikh and a Taoist. Most of the rest are Catholic or some flavor of Protestant. I'm a Unitarian. We have Episcopalians, Baptists, Methodists, and a few Pentecostals."

"What would my duties be?"

"Same as any police chaplain. Provide comfort and counseling to officers and their families in times of crisis, offer nondenominational prayers on appropriate occasions. Support health and welfare activities. And every now and then, preside over a wedding or a funeral."

Ben nodded. "I can do that. What's the second job?"

"Captain Peters is about to become acting chief—Chief Sinclair has forty-two years on the job and he's retiring. It will be a few months before we find a new chief and between you and me, Peters has the inside track. He wants you to be on call as a consultant for major cases—murder, kidnapping, rape and so forth, as well as complex white-collar crimes when they occur. He thought that it might amount, on average, to maybe ten hours a week or less.

"That got me thinking. We're one of several small cities in the northern part of the state. I supposed that there might be one or two others that might want your help sometimes. On big cases. I know quite a few of the city managers and mayors in this part of the state and as it happens, there were three that are interested in a sort of time-share arrangement for a top consultant. We worked things out, if you agree, to reserve an office and a phone with the same number for you in all four cities and have you split your time. We'll pay half your salary and the others will split the rest. You would be on call by all four departments but you'll work out of Steins unless called away."

"Interesting," Ben said. "What does the State's Attorney think about that?"

"He's on board. You'll be appointed an Illinois State special investigator with the rank of lieutenant, which would give you legal authority for anything that you might get mixed up in."

Ben said, "I see a possible conflict of interest: What happens if a police officer or someone else, confides to me in my capacity as a chaplain that he committed a crime? Or violated orders? As clergy, I'm obliged to keep this information confidential."

Rodenstock scratched his head. "We'll have our city attorney take a look at that."

"What are the cities?"

"Steins, of course, Illini Falls, Briarcliff and Moffets. Moffets is thirty miles from here, all of it expressway. Illini Falls is practically next door and Briarcliff is about eight miles southwest."

"While you're working out the clergy privilege issue, I'll need to discuss this with my fiancé."

"You haven't asked about salary?"

"I prefer to let you bring that up."

"Okay. The median salary for a police lieutenant in this part of Illinois is around $90,000 a year, plus benefits. Our last chaplain was Sergeant Bill Johannson. Came from a family of devout Lutherans and joined the department after dropping out of the Lutheran School of Theology, in Chicago. He went to night school here while he was on the job, got himself a Master's Degree in psychology and became a licensed marriage and family counselor. That was about eight years ago. He retired this year and moved to Florida."

Ben said, "Is that typical for police chaplains?"

Rodenstock nodded. "Very typical in these parts. Most of the chaplains I've met are sworn officers, usually a sergeant, either ordained or trained in counseling. It's an extra duty that brings them between $20,000 and $40,000 a year in overtime. The year I came to Steins we had a big fire—an old warehouse on the north side caught fire. Couple a hundred kids—teenagers—snuck in and held a rave. Sixteen dead, about forty disfigured for life. Two of the dead were police and one was a firefighter. Sergeant Johannson worked fulltime on that for months. His overtime on that one incident came to almost $70,000. Old Mr. Finkelstein—that's Randy's late father—was the owner of that building. The kids didn't have permission to use it but Finkelstein's insurance covered most of the liability losses. Aside from that, he donated $50,000 to the Police Welfare Fund. Some of that went to Johannson."

"Then having a full-time chaplain on call might actually save money?"

"That is our hope. And frankly, it would leave you a lot of free time. We have a very limited overtime budget in Steins and most of our sister cities are the same. Hiring you would help us by shifting sworn officer overtime to the salary budget, where we have more control."

Ben thought for a moment. "What are you offering?"

"We'd like to bring you in at $120,000 a year, with semi-annual reviews. Health insurance, life insurance, Illinois State law enforcement officers pension plan and so forth. Our budget and hence our salaries are subject to the city council's annual review. They have approved your salary for this year and next. I don't know about the other cities."

Ben nodded. "If I understand the jobs, I'd basically be on

call 24/7?"

"That sounds about right."

Ben shook his head. "I can perform the duties of a rabbi or chaplain, any time. But my religion and beliefs require me to observe the Sabbath, which for Jews begins at sunset Friday and ends an hour after sundown Saturday. I cannot travel or do crime consulting on the Sabbath. The only exception would be to save a life."

Again, Rodenstock nodded. "That won't be a problem. We can write that into your contract. Realistically, I'd expect that the investigative part of your job would hinge on consulting on cases that give one of the departments more than they can handle or stump their best detectives."

"Sounds okay— but we also must agree in advance on *when* I could be called into work. Unless it's truly an exceptional case, I shouldn't be a first responder. I don't want to work every murder case, every rape or grand theft. I should be notified only when investigating officers run into an issue they're having trouble with or need an outsider's insights. In other words, I'm not going to be an ordinary police detective."

"We'll spell it all out in your contract. Oh, one more thing, Rabbi."

"Go ahead."

"The chiefs of our sister cities would like to meet you."

"You mean before they hire me."

Rodenstock chuckled. "Yeah. They don't want to buy a pig in a poke."

Ben said, "Or as we say in Hebrew, 'A cat in a sack."

Rodenstock chuckled again.

Ben said, "And that reminds me of an old Jewish joke."

"Go on."

"By defeating the Austrians and Russians in the Battle of Austerlitz, Napoleon dissolved the Holy Roman Empire and created the Confederation of the Rhine, a vast expansion of his empire. After this battle, the Emperor summoned his commanders to a celebration. He said, "As a reward for your courage, I grant each of you a wish. Ask, and it shall be granted.

The Bavarian commander said, "I ask for Bavaria's autonomy."

"So it shall be!" Napoleon replied.

The Slovakian commander said, "Liberty for Slovakia?"

"So it shall be!"

And so it went for each of his generals.

Finally, the commander of the Jewish legion stepped forward.

"And what for you, my loyal friend?"

"I would like a cup of hot coffee with milk and sugar, two bagels with cream cheese, and some smoked salmon on the side."

"Bring my friend his breakfast immediately!" ordered the Emperor.

As the Jewish commander sat down to eat, the other generals surrounded him.

"You fool!" said the Bavarian. "Why such a modest request? You could have asked for a province, for riches and power! Why waste your wish on a plate of food?"

The Jew took another bite from his bagel. "True. But at least I got what I asked for."

Rodenstock roared with laughter. "Are you actually a rabbi?"

"Hath not a rabbi eyes? Hath not a rabbi hands, organs,

dimensions, senses, affections, passions; fed with the same food, hurt with the same weapons, subject to the same diseases, healed by the same means, warmed and cooled by the same winter and summer as a Christian is? If you prick us, do we not bleed? If you tickle us, do we not laugh?"

"You're quoting Shakespeare?"

"After a fashion. And as Shylock, the Merchant of Venice, *might* have said, "Do we not have a sense of humor?"

"I just thought that being a clergyman and all…"

"I think you should make it your business to get to know a priest or a minister, or both. You'll find that we're all just like everyone else—except that probably we all try to exercise more self-control, that we avoid responding to what the ancient rabbis called 'evil impulses.'"

"It's an education, this job," Rodenstock said. "So you'll meet with the other police chiefs?

"I'd be delighted to. Is this one meeting or three?"

"One. In Illini Falls. How does tomorrow afternoon sound?"

"I have an appointment with a wedding caterer tomorrow afternoon."

"You're getting married! That's great. How about next Monday, about 2:00?"

"Sure. Very nice meeting you, Mr. Rodenstock."

"It's Gil. I'll be in touch, Rabbi."

Chapter Seventy-six

Chicago

An Uber car took Ben into Chicago and to one of the enormous furniture emporiums on North Avenue. Inside he found Miryam sitting on an ottoman, her legs tucked under her, in earnest discussion with a slim, fifty-something woman in a designer dress.

Miryam leaped up and almost squealed with delight when she saw Ben.

"Lenore, this is my fiancée, Rabbi Maimon," she said, beaming.

Ben took the proffered hand and decided to shake it instead of kissing it.

"Lenore is the director of sales and we were discussing furnishing our new home."

Ben smiled. "How far have we gotten?"

Lenore made a face. "Miryam is quite charming and surprisingly knowledgeable about furniture. But I think that she's making a mistake."

Ben said, "How so?"

"I understand that you're buying a century-old house near the university?"

Ben smiled again. "That's right."

"She also tells me that you presently own several pieces from the Federal era of American furnishings? Genuine antiques?"

Ben nodded agreement.

"Why not complement those pieces with contemporary copies of complementary pieces—tables, chests, cabinets, and chairs? A fainting couch, sideboards and all the rest?"

"I hadn't thought about it, Lenore but my first thought is that we have so few of these antiques—only enough for a small bedroom—that there is no reason to lock us into that style for the whole house. Also, I may decide to keep my place in Cambridge, Massachusetts —it's paid for and if so I'll want to leave my furniture."

"Exactly what I've been telling her," Miryam said. "Our house was built in 1924. It was the Jazz Age, the Roaring Twenties. Art Deco ruled among the moneyed. And the Craftsman movement made houses convenient and easy to live in."

"I yield to your vision, young bride," said Lenore.

Ben said, "So, Craftsman, with maybe a touch of Art Deco?"

Miryam shook her. "Craftsman. Or Mission. Simple, functional, beautiful. I came today just to look around, to see what's available. Now that I have some idea, I need to go back to our new house and see what we should get and what would go where."

Ben smiled. "The lady has spoken. Shall we get some lunch?"

As they got into the Toyota, Miryam said, "Why would you keep the Cambridge place? Are you planning on leaving me?"

Ben shook his head. "Neither of us knows what the future holds. In two or three years you will have a doctorate. I might be offered a pulpit somewhere and we might leave Chicago. Even if we stay for the rest of our lives, it'll be nice to have a place in New England as a vacation home—or just to get away for a long weekend. I still have a lot of friends in New England and it will be good to see them now and then. Especially Bert Epstein, my doctor.

"So you don't have any girlfriends tucked away in Cambridge?"

"Only a few."

Miryam socked Ben's shoulder, hard.

"But none to compare with my Marita."

"Don't tease me that way, Romeo Ben. I can hardly believe, still, that you want me above all the beautiful women in your life."

"Above all the women in the world, Miryam. There is nobody but you for me."

She clung to him for a long moment. Then punched his shoulder again.

"*That* is for scaring me," she said.

Chapter Seventy-seven

Steins

As the eight days of Passover approached, Ben made a call that he had been dreading since he came to Chicagoland: To Esther and Murray Ickovitz of Evanston, the parents of his late wife, Rachel.

He had not spoken with the couple in more than two years, when he was passing through Chicago on the way from his home in Cambridge, to a client's synagogue in Burbank, California. That call had been brief but cordial and had left Ben feeling that even speaking with him was a painful experience for the couple in that it evoked sadness and memories of their beloved Rachel.

This time was different. Murray was effusive in his greeting and when Ben explained that he was about to be married, they surprised him by inviting both Ben and Miryam to join a Passover Seder at their home.

A few hours before setting out for the Ickovitz home, Ben took Miryam to an Evanston cemetery and found the graves of Rachel and Mark Moses Glass, the son who had survived just a day after his birth by an emergency Caesarian.

Hand-in-hand Ben and Miryam recited the *kaddish*, a prayer for the dead, then walked silently among the gravestones, still holding hands but each alone with their thoughts.

They found the rented Toyota where they had left it and climbed in.

Miryam said, "If this is a bad time, this can wait. We need to talk about transportation."

Ben smiled. "It's okay. Tell me what's on your mind?"

"We're going to need two cars. But you have an almost-new Prius in Cambridge."

Ben smiled again. He had also been thinking about that car. For several years, he had leased parking space in a public garage near his place. The lease would be up in June.

In a few sentences, he explained all this to Miryam.

"If there's nothing keeping you here after Passover, why don't you fly back to Boston and get your car?"

"And then turn in this car? Won't we need it?"

"Can you keep a secret?"

Ben smiled. "Probably."

"I'm buying you a car as a wedding present. I'll drive the Prius."

"What kind of a car?"

"That's the secret."

Chapter Seventy-eight

Evanston

Esther and Murray seemed genuinely glad to meet Ben and Miryam.

Esther said, "I hope you know how lucky you are to find a man like Ben. When he married our Rachel, we were a little skeptical—he's kind of short and he was still in rabbinical school. But as we got to know him, we realized that there wasn't anyone who would have been a better husband to our daughter."

Ben said, "It's very kind of you to say that, Mrs. Ickovitz."

Esther said, "Please Ben, after all these years, you should call us Esther and Murray. Our Rachel is gone but we still think of you as family."

Murray said, "Miryam, how did you two meet?"

Ben and Miryam exchanged glances.

Miryam said, "He was working a case in Brooklyn, where I grew up and we met during his investigation."

Murray said, "Ben, you're still some kind of private eye? I never understood exactly what you do and why you didn't find a pulpit?"

Ben said, "I was infected with a virus from someone's blood—in the aftermath of the bombing in Jerusalem. I had a lot of trouble finding a pulpit. No congregation was willing to have an HIV-positive rabbi interacting with their children. Or at least the boards of directors that interviewed me seemed to believe that.

"I gave that idea up and became a sort of roving troubleshooter for synagogues, museums, nonprofits and so forth. Now, I think, my virus is cured."

Miryam said, "What do you do, Mr. Ickovitz?"

Murray smiled. "It's Murray to you, too. I'm a lawyer. Mostly estate work."

Ben said, "We'll need new wills, as soon as we're married."

"Did you buy a house yet?"

"Near the University. It's in escrow.

"Then call me and we'll talk about a trust, so you'll never have to deal with probate."

Esther said, "You bought near the University? On the South Side?"

Ben said, "It's not a bad neighborhood. Used to be but it's much better now."

The doorbell rang, ending the conversation.

Murray said, "Don't forget—call me when you're settled and we'll draw up your estate plan."

Chapter Seventy-nine

O'Hare International

The Sunday afternoon before their wedding, Ben waited at the curb while Miryam went into the United terminal to find Deborah HaCohen, her childhood friend in Brooklyn's Bensonhurst neighborhood. Miryam had asked to be her maid of honor. After a few minutes, Miryam appeared, towing a suitcase and a moment later Deb, a tall, slim, elegant redhead, followed, carrying a second, smaller one.

A spot at the curb opened in front of Ben and a taxi swooped in to slowly disgorge five large men with armloads of carry-ons and a trunk jammed with suitcases.

Ben popped the Prius's hatchback and took suitcases from Miryam and then Deb, placed them inside, then closed it.

As he headed for the driver's seat, a tall, heavy, clean-shaven man with pale cheeks, a sunburned forehead and what looked like a glass eye under a gray fedora and wearing an expensive camel's hair overcoat strode past the other side of the Prius and got into the taxi. There was something familiar about him but Ben couldn't place his face.

Ben was halfway to Steins when it hit him: The man was Rabbi Meir Farkas, a long way from home and definitely not wishing to be recognized. Farkas didn't see Ben because he was on the side of his glass eye.

As Ben pulled into the circular driveway of Hotel Ohelim, a Skokie inn that Miryam's cousin Avi Benkamal had rented—every room—his cell phone buzzed. He let it go to voicemail.

He dropped Miryam and Deb in front of the lobby and then parked.

His phone buzzed a second time.

"Hi Pat," he said.

"We're tracking Rabbi Farkas," Gilmore said. "If you'd care to join our stakeout, find the Northern Illinois Municipal Power van near the corner of Finkelstein and Epstein. Get here before dark or don't bother— your call."

"I'm on my way."

Chapter eighty

Steins

It was almost dark as Ben approached the utility van and parked. The door opened a few inches and Agent Ed Roberts smiled and stepped back to let Ben hop inside.

One interior wall of the van was high definition video screens in two rows of four each. FBI technicians with headsets sat at a narrow table under the screens.

"He just checked into the Gurnee Holiday Inn," Gilmore said.

One of the eight screens lit up and showed Farkas at the main desk.

"He's using one of his aliases, Gustavo Villareal," Roberts said. "He made the reservation day before yesterday, from New York."

"And you just happened to know this alias?" Ben said.

"Shin Bet was happy to provide three of his known aliases."

Ben said, "Let me guess: He's got powerful friends in Israel that would make prosecution difficult and embarrassing, so they were happy to let us have him. Did they freeze his accounts?"

"Four days ago. He left for New York the next day."

"Now what?" Ben said.

"Now we wait. He'll probably want to kill a few hours in his room."

"You have a camera in there?"

"Just one. Very cooperative manager at that place."

"Who is he talking to?"

"A rabbi in Rio de Janeiro, a hotel in Nassau—the Bahamas—someone named Jonathan in Curaçao and someone named León in Panama City."

"He's going to the Bahamas to wire cash to Panama City, then visit Curaçao before he gets to Brazil, which puts him safe from extradition?"

"Looks that way. We will have someone at every stop along the way."

"So now?"

"We wait. Let your girlfriend know that you'll be here indefinitely."

"She knows."

§

Ben dozed in a corner. Roberts was out for a walk and a smoke.

Two of the three technicians slept, heads on the desk.

As Roberts returned, Gilmore said, "He's moving."

In seconds everyone was alert and watching a middle screen, which showed the back end of a dark Ford Escape rolling out of a parking lot into a well-lit street, then turning onto Interstate 94 to head north. The chase car moved into a faster lane and passed the Escape slow enough to confirm that Farkas was behind the wheel.

"Heading this way," Gilmore said.

Eight minutes later the Escape passed the utility truck, which had by then put a pair of ladders next to a pole. One of the agents, wearing a hard hat and a tool belt, was climbing the pole.

All eight screens flared to life. A camera on a light pole in the temple parking area showed the Escape turning into the Beth Ohr lot to stop near the front door.

Farkas left the car carrying a folded duffel and approached the front door. A key got him inside and when the alarm didn't sound thirty seconds later, Ben knew that Farkas had somehow obtained the security code. Maybe he had it from Rubin before he was killed.

A minute dragged by before Farkas appeared on the four top screens, which showed feeds from cameras hidden in the ceiling above all four walls in Rubin's office.

Farkas came through the door, locked it behind him, set the bag on the desk and turned on the light. He went to the last file cabinet, lifted the front an inch or two and dragged the cabinet away from the wall until he could rest the back end of the top against the wall, leaving a small space above the floorboards.

He dropped to his knees, then found the juncture of two floorboards. He pushed one floorboard down about a quarter-inch, then pulled the end of its mate up. He slid this board out of the grooves, opening a space four inches wide and six long.

From this, he removed a small loose-leaf notebook, which he tucked into a pocket. He slid the loose board back into place and restored the other to its original position.

Farkas tipped the cabinet forward, pushed it back into place, then moved to the first cabinet, against the wall near the door. It was somewhat wider than the other cabinets.

He pulled out the bottom drawer and laid it aside.

Then he lay supine on the floor in front of the hole left by the vacant drawer, put his arms over his head and using hips and heels, pushed himself into the hole as far as he could. After a long moment, he pulled himself back out and stood up, holding a cardboard box about 15 inches wide and twice that long.

He put the box on the table, restored the drawer to its former position, then took out a folding knife and opened the sealed box.

In the van, Ben and the FBI crew saw that the box was full of $100 bills in banded stacks. Farkas transferred all of it to the bag, zipped it shut and left the empty box. He turned out the lights and locked the door behind him.

On a lower screen, Ben saw half a dozen agents in SWAT gear position themselves on either side of the front door.

It was five minutes before Gilmore ordered them to go inside and find Farkas.

§

Silence filled the inside of the van.

The tactical radio crackled to life.

"Got him."

A few minutes later the door opened and two agents came out, one holding Farkas's bloody head and the other his feet.

"No sign of the box," said the team leader over the radio.

"What about the notebook?"

"No. Not in any of his pockets."

"Is he alive?" Ben asked and Gilmore relayed the question to the team leader.

"He's breathing. Looks like he was mugged—big gash behind his right ear and another on his jaw and mouth."

Roberts said, "I'll call an ambulance."

Gilmore said, "Search the building. Exigent circumstances."

Two agents stood watch over Farkas while the rest went inside.

Ben said, "I have keys that will be helpful."

Gilmore keyed her radio "I'm sending the rabbi with keys."

"Go," said Gilmore and Ben left the van and jogged to the

front door, where he went into the building with an agent.

For half an hour they searched every room and closet but found no one. Behind the rear fire door, in a dumpster, an agent found a well-used wooden baseball bat with streaks of blood on its business end.

Ben jogged back to the van. "I need to get back to the hotel for Miryam and then I'm back here to spend the night."

"You still live here?"

"Until we close escrow on a house."

"Before you go, any ideas on what just happened?"

Ben shrugged. "I'd say someone knew he was coming and either suspected or knew that he'd go to that room."

"Any idea who that could be?"

"It breaks down into a short list of who might know there was money hidden there and who might know that he was coming. I can think of only two people who might have known about the money but I'd be very surprised if either of them would have been up to mugging him."

"Names?"

"Rabbi Manny Shevitz and Mrs. Leah Shevitz."

"One more thing, Rabbi," said Roberts. "Any ideas about how the mugger escaped the area?"

"I'd say on a bicycle," Ben said.

Roberts said, "If Farkas recovers consciousness, we'll find out who might have known he was coming and how they got into the building without tripping the alarm."

Chapter Eighty-one

Illini Falls

Ben shook hands in turn with Chiefs Dougherty, McConnell and Cone of Illini Falls, Briarcliff, and Moffets, respectively.

"Have a seat, Rabbi," said Dougherty.

Ben said, "Have I stumbled into a meeting of the Sons of Ireland?"

All three chiefs laughed, genuinely amused.

Chief Cone said, "How did you know I was Irish and not one of your tribe?"

Ben smiled. "I'm guessing it used to be McCone but one of your grandfathers, worried about anti-Irish sentiment, changed it. Anyway, C O H E N or C O H N are Jewish names. If you keep up with baseball, you might recall David Cone. He pitched for the Mets in the late 1980s and early 1990s. Many Mets fans thought he was Jewish. But the Irish knew better.

"Actually, it was my great-great-grandmother, Erin," said Cone. "They lived in Boston for a time, back when being Irish was like being a leper."

Ben nodded. "Well, gentlemen, how can I help you today?"

McConnell said, "You come very highly recommended. I had one of my sergeants read your FBI file and write a summary for me."

Ben said, "There's another file. It's my father, the same name. He left town when I was an infant and I never met him."

Daugherty smiled. "I started to read that one and was ready to call Peters and yell at him until I saw his date of birth and then his death certificate."

Cone said, "We have a case that has stumped us. Kind of a locked room deal, except, it was a whole house."

"I'd be happy to read the file but why don't you give me the short version?"

Cone said, "Well, there's not much to tell. Man name of Arthur Zich, sixties, well-to-do real-estate developer. Found dead in his kitchen, hacked to death with one of his own kitchen knives. No sign of forced entry, all doors deadbolted and all windows closed from the inside. Bars on all windows. No fingerprints on the knife."

Ben said, "Did you find traces of blood in the bathtub?"

Cone nodded. "In the drain. Same DNA as the victim's."

"So, the killer was allowed into the house and was, therefore, someone Zich knew. After he killed Mr. Zich, he cleaned himself up in the bathroom, then left without disturbing the deadbolts."

"But how did he get out of the house?"

Ben said, "What time of year was this?"

Cone said, "Just before Halloween."

"Can I take a look at the house?"

"Right now?"

"If it's convenient."

§

The house was a spacious split-level with five bedrooms, four baths, an office, kitchen, formal dining room, utility room, and living room. As Cone had described it, the windows were barred and there were deadbolt locks on all the doors. The garage, a separate structure, was ten feet from the back door, with a portico between.

Ben walked all the way around the house, peered closely at the bars, then stopped, thinking.

"Where are the window screens?'

Cone shrugged. "Let's try the garage."

The window screens were there, neatly stacked on plywood shelves. Ben examined the top one, then replaced it on the pile.

Ben asked to see the inside of the house.

"Where did the murder take place?" he said.

"In the master bedroom," said Chief Cone.

Bent went first to the living room, a large, well-lit space with a sofa and twin easy chairs upholstered in a light gray material. A deep pile rug of matching color covered most of the floor.

Ben satisfied himself that all the windows were locked. He pushed a button that unlocked the window, raised it, then pulled it down until it clicked shut.

Ben said, "The killer came in the front door, stabbed Zich—evidently a crime of great passion because he was stabbed several times. So, he was someone who knew Zich. Likely he'd been in the house before.

"After the murder, he cleaned up in the bathroom and returned to the living room. He bolted all the doors. He came to a window—maybe this one, maybe another one. He opened the window.

"Then...." Ben hunted with his fingers for the bottom part of the window frame, slid the front panel of the window frame's apron to the left and found a small lever under the panel. He pulled it from right to left.

Ben slid the apron back to its original position.

He opened the window, grabbed the bars and pushed them out and up until there was room for him to step through the open window.

A chorus of amazed ahs and ohs followed him.

Outside, Ben closed the window until he heard it lock into place.

Then he pulled the bars down until they locked.

He waited, smiling, while the three chiefs let themselves out of the house through the front door.

McConnell said, "How did you know?"

Ben shook his head. "I didn't. I suspected that a housing developer would never live in a house with locked doors and bars on the windows unless he had an emergency exit or a way to open the bars. The screens, which were very dirty, provided a clue: No one with a living room as light in color and almost pristine as this one would want to bring those dirty screens into the house.

"When I examined the bars, I saw a tiny hinge almost hidden on the inside of the top bar. Why bother with a hinge unless you wanted to swing the bars up out of the way? How to unlock the bars? A lever or button has to be somewhere in the window frame or near it.

"So now your detectives need to find someone with a grudge against Zich or some other reason to kill him. Someone he wouldn't fear to let in his house when he was home alone. Among those people, see who doesn't have a solid alibi."

The chiefs crowded around Ben, shaking his hand.

"One more thing, gentlemen," Ben said.

"When I walked through the kitchen, I saw that all of the kitchen knives were exactly where they were supposed to be. Why isn't at least one of those knives in an evidence locker?

"And Chief Cone, I noticed that when you unlocked the front door, the key was one of several on a ring that also included the coat of arms for the city of Moffets.

"I conclude that no murder took place in this house and that it likely belongs to the mayor or some other leading official in your city."

Cone had the grace to blush. "It's my son-in-law's house. He's the city controller. There was no murder here."

Dougherty and McConnell laughed and after a moment Cone joined in.

"It doesn't matter," Ben said. "And I'd like to think that discovering whose house this is was surely part of Chief Cone's test. So, do I get the job?"

The three men exchanged glances.

Dougherty said, "We want to hire you. But now we each have to go to our city manager and see if they'll bump our budget up a bit. If not, we'll have to go through our budget and see what we can cut to fund our share."

"I understand."

"Assuming all goes well, when can you start?"

"I'm getting married soon. Then we'll go someplace for a few weeks. Let's say the first of July?"

§

Division X of the Cook County Jail is on South California Avenue on the Lower West Side, just north of the Stevenson Expressway and the Chicago Sanitary and Ship Canal. Most of the 768 beds on its four floors of maximum security are devoted to sick, injured, mentally disturbed or addicted detainees. Charged with fifty-two counts of money laundering, fraud and evading federal and state taxes, after first-aid treatment by ambulance paramedics, Rabbi Farkas was examined by a police physician and assigned to a third-floor ward. When he awakened several hours later he demanded to see the Israeli Consul-General and that he be served only kosher food.

The Consul-General send a junior consular employee to the jail but Farkas refused to see him. That evening, when the night shift nurses came on duty, they found that one of their number had called in sick and was replaced by a male nurse who called himself Stanley Kübler and was employed by a well-known nurse registry.

About midnight, an order appeared on the ward nurse's computer that prisoner Farkas was to have an enema. The job was given to the replacement nurse, who took a Fleet enema from the nurse's expendable items cabinet and as he made his way back across the ward replaced it with one concealed in a pocket. He administered the enema, cleaned up the patient's bowel movement and left the floor.

At the employee exit, the nurse's genuine ID was not challenged. He left the facility and was picked up a block down the street by two men in a dark SUV.

At dawn the following morning, his body was found floating in the Sanitary and Ship Canal. He had been strangled with a length of piano wire, which remained in the wound.

Chapter Eighty-two

Skokie

The rented hotel was filling with Benkamals from Israel and Moshons from Argentina, a few old enough to have known each other from Damascus or Aleppo before 1947, when most of Syria's Jews fled or were expelled and sought refuge abroad. Ben's guest list had grown to nine couples and all had made travel arrangements or were living in Chicagoland. All five of Miryam's bridesmaids and Deb, her maid of honor, had arrived and were fitted with matching dresses, courtesy of Levi Moshon, one of Miryam's Buenos Aires cousins. The caterer had been given a headcount. The Skokie Banquet and Conference Center knew how many guests to expect.

As the day before the wedding was *Shabbat*, Bachelor and Bridal parties would be held on the Thursday evening prior.

A little after 3:00 that afternoon, minutes after the wedding party's final rehearsal, Ben and Miryam got into the Prius and prepared to return to Ben's tiny apartment for a nap before their respective parties.

Ben's phone buzzed: A text from Lilly:

URGENT THAT WE MEET ASAP. WOULDN'T BOTHER YOU BUT HAVE NO ONE ELSE TO TURN TO.

Ben replied that he would meet her in the office at Beth Ohr in an hour, then showed the text to Miryam.

"This better be important," she said.

Ben shook his head. "She seems like a fine woman. I can't imagine what her problem is but she had been very forthcoming with me. It shouldn't take long."

Ben switched on the car and silently left the lot. Before he reached the Interstate, his phone buzzed again: Pat Gilmore.

He let the message go to voice mail.

Twenty minutes later at Beth Ohr, Ben and Miryam went upstairs. As Miryam was changing into sleepwear, Ben played back the voice mail message.

"Ben—Pat Gilmore. Thought that you should know that Rabbi Farkas was murdered in the Cook County Jail. He was injected with battery acid. And get this: The injection was made through his anus. He died in the prison hospital this morning."

Ben shuddered, then wiped the message. Miryam didn't need to hear it.

Chapter Eighty-three

Steins

Lilly was waiting in the office when Ben came downstairs.

"We can't talk here," she said. "Let's go to your office."

"You mean what used to be your brother's office?"

She nodded, yes and followed Ben up two flights to the office. Ben unlocked the door and they went inside.

"What's going on?" Ben said.

"I hardly know where to begin."

"Start anywhere," he said,

"Okay. Uh. Okay, you know that Randy, my husband suffers from dementia?"

"Early-onset Alzheimer's, you said."

"That's what I thought. Yesterday he was hospitalized. He's near death. His doctor told me that Randy's blood showed a very high level of lead. They repeated the test—the same result."

"Someone poisoned him?"

"It has to be Naomi. His daughter. She prepares his meals."

"What about *your* blood?"

Lilly shook her head. "He has a special diet. I don't eat with him. But I gave blood and had it checked just the same—I'm okay."

"This is a very serious accusation," Ben said.

Lilly nodded. "There's more. For the last few months, even as Randy got worse, he had a few lucid times. A minute, five minutes. And twice he told me that he thought that Naomi was selling off his company's properties."

"What do you mean?"

"I checked—it's true. In the past year, Naomi has sold off seventeen buildings. Office buildings, apartments, retail shops with apartments over them. The company has only six properties left."

"Why is that distressing?"

"Because she's moving the money from those sales out of the country."

"Does Randy know that?"

Lilly shook her head, no.

"I can see that this would be disturbing but why the urgency?"

"I haven't got to the worst part yet."

"Go ahead."

"Randy's doctor called and asked for a copy of his advanced directive—instructions on how he wants to be treated as his illness progresses. I went looking for it in Naomi's office—she was out somewhere with her girlfriend—and the first thing I found was *this*."

Lilly fumbled open her purse and handed Ben a small loose-leaf notebook. There was dried blood on the cover. Inside were several pages of notes: Bank information, including coded account numbers and passwords.

It looked like the notebook that Farkas had taken from beneath the floorboards in Rubin's office.

"That's my brother's handwriting," Lilly said. "I went fishing in her desk and found that she has been laundering money for about a dozen people. She charges fifteen percent."

"Fifteen percent," repeated Ben and immediately something

bothered him about that number.

Ben said, "How do you know that she's laundering money?"

"I was L'Dor v'Dor's treasurer for years. The notations in my brother's notebook are the same kind that Naomi made in her own notebook, which she kept in another desk drawer."

"What did you do when you found that notebook?"

"I left the house and called you from my car."

"Where is Igor? Mr. Falkenberg—your chauffeur? Your bodyguard?"

"Naomi fired him the day before yesterday. No notice, no severance."

"Why?'

Lilly shrugged.

Ben thought for a few moments.

"Are you sure that Randy will die soon?"

"His doctors give him a few days, maybe less."

"Is there anything you can do here to ease his death?"

Lillian shook her head, no.

"Where's your passport?"

"With my papers—in Randy's house."

"Get your passport, take what you can carry in a small bag and get on a plane for Israel. By the way, Rabbi Farkas died this morning in a jail hospital."

"I hope you won't think less of me but I'm not sorry. Will you come with me to get my things?"

"I'm getting married this Sunday and my bachelor party is this evening. Why don't you ask Rabbi Shevitz?"

"When my brother was murdered, Shevitz ran away. But

when my car caught fire, you ran *toward* the flames and pulled me out. I need someone I can trust. Besides, it shouldn't take long. I'm worried about what Naomi would do if she found out that I was snooping."

"Let's make it fast," said Ben.

Chapter Eighty-four

Steins

Ben stopped in the first-floor and went into the office. He asked Tracy Washington for a number ten envelope, then addressed it to Pat Gilmore at the FBI in downtown Chicago. He put his own name and Beth Ohr as the return address. Then he took the small notebook from his pocket and slipped it inside before sealing the envelope.

"Do we have any postage stamps?" Ben asked.

"We use a meter," Mrs. Levy said. "Postman will be here any time now to pick up."

Ben handed the envelope to Levy. "Can you make sure this goes out with today's mail?"

"What's in it?" she asked.

"Better that you don't know. Just promise me that it will go out this afternoon."

"Of course," Levy said. "I'll hand it to the postman myself."

"Thank you," Ben said and followed Lillian outside to her SUV.

With Ben beside her, Lilly drove north on Finkelstein Boulevard and then turned into a narrow driveway between three-story apartment buildings with ground-floor shops. She came to a large door that seemed to stand alone in the middle of the driveway. She took a remote from her sun shield and punched in a four-digit code. The door slid downward, revealing the entrance to a tunnel. She eased into the steep tunnel, which dropped twelve feet as it traveled westward about a hundred. Another door slid open and they were in a small parking garage, with room for about a dozen cars. She parked in a marked space and Ben followed her into a small elevator, which took them up to a brightly-lighted foyer. Across from the elevator was a glass door leading to a street.

"I've always found this creepy," she said.

Ben grunted and nodded his head. He found it more than creepy: It spoke volumes about those who used this home and their obsession with privacy.

Lillian used a key to open an ornate wooden door and Ben followed her inside to a second foyer with corridors leading off in three directions. She went straight ahead toward a kitchen and then through a door off the kitchen into a small bedroom.

Ben followed her inside and watched as she took her passport from a dresser drawer, a large manila envelope and then some underwear and a pair of slacks and stuffed everything into a carry-on bag. She went into the bathroom and came out with a bag of toiletries. She dropped it all in the bigger bag.

A door slammed outside and footsteps approached. Lilly quietly closed and locked the door and they stood next to it, listening.

At first, there was no conversation, just a faint hum. Then an unfamiliar woman's voice.

"I saw Lillian's car downstairs," she said. "Is she in her room?"

Ben tiptoed into the bathroom and quietly closed and locked the door behind him.

He looked around. The only other way out of the room was through a barred window that looked out onto a furrowed field. An eight-foot Cyclone fence ran along the city street beyond.

As Ben searched with his fingers for a sliding panel that might conceal a hidden latch, he heard Lilly and the unknown woman speaking in the bedroom.

"Where have you been?" the woman said.

"I was at the hospital. Randy is just barely holding on."

"Are you going someplace?" said the woman.

"Back to Israel," Lilly said. "Nothing can be done for Randy, he doesn't even know I'm there and I just can't stand to watch him die, day by day."

Another woman, her voice somehow familiar in its low pitch and slight rasp, said, "Have you seen a little notebook? With a yellow cover?"

"No. Maybe. I can't remember if I did," Lillian said.

"But you were poking around Naomi's desk, weren't you?" said the woman and with a shock, Ben realized that the speaker was Leah Shevitz, Manny's wife.

Ben heard the unmistakable sound of an automatic pistol being cocked.

In a quiet, conversational voice, Leah said, "Don't make me shoot you."

"Put that away," Lilly said. "Doctor Nakamura called and asked if I could get him a copy of Randy's advance directive. So I looked through the desk drawers for it."

Leah said, "Naomi, do you believe her?"

Naomi said, "I think she's lying. I think she took the notebook."

"No, no, you're wrong," Lilly said.

In the bedroom, Leah grabbed the carry-on bag and dumped its contents on the bed and rifled through it.

In her mid-twenties, Naomi was a slim-hipped beauty; her flawless complexion imperiled by piercings and tattoos running up her right arm and shoulder and onto her cheek, and gunmetal gray eyes now blazing with unnatural passion.

She raised the bottom of her sweater and took out the gun

tucked into her waistband.

"You're not going to shoot me!" Lilly said.

Naomi said, "You're not leaving until we find that notebook."

"But I have no idea where it is!"

Leah said, "You've been eavesdropping on us, haven't you."

Lilly burst into tears. "What's wrong with you? Both of you? What have you done that makes you so suspicious of me? What's in that stupid notebook, anyway?"

"We can make you talk," Leah said. "Remember your brother's pay-for-play girlfriend?"

Lillian said, "I don't know what you're talking about."

Leah said, "Of course you do. He was sending his pension checks to that Russian whore through your bank account."

"I don't have a bank account in the States."

Naomi slapped Lilly's face twice. "You're a liar. You had to know. And if you know what we did to her before we let her die, you'll quit stalling and give us that notebook."

Lilly screamed. "I don't have your notebook!" she said.

Leah said, "If you don't tell us what you did with that notebook, you'll *beg* us to shoot you before we're finished."

In the bathroom, Ben weighed his choices. He could try to burst into the bedroom and disarm both women or he could quietly leave and come back with the police.

He decided that the odds were much against disarming both before one of them got off a shot.

Maybe he could try to call for help. After a moment's thought, he dialed 911 and then slipped the phone into the medicine cabinet and closed it. Then he returned to the window.

A moment later, his fingers found the bar release. As quietly as he could manage, he slowly pushed the bars up and away.

He climbed onto the tank and was halfway through the window when Lilly screamed.

"You! You killed my brother!" she shouted.

Leah said, "We gave him every chance to cut us in. We even promised to bring in new clients. All he had to do was stop pretending he was raising money for charity, cut his commission to fifteen percent and we could all get rich."

Ben's phone rang.

He went out of the window and ran through the field toward the fence.

In the bedroom, Naomi rushed to the bathroom door.

Locked.

She tried to kick it open but when that didn't work, she aimed her pistol at the door and fired five times.

As Ben leaped onto the fence, a burly man ran up behind him and swung an ax handle at the back of his head.

Ben's world went dark.

Chapter Eighty-five

Steins

Miryam awoke with a start. She peered at her tiny wristwatch.

A little before 5:00—but where was Ben?

She put on jeans and a sweatshirt, slipped barefoot into sneakers, grabbed her purse and ran down the steps.

He arrived on the first floor as Mrs. Levy was locking the office.

"Have you seen Ben? Rabbi Ben?"

Mrs. Levy smiled at Miryam. They had not met previously but she had heard plenty about the beautiful young woman sharing his apartment.

"You must be Miryam," Levy said.

Miryam smiled. "Yes, Ben's fiancé. The wedding is on Sunday and our parties are tonight but I can't find Ben."

"He left with Mrs. Finkelstein."

"Do you know where they went?"

"No, sorry. But he mailed something to the FBI before he left."

"The FBI? Do you know what it was?"

"It was in an envelope. Felt like a small notebook."

"Thank you," Miryam said.

She went through the front door and saw that Ben had left the Prius.

Sitting behind the wheel, she pondered her next move.

She punched in Ben's number but the call went to voicemail. She left a short message: "Don't forget your bachelor party! If you don't get back to Beth Ohr by 7:30, I'll take a cab and leave you the Prius."

Then she dug through her purse until she found Agent Gilmore's business card and after agonizing over the decision for several minutes, called her.

Chapter Eighty-six

Steins

It took only five applications of Naomi's hot curling iron to the most sensitive areas of Lillian's breasts for the older woman to break. "No more! I'll tell you! I gave it to Rabbi Ben and he mailed it to the FBI," she said, sobbing.

"See, that wasn't so hard," Leah said.

Naomi said, "Where did he mail it from?"

"The box outside the post office."

"Just across the street from our parking entrance?"

"Yes. That one."

"She's lying," Naomi said. "Give her the iron again."

"No!" screamed Lillian. "I'm telling the truth."

Leah said, "How did the rabbi get that notebook?"

"I gave it to him. I asked him what to do with it and he borrowed an envelope from the office and put it in there. Then he ran it through the postal meter. We took it to the post office on our way here."

"Where is he now? Where did he go?"

Lillian shrugged. "He left just before you came home."

Naomi grabbed Lillian's hair and applied the hot iron to her cheeks until she screamed for mercy.

"Your pal the rabbi was in the bathroom listening to us. Now he's downstairs in the garage. When he wakes up, we'll see if his story is the same as yours."

Leah and Naomi left Lillian in the small bathroom where she

lay on the floor with her arms knotted behind her with pantyhose.

They went into the corridor. Naomi said, "Run across the street and see when they empty that box. If it's still there, we won't have to torch the whole building."

Leah smiled. "Right. All we'd have to do is pour some gasoline in and set it afire."

Naomi said, "I'll have somebody put that together."

Leah said, "What are we gonna do with Lillian and that pest, the rabbi?"

"I'll call Joe Stern and ask him to send Simon and to call that cop buddy of his, the one with the boat."

Chapter Eighty-seven

Skokie

Miryam was waiting in front of the Hotel Ohelim when Gilmore and Roberts arrived in their SUV.

"Get in," he said and Miryam climbed into the back.

"Miryam, tell me one more time what you said on the phone," Gilmore said.

"I said that I can't find Ben. He's not answering his phone. The lady in the temple office said that he put something—a small notebook, she said it felt like—into an envelope and they ran it through the postage meter and the postman picked it up about a quarter after 2:00. The envelope was addressed to an FBI agent, she said. She couldn't remember the name."

Roberts said, "Has Ben ever said anything to you about a notebook?"

Miryam shook her curls. "Not a word. When he's on a case, he usually doesn't talk about it."

"Here's a couple of things that I know about Ben today," Gilmore said. "His phone was at 356 Second Street, Steins. He dialed 911 from there but didn't respond to the operator, so she rang back. He didn't respond to that either. Now that phone is off. The back of 356 faces an alley and on the other side of that alley is a three-story building at 347 Finkelstein Boulevard. It's directly across from the post office. In front of that post office is a steel post box. Someone dropped burning gasoline inside that box around 2:00 p.m."

Miryam's eyes widened. "You don't think Ben—"

"It wasn't Ben," Gilmore said. "There's a security camera on the post office. Postal Inspectors accessed that camera's storage device. On the way here, I had them upload it to my phone."

She passed her Samsung phone to Miryam. "Push the arrow on the screen and watch."

Miryam did as she was told and watched a slim figure carrying a shopping bag approach the post office. It knelt in the building's shadow and took a wine bottle with a rag for a stopper from the bag. This person wore gloves. He or she produced a lighter, set the rag afire, then ran to the postbox, opened the pull-down door at the top and dropped the bottle inside.

After a few seconds, flames came out of the open door. The arsonist abandoned the shopping bag and dashed across the street and disappeared in the space between the buildings.

"Wow," Miriam said.

Roberts said, "Do you recognize the person who threw the bottle?"

"I think so," Miryam said. "I'm pretty sure that's Leah Shevitz, Rabbi Shevitz's wife."

Roberts said, "Do you know where she lives?"

"In Steins, with her husband."

"One more thing," Roberts said. "Three people living within a block of that post office heard multiple gunshots around 3:30 this afternoon."

Gilmore said, "I'll check with the Steins police and then I'm going to ask the postal people to send a team to arrest Mrs. Shevitz. Then I'll have a S.W.A.T. team meet us near 356 Second Street. If Ben is still there, he's probably in trouble."

Miryam said, "How long is that going to take?"

Roberts said, "A few hours, probably."

"I've got a bad feeling about this."

Chapter Eighty-eight

Steins

Gilmore said, "Agent Roberts will wait here with you."

Miryam said, "Please don't hurt my Ben. He means everything to me."

"He's a good man," Gilmore said. "If he's in there and alive, we'll get him."

Gilmore stepped back from SUV, tightened her Kevlar vest and pulled on a helmet.

She went around the corner, where eight men in similar garb waited.

Two of these men pushed open the front door and the squad moved into the foyer. There was a single bell, with a nameplate: R. Finkelstein & Co.

"The door to the stairs is locked," said an agent.

"Crowbar," said the team leader and another agent produced one, jammed it into the crack between the door and the frame and ripped the door open.

A loud, wavering siren sounded.

The team rushed up the stairs to a second door, battered it open with a single blow of a battering ram and cautiously pushed inside.

The house was deserted.

Gilmore found Ben's phone, wallet and keys in the bedroom off the kitchen.

Agents found several long strands of gray and black hair on the floor of a bathroom. Lillian's passport, a thick envelope of sketches and her purse were on a bed in the bedroom next to the bath with the hair.

§

"They were here," Gilmore said as he pulled off her vest. "Ben and Mrs. Golden."

"Where are they now?" Miryam whispered.

"We'll find them," she said.

Chapter Eighty-nine

LAKE MICHIGAN

Ben awoke to a splitting headache. His hands were cuffed behind him and he lay sprawled on a floor that seemed to move from side to side. A low-pitched roar filled the room.

The floor tilted again and Ben realized that he was on a boat.

He rolled over. Three feet from him lay Lilly, also handcuffed.

Ben began to stretch his muscles, starting with his legs. After a minute or so he rolled on to his left side, folded both legs tightly against his buttocks and bent backward and pushed his hands down until he could find the lock picks hidden in his pant cuff.

It took several minutes before he had them. After a few deep breaths, he used the picks to open the lock on his left hand. Then he brought his hands in front of him and opened the other lock. Then he moved behind Lilly and whispered, "Are you awake?"

"Yes," she whispered.

"Hold still. I'm going to take your cuffs off."

With a few quick moves, Ben unlocked both bracelets.

"Are you hurt?"

"They burned my breasts and they ache," she said.

"Who burned then?"

"Mostly Naomi. But Leah as well."

"Listen carefully," Ben whispered, switching to Hebrew.

"Cain," she replied. "Okay."

Bride of Finkelstein

"I see a couple of bags of cement and one of sand. On deck, they probably have a couple of washtubs or something similar."

"Why? What are they planning?"

"Not sure but probably they will put us in cement overshoes and throw us over the side."

"I can't swim!"

"Stay calm. I won't let you drown but before we get to the water, I have some questions."

"What do you want to know?"

"How strong are your arms and shoulders?"

"Pretty strong. I worked out in Randy's exercise room almost every day."

"Can you lift your own weight a foot or two?"

"I think so. If I had to."

"Okay. Let's put the cuffs back on but leave them unlocked."

"Why?"

"Surprise is our biggest asset."

Only a minute after Ben had replaced his own cuffs, the engine slowed, then stopped.

§

"It won't hurt as much if you just inhale the water an' get it over wit," said Simon as he poured concrete from a bucket around Ben's feet into a wooden milk box.

Ben's hands remained cuffed behind his back.

He looked around the rear deck of a fifty-foot cabin cruiser, bobbing on the lake waves. To his right, in the distance, the brilliant lights of downtown Chicago shone through the darkness.

Simon straightened up with a groan and set the bucket down.

Seated on the transom to Ben's left, just within his peripheral vision, was a second goon, a Chicago cop that Simon had called Matthews. He cradled a twenty-gauge Remington 870 auto-loading shotgun in his left arm.

Wearing only a T-shirt that was much too small and panties, Lilly stood in a similar box between Ben and Matthews.

"Stay still, it'll only be a few more minutes," Simon said.

Ben wiggled his ears and while the two thugs were giggling over that, he furiously moved his toes back and forth, pushing at the insides of his loafers and pushing up on his toes. But he needed another distraction.

Ben chanted the opening verse of the Aramaic prayer for the dead *"Yitgadal v'yitkadash sh'mei raba b'alma di-v'ra shirutei.* Instead of the usual cadence, he raised his voice and changed his tone to something akin to a snarl.

"You picked the wrong man," he said. "I'm not just a rabbi, I'm a *kohain*, a Jewish priest. *"Yamlich malchutei b'chayeichon uvyomeichon uvchayei d'chol beit Yisrael."*

"I curse you and your children, your children's children. For seven generations they will find no home. They will be forever strangers in a country not their own. And my spirit will haunt them until the end of time."

Simon shrank back in horror. Matthews frowned, wondering if he could believe what he was hearing.

"Why you gotta be like that," said Simon. "We just the little guys. The bosses want you dead, somebody gotta do it. Curse them, not us."

"The bosses? You mean Joe Stern?"

"He jest *my* boss. He work for dat lady, Naomi. Now that Randy sick, that bitch be the big boss and dere nuttin that ever change her mind."

"Then give me a swig of that whiskey," Ben said, pointing with his chin toward a half-empty bottle of Crown Royale on the bulkhead. "Maybe I'll change my curse."

"Sure, have a drink," said Simon, holding up the pint bottle. "Maybe help a little."

"Sure," said Ben, letting his voice tremble.

Abruptly the land breeze, faint but redolent of a huge landfill, died. The faint throb of diesel engines came across the water.

Ben felt the swell change directions beneath the boat.

A huge ship was approaching, its bulk displacing a vast underwater wave before it. In a few moments, Ben knew, the cabin cruiser would be rocked.

Simon unscrewed the bottle top, approached Ben and held out the bottle.

Ben took several deep breaths in quick succession, then opened his mouth. Simon poured whiskey into it.

A gigantic ore carrier converted to a container ship passed less than a hundred yards to landward.

The cruiser rocked from side to side in the boat's wake.

Ben spit a short stream of whiskey into Simon's eyes.

Lilly pulled her hands apart, sending the cuffs flying. She bent over.

Ben snapped his head left and shot a long stream of whiskey over her into Matthews' face.

Pushing down on both sides of the box with her hands, Lilly pulled both feet out of the cement.

Ben shed his cuffs, hopped sideways, twisting as he closed on Simon.

Wiping his eyes, Matthews charged forward.

Lilly ran at him, shoulder down, and bowled him over.

Ben punched Simon's throat with all his strength.

Inhaling deeply as he hopped forward, lifting the hardening cement and the box once, twice and feeling his left heel come loose, Ben threw himself over the rail just as the shotgun belched fire.

Lilly went headfirst over the gunwale.

The lower lip of the heavy box caught on the rail and Ben's face bounced off the fiberglass hull.

The shotgun fired again.

Ben raised his legs, his feet still encased in concrete, brought the box down on the rail and dropped headfirst into the dark waters.

Chapter Ninety

Lake Michigan

Don't panic, Ben told himself as the heavy box pulled his legs down.

Descending into colder and colder water, Ben lifted and dropped his legs. Lifted and dropped, all the while moving his toes and waving his outstretched hands, trying to slow his descent.

Too late, he thought and then a fierce, electric pain raced from the big toe on his right foot up to his buttock.

His bare right foot came out of the box.

He pushed his right foot against the edge of the box and pulled his left upward.

He pushed again and again almost unbearable pain stabbed his leg and hip.

He pushed again and his left foot came out.

It was pitch dark.

A moment later a brilliant light appeared above him for a few seconds.

Silhouetted at the edge of the bright area was Lilly, struggling in the water.

Arms outstretched, Ben pulled water and kicked. Pulled water and kicked, meanwhile bending and straightening his whole body, writhing in a rhythm like some huge otter.

His lungs were afire.

He knew that he was about to drown and for an instant

pondered the benefit of getting it over with.

A vision of Miryam appeared before his tightly shut eyes.

Never.

Ben let a little air out of his nose.

A little more.

More.

He could hold his breath no longer.

His head broke the surface and he gulped air.

A brilliant light painted the water near his head.

Ben went under just as the shotgun fired.

The light winked out and Ben surfaced, looking around in the dim light.

Treading water, he caught his breath. The cabin cruiser raced away, its engine a faint growl on the water.

He swam toward the spot where the boat had been.

On his fourth downward stroke, his left hand touched something that felt like silk threads.

Hair.

Lilly!

Down he went until he could feel her hair with both hands. One hand filled with long strands and he closed his fist, kicking and battling with his free hand until he broke the surface.

Treading water and gasping for air, he pulled Lilly up.

She wasn't breathing.

Somehow, she had lost the shirt. Her huge breasts bobbed in the water as Ben came face-to-face with her. Treading water, he put pinched her nose with his left hand, put his mouth over hers, parted her lips with his tongue and blew his lungs empty into her.

Again. Again, Again.

She didn't stir.

Filled with dread, he turned her shoulders until he could grasp her upper left arm and move her almost perpendicular to his own body. He relaxed back into the water, Lilly following atop him. Holding his right hand open, he aimed a blow between her breasts and struck her sternum with the heel of his hand as hard as he could.

Nothing.

He struck her again. And again. And again.

Lilly stirred, coughed water once, twice and Ben turned her toward him. She opened her eyes. "I'm alive?" she gasped.

"Back from the dead, I think. Lilly, I had to hit you very hard. You'll have bruises on your chest. I'm very sorry but it was the only way."

"Silly man," she said and pulled him to her.

After a beat, she released him.

"Lilly, I'm going to teach you to swim."

"Here? Now? I'm freezing. What happened to my shirt?"

"Gone. It was too small anyway."

Ben said, "Can you ride a bicycle?"

"If I had one to ride."

"Pretend you're on a bike. Now move your legs, push those pedals."

Ben moved a short distance away and watched as Lilly remained upright, moving up and down with the swells.

"You're treading water," he explained. "Now you know how to

keep from drowning. Just ride your bike."

"I can do this," she said.

"Slow down. Just barely move the pedals."

"Got it," Lilly said.

"Now let's blow bubbles," Ben said and took a breath of air, put his head sideways in the water and blew bubbles. He lifted his head to grab more air, switched cheeks and put his head in the water again and blew more bubbles.

Five times he lifted his head, blew bubbles, switched sides, blew bubbles and switched sides.

"Now you," Ben said.

"I'm so cold," Lilly said. "Do we have to do this now?"

Ben shook his head. "I can leave you here treading water and try to swim for help or I can teach you to swim and we'll go together," he said.

"What's it gonna be?"

"I guess I blow bubbles," she said.

Ten minutes later, side, by side, they began swimming toward the bright lights of downtown Chicago.

After a few minutes, Ben felt a cramp growing deep within his right thigh.

"Cramp!" yelled Ben. "Tread water for a while."

Ben lay back in the water and willed himself to relax his thigh muscles, his back and then arms and legs. Floating in the cold water, for a few seconds he felt a sense of serenity as his muscles softened.

"How do you feel?" Ben asked.

"I've never been so tired in my life."

"Me too. But we can't stop now. Let's just push through the

wall, get some endorphins flowing and go on. We'll try another stroke and rest some of our muscles."

Ben had never learned the breaststroke but he'd watched Olympic athletes pulling themselves across the water.

Holding his cupped hands in front of him, he pulled water, lifting his chest out of the water and kicked, head down he flattened his arms against his side and moved them upward for another stroke.

Again. Again. Again.

After what seemed like a very long time, Ben had to rest. The lights seemed no closer.

Side by side and panting, Ben and Lilly tread water until they could resume their swim.

Tired beyond anything he had experienced. Ben swam until he realized that Lilly was not with him. He turned around and swam several strokes to find Lilly, deathly pale, barely able to keep her head above water.

"Leave me," she sighed. "Save yourself."

Ben moved behind her, put his left arm under her shoulder and as he had learned during his two weeks of childhood summer camp and with his right arm began the side stroke toward the lights. "Relax," Ben said. Let your legs trail as I swim. Don't fight me, don't grab me. Or we'll both drown."

"Okay," she whispered, obviously exhausted.

He began swimming but after what he estimated as ten minutes, he had to stop. He lay on his back, panting until he could tread water. Then he pushed himself out of the water and turned himself around.

There! To his left, not far away, was a light.

No, two lights, moving.

A car!

Still holding Lilly, he resumed his sidestroke, angling away from the bright lights of Chicago, moving to his left, toward the car lights.

The lights winked out.

Keeping downtown Chicago on his right, dipping into reserves of energy and will power that he had never imagined possible, Ben slowly closed on the spot where he had seen the lights.

He dug down.

He kicked.

He dug down.

He kicked.

He dug down.

He kicked—and his feet struck the bottom.

"Lilly?"

"What now?"

"We're going to stand up and walk now."

He released his hold.

Cautiously she put both legs under her and still clutching Ben, began to walk across the uneven lake floor. After several minutes, now breathing almost normally, he saw something looming ahead in the glow of city lights dimly reflected from clouds.

Cautiously they approached a wall of huge rocks, each as big as a truck.

Even warm and rested, he knew that neither of them would ever be able to climb them.

"Which way" Lilly said, leaning against Ben.

"Left, I think,"

As the water grew shallower, the wall began to diminish. After several yards, they saw what might be a footpath, a narrow, stony way through a break in the wall.

Stumbling on small rocks, stubbing their toes, almost falling, they found himself on grass. Just ahead was a sidewalk and as Ben set foot on cold, smooth concrete, he was blinded by a pair of approaching lights.

Lilly sat down on the grass and leaned against Ben's legs.

A car stopped directly in front of them, perhaps fifty feet away.

The lights winked out.

A door slammed shut.

Spent, Ben dropped to his knees. He needed to rest. Darkness enveloped him as he lost consciousness.

But only for a few seconds.

He felt hands on him. Voices.

"Get them inside, quickly," said a woman in an authoritative voice.

"He's got handcuff marks on both wrists," said a man's voice.

"We should call the police," another woman said.

"No!" Ben croaked, barely able to speak above a whisper.

"No police. FBI...Agent Gilmore," he said and found the mercy of unconsciousness.

Chapter Ninety-one

Chicago

"And how are we feeling this morning, Mister... Mr... What is your name, sir?"

Ben smiled. "Call me Ben. I wish to speak with FBI Special Agent Pat Gilmore," he said and recited her phone number.

The nurse frowned. "Whom shall I say wishes to speak with her?"

"I just told you: Ben."

"I'll tell the doctor," she said. "In the meantime, Ben, how are you feeling?"

"I've been better," he said.

"Your right big toenail was torn off. Do you know how that happened?"

Ben nodded. "I think so."

The nurse stared. "Do you know what day it is?"

Ben shook his head. It hurt. "I was clubbed in the head Thursday afternoon. I don't know how long I've been here. How could I possibly know what day it is?"

"Do you know where you are?"

Ben looked at the IV bottle hung from a stand with a line going to a bandage near the inside of the elbow joint in his left arm.

Ben said, "Some kind of hospital. Where is Lilly?"

"The woman you came with?"

"Yes. Lillian Finkelstein."

"She's sleeping in another ward."

He looked around the room, at the bright colors on the walls, the cartoon characters. He looked at his bed, which was short and narrow.

"A children's hospital?"

"Very good! This La Rabida Children's Hospital. You were found, soaking wet, on the sidewalk outside, about 3:00 this morning. You were severely dehydrated, your blood sugar was dangerously low, as was your blood sodium and potassium, You have bruises all over your body. In addition to your lost toenail, there are shrapnel wounds on your right leg and buttock and you were suffering from hypothermia. You have scratches on your legs and wrists. We also found small amounts of concrete under your remaining toenails. Can you tell us how this happened?"

"Who is 'us.'"

"Tell *me*, then."

"I'll speak to Special Agent Gilmore. In the meantime, I'd like to see the hospital administrator."

§

Half an hour dragged by and Ben dozed off. He was awakened by the entry into his private room of a tall, distinguished-looking man who appeared to have been sent by Central Casting to play the role of a hospital administrator.

"I'm Doctor Henry Weiss," he said. "Chief of Medicine. I understand you want to speak to the Administrator."

"You'll do. But first I need you to confirm your identity."

The man frowned, then fumbled out his wallet. He produced a driver's license and an Illinois license to practice medicine.

"Okay, Henry—may I call you Henry?"

"If you like. Why are you being so secretive?"

"The short answer is fear."

"What are you afraid of?"

"Anyone connected to Chicago PD."

"Will you tell me why?"

"Yesterday a couple of goons, one of them a Chicago police officer, took me and Mrs. Finkelstein out on the lake in a boat and fitted us with cement overshoes."

The doctor frowned again.

"Cement overshoes?"

"I was held at gunpoint on a cabin cruiser, made to stand in a wooden box, which was then filled with cement. Before it dried, I hopped to the rail and went over, head first. They tried to stop me, of course.

"The rest you can guess."

"Who did this to you? Why?"

"I have the names of the two men and I will tell them and the reason for it to Special Agent Gilmore when she gets here. But first, I need someone to call her."

The doctor closed his eyes for several seconds. "Mrs. Finkelstein is still unconscious. She had recent bruises on her chest and burns on her breasts. Can you explain how that happened?

"She told me that someone used a hot curling iron on her breasts to get her to tell them something. As for the bruises, I had to resuscitate her while treading water—we were a long way from shore. I tried mouth-to-mouth but it didn't work."

"She may press charges against you," Weiss said.

Ben laughed.

Weiss said, "Your injuries and hers are consistent with your explanation. But why don't you want the police?"

Exhausted and ill-tempered, Ben lost it.

"Are you really a doctor?"

"Of course I am."

"Can you add two to two?"

"Go on."

"I just told you that I was held prisoner by a Chicago police officer. He held a shotgun on me while his partner poured the cement. The Chicago police cannot be trusted."

Weiss nodded. "Ah. Now I understand Mr.– "

"Rabbi. Rabbi Ben Maimon. What day is it?"

"Sunday."

"What time?'

Weiss glanced at his wristwatch.

"Nearly 11:00 a.m."

Ben sat up and threw his legs over the side.

The doctor gently pushed him back down. "You're in no condition to go anywhere."

"In four hours, I'm getting married in Skokie. Weak as I am, I won't let you stop me."

"I see," said the doctor. "If I let you call this FBI agent, will you talk to one of my doctors?"

"A psych exam? Sure. But after you speak to Special Agent Gilmore, you'll believe me."

"What's that number?"

Ben recited the number, then sank back on the bed, exhausted.

Weiss took out a cell phone and haltingly punched in the number.

The phone rang four times on the other end before Weiss heard a woman's terse voice say "Gilmore."

"Special Agent Gilmore? This is Dr. Henry Weiss at La Rabida Children's Hospital. Do you know a short, red-headed man named Ben who says he's a rabbi?"

Chapter Ninety-Two

Chicago

A nurse entered Ben's room and removed the IV taped to his arm.

A second nurse brought an electric razor and shaved the four-day beard on his cheeks.

He went back to sleep.

Half an hour later, Dr. Weiss returned and awakened Ben. "You're still very weak. I think we should transfer you to a general hospital but I've agreed to release you into the custody of your family doctor."

Ben closed his eyes and went back to sleep.

A minute later the door burst open and Miryam flew across the room.

She lay down beside Ben and gently hugged him.

Ben opened one eye, then the other.

"Have I died and gone to Heaven?" he whispered.

"Silly man. *I'm* in Heaven."

And she burst into tears.

"I thought—*we* thought, that you were dead. That Naomi or one of her goons had killed you. Nobody seemed to know where you were until about two hours ago. What happened to you?"

The door opened again and Agents Gilmore and Roberts strolled in.

"It's a long story," Ben said, sitting up, still holding Miryam. "But it'll have to wait. Agent Gilmore, do you have lights and sirens in your vehicle?"

The room door burst open and there stood Lilly Golden, clad in ill-fitting green scrubs. "Ben!" she shrieked, then flew across the room, pulled Ben from the bed and hugged him tight, his feet dangling several inches off the ground. Then she held him at arms-length and smothered his face with kisses.

"What a man!" she cried. "He saved my life, twice."

Still holding Ben in a death grip, she peered at the others. "You must be Miryam. Do you have any idea who this man you're marrying really is?" she shouted. "It isn't fair, I know but I want to steal him from you."

Ben gently but firmly pushed her arms down and stood barefoot on the tile floor. "May I introduce Lillian Golden, born Deborah Lillian Ruben and now the wife-in-name-only of Randy Finkelstein.

Miryam said. "I know exactly who I am marrying and what he is. Not another word about taking my Ben or I'll tear you to pieces."

Ben and everyone except Miryam laughed.

"Miryam," Lilly said, "When I was so tired—exhausted—that I couldn't swim another stroke, Ben put his left arm around me and swam with one arm for what seemed like hours. And every time he dug down for another stroke he mumbled 'Miryam.' I was only kidding. Please don't hate me for teasing you."

Miryam said. "I'll think about it."

Roberts said, "Enough. Now we have a story for *you*. Yesterday, the Coast Guard found a cabin cruiser that had run aground on Big Sable Point on the Michigan shore. In it was Simon De Leon, a.k.a. Big Simon, a gigantic black man from Curaçao, along with a Chicago cop that he'd strangled. He told the Coast Guard that a red-headed Jewish priest put a curse on him and his children for seven generations. De Leon is in every U.S. criminal database, so the Coast Guard called us. We knew that Simon worked for the Stern brothers and that they worked for Randy Finkelstein—"

Ben said, "Whoa. Randy Finkelstein was a mob boss?"

Pat Gilmore said, "Oh yeah. Until he began to lose his mind, he was the Big *Makker* of Chicagoland crime."

Ben said, "Then his daughter, Naomi, fed him enough lead to kill him and took over the enterprise."

Gilmore said, "Simon said he fitted you with cement overshoes and threw you into the lake. Is that true?"

Miryam gasped.

Ben said, "No, not exactly. I jumped."

Gilmore said, "And yet, here you are. How does that happen?"

Ben said, "Have you heard of Jewish White Magic? The Kaballah?"

Gilmore shook her head.

Ben said, "Well, that's a conversation for another day. Right now, I've got to get out of here."

Roberts said, "Your girlfriend here told us that you were last seen leaving your temple with Randy's wife. We found your wallet, keys, and phone in Mrs. Finkelstein's room in Randy's house. Randy is in the hospital, so we put out a BOLO for his daughter. We found Naomi Finkelstein with Leah Shevitz in TSA custody at O'Hare. They were just about to board a flight to Miami when a man named Igor Falkenberg—a hunchback, we're told—told a TSA supervisor that he had followed them to the airport and that they were wanted for murder and money laundering. They had checked a suitcase full of hundreds. Naomi Finkelstein's carry-on had a hard drive that nobody can read. They are now busy blaming each other for several murders.

"And by the way," Gilmore continued, "that little notebook you sent me implicates twenty-two people in Rabbi Ruben's money laundering enterprise. We'll want your statement but I guess we have the broad strokes."

"That's really great," Ben said. "But right now, we need to get to Skokie. Do you have a fast car with lights and siren?"

Roberts shook his head.

Miryam said, "Ben, my darling, they won't start without us."

Ben said, "Most of our guests have come halfway around the world. We shouldn't keep two hundred people waiting."

Mitch Katz, MD, Ph.D., pushed into the room wearing a big grin and holding an overnight bag in one hand and a plastic-shrouded tuxedo in the other. He was followed by Deb HaCohen and one of the bridesmaids, both in wedding attire.

Deb said, "Miryam, come with us. We'll do your makeup in the nurse's lounge."

Ben said, "Pat, please tell me you can find us a car that can get us to Skokie by 3:00?"

Gilmore shook her head.

"If you can squeeze in two more wedding guests, we've got something better," she said. Further conversation was drowned out by the sound of a big helicopter landing in the parking lot next to the hospital.

"Make it *three* more," Miryam shouted. "Lilly, come with us. We'll find you something to wear."

-the end-

AUTHOR TO READER

Only those who have lived the lonely and often underappreciated life of a writer can truly understand the satisfaction that we get from knowing that our work is read. Whether this book made you regret the waste of your time or grateful for the temporary transport to another, mostly mythical cosmos, please understand that *you*, singular and plural, are the reason that I write. Thank you for buying and reading this book. It pleases me far beyond mere words.

Rabbi Ben is a mythical creature. He doesn't look like anyone that I've met or seen but I have a clear picture of him in my mind's eye. He grew out of a series of experiences widely separated in time and space. As a young man, I had the privilege of serving my country in the U.S. Army. During my thirteen years in uniform, I met many chaplains, a few of them Jewish and without exception, they were bright, inquisitive, learned men who worked to serve their God, their country and their fellow humans.

Three of these chaplains, in particular, stick in my memory. One was Harry Schreiner, the "Rough-Riding Rabbi" of the Korean War, who wore out three jeeps and several chaplain's assistants as he drove all over that embattled peninsula, often under fire, looking for Jewish men or women—more than a few nurses were of that faith—to whom he could offer a little spiritual or temporal comfort. After the war, he returned to his congregation in Morristown, NJ. More than a decade later, he fought to return to active duty for a year to serve Americans in Vietnam. That is where I met him, very briefly and in an instant felt the calm good cheer and saintliness that he radiated.

Years later, in South Korea, I met Rabbi Harold Wasserman, the Running Rabbi. Compact and muscular, the only Jewish chaplain to graduate from the Army's tough and dangerous Ranger School, he ran five miles a day, maintained a strictly Kosher diet and projected a bearing that was both martial and sympathetic, thus earning the admiration and respect of all. Based in Seoul, he traveled the country constantly, seeking out homesick Jewish soldiers and offering them sympathy, a path to Godliness and a taste of home. I was pleased to call him my friend.

I met Rabbi Howard Kosovske in Frankfort, Germany and was astonished to learn that our paternal grandmothers were sisters; we are second cousins. Many years later we renewed our acquaintance when his daughter, then a rabbinical student and now a rabbi, became a member of my synagogue. When Howard retired from his congregation in Salem, MA, he became a visiting rabbi, filling in around the country and around the world for short periods to allow other rabbis to go on sabbatical or to help keep a congregation together as they sought a full-time rabbi.

If you have read this book or any of the others in the Rabbi Ben series, you will perhaps appreciate how these three men led me to create a roving rabbi, doing his thing under a different sky in each book. For the rest, I was privileged to observe my friend, Rabbi Daniel Shevitz, of Congregation Mishkon Tephilo, in Venice, California, for over two decades. I imbued the fictional Rabbi Ben with Shevitz's exhaustive knowledge of the Torah, Talmud and other Jewish writings and with an expanded version of his artistic and scientific gifts. To prevent him from seeming too perfect, I injected a twisted and shameful family history that he unconsciously strives to understand and live down.

A decade spent in a variety of positions on Mishkon Tephilo's board of directors provided insight into how a synagogue is run and how rabbis fit into the business plan. The rest came from my experiences writing about crime, during which I met many criminals, some entertaining, some frightening, others quite puzzling. Finally, in my early sixties, I segued from writing nonfiction books to penning screenplays, always with the aid and inspiration of my friend and collaborator, Larry Mintz. As I learned how to fashion scenes, I realized that I need not limit myself to writing books about factual matters. The first Rabbi Ben book came out of a real-life event: Rabbi Shevitz discovered a long-forgotten safe in his office. In it were the ownership documents of a score of burial plots in three different Jewish cemeteries.

Were these cemetery plots still empty? How could we know?

A book was born and a character named Rabbi Ben emerged to move the story forward.

This book, the fourth in the series, had a different sort of birthing. I was asked to consider writing a nonfiction history of Chicago crime, in the vein of my previous histories of crime in Los Angeles (*Fallen Angels*) and New York (*Rotten Apples*). Preliminary research revealed that the infamous organized crime of earlier eras, chiefly the Italian Mafia, was a shadow of its former self. Meanwhile, however, the Chicago area has grown enormously, spilling out of the city where I was born and raised and into a confusing host of small suburban townships, cities, and villages. I suspect that organized crime had followed this population shift and that newer immigrants, often Russian, had taken the place of the old Mafia. Joining that slender thread came another: more modern types of crime that evolved to protect criminal enterprises from the sort of laws that had brought down the old mafia. From the haze of the lucid dreaming that is my usual mode of creative writing came the story that you have just read. As always, if you enjoyed it or if you didn't, I'd like to know. Please contact me through my Website: www.marvinjwolf.com.

Marvin J. Wolf

Asheville, NC

2019